TRICK OR TREAT

"Leroy!" Hayley called out.

But the puppy didn't answer. He was too preoccupied with something.

Hayley rushed forward. She was practically on top of Leroy now, still shining the flashlight down on him. "Leroy, what in the world have you been up to?"

And then her eyes rested on something she couldn't quite make out at first. Leroy was busy digging something up from the soil. Hayley looked closer, not sure what it was, but as she crouched down to get a closer look, her eyes widened in horror.

Sticking up from the dirt was a fingernail painted with pink nail polish. It was a woman's finger and Leroy was hard at work digging up the rest of the body that went with it . . .

Published by Kensington Publishing Corporation

HAUNTED HOUSE MURDER

Leslie Meier
Lee Hollis
Barbara Ross

KENSINGTON BOOKS
www.kensingtonbooks.com

KENSINGTON BOOKS are published by

Kensington Publishing Corp.
119 West 40th Street
New York, NY 10018

All Kensington titles, imprints and distributed lines are available
at special quantity discounts for bulk purchases for sales promo-
tion, premiums, fund-raising, educational or institutional use.

Special book excerpts or customized printings can also be created to fit specific needs. For details, write or phone the office
of the Kensington Special Sales Manager: Kensington Publishing Corp., 119 West 40th Street, New York, NY, 10018. Attn. Special Sales Department. Phone: 1-800-221-2647.

Kensington and the K logo Reg. U.S. Pat. & TM Off.

ISBN-13: 978-1-4967-1997-3
ISBN-10: 1-4967-1997-2
First Kensington Hardcover Edition: September 2019
First Kensington Mass Market Edition: September 2020

ISBN-13: 978-1-4967-1998-0 (ebook)
ISBN-10: 1-4967-1998-0 (ebook)

10 9 8 7 6 5 4 3 2 1

Printed in the United States of America

Contents

HAUNTED HOUSE MURDER

Leslie Meier

Chapter One

"**B**ut that place is a death trap! Someone's going to die in there!"

There was no mistaking the emotion in the speaker's voice, which rose above a hum of other, discontented voices. Reporter Lucy Stone found herself quickening her steps as she carefully negotiated the steep cement steps that led from the parking lot to the basement meeting room in the town hall. As usual, she was running late, which was rarely a problem when she was covering meetings in the tiny coastal town of Tinker's Cove, Maine. Experience had taught her that nothing ever started on time, so she had developed the habit of planning to arrive at least fifteen minutes late. She was a busy wife and mother and she didn't have fifteen minutes to spend twiddling her thumbs while waiting for a meeting to start.

Truth be told, the weekly selectmen's meetings were usually poorly attended, as the five members debated mundane matters such as adding storm windows to the harbor-master's shed or arguing whether it would be more cost effective to repair or replace the oldest of the town's two police cruisers. The meetings were televised on CATV, but hardly anyone watched, and only a few regulars bothered to attend. Those included Stan Wysocki, the town's resident curmudgeon, and fussbudget Verity Hawthorne, who always brought her knitting. And the media, of course, in the person of Lucy, who worked part-time for the town's weekly paper, the *Pennysaver*.

Today, however, she seemed to have miscalculated. That realization hit her when she stepped inside the cement block walled meeting room, which even yellow paint couldn't brighten, and found that every single folding chair was occupied. Well, taken, not exactly occupied, because emotions were running high and most people were on their feet.

Selectman chairman Roger Wilcox was banging his gavel, attempting to call the meeting to order, but nobody in this crowd of agitated citizens was about to settle down.

"Think of the children!" cried Anna Keller, who had her youngest, barely four months old, nestled against her chest in a Snugli baby carrier. "That place is right across the street from the elementary school!"

"I dread to think what would happen if some kids ventured inside," added Lydia Volpe, who was a retired kindergarten teacher. "What if the floor gave way, or the stairs?"

"And often, too often, there are kids hanging around the fields, waiting to be picked up after soccer practice or after-school programs," said Janet Nowicki, who coached a youth soccer team. "You know the town meeting refused to fund a late bus for those kids."

"It's up to the town to do something! They should raze it, or let the fire department do a controlled burn," declared Lori Johnson, whose husband was a firefighter. "It's not only dangerous, it's an eyesore!"

"And I'm afraid it's going to bring down property values," predicted Franny Small, a former selectman who happened to live next door to 66 School Street, which Lucy suspected was the property in question. She had often wondered about the house, a once impressive Victorian mansion which now had peeling paint, a sagging porch, and curling shingles. And with Halloween approaching, she wouldn't be at all surprised if a ghost or two had taken up residency in the tall tower that stood on one side of the formerly stately home.

It was Franny's dire prediction about property values that caught everyone's attention, and the chairman was able to seize the moment. "Order! Order! Sit yourselves down," Roger bellowed, pounding the gavel on the bench. "This is unacceptable. I suggest you organize in some fashion, choose a spokesperson, and put your issue on the agenda for our next meeting." He banged the gavel again. "We have business to attend to. Item one: Repairs to the bandstand on the town common."

Franny Small raised her hand.

"Do you have something to say about the bandstand?" asked Roger.

"No." Franny stood up and smoothed the autumnal silk scarf she'd added to her Talbots cashmere twin set. She was now retired from the costume jewelry company she'd created and sold, for what was reputed to be more than two million dollars, and was considered the town's wealthiest year-round resident, although she played down that fact pointing out that there were several much wealthier summer residents. "As a former select-person I would like to remind the chairman that the first item on the agenda is *Citizen Concerns*. These good people deserve to be heard."

"Um, yes," said Roger, looking extremely annoyed. "And I think they've made themselves perfectly clear."

"But *you* haven't," countered Franny. "We haven't heard a response from the board. What exactly are you going to do about this problem?"

There was a definite buzz from the concerned citizens, who wanted answers from the five members of the town's governing board.

"Dodging the issues, as always," muttered Stan.

"If I may," said Joe Marzetti, a longtime board member who happened to own the town's grocery store. "I think that since these concerned citizens have gone to the trouble of coming to the meeting that we can tweak the agenda and accommodate them."

"I don't . . ." began Roger, but sensing a certain resistance from the other board members, he changed his tune. "Well, if we're all agreed?"

Receiving nods from the other board members, he turned to insurance broker Jim Moskowitz, who was seated next to him. "What do you think, Jim? Is the town liable?"

Lucy was especially interested in Jim's response, as her son, Toby, was married to Jim's daughter, Molly, and they shared a grandson, Patrick, who unfortunately lived in Alaska with his parents.

"I know the property in question and I think it is certainly what we in the business call an attractive nuisance. First things first. Let's have the building inspector conduct an examination and determine if the building is dangerous, and what should be done about it."

Lucy found herself nodding along in agreement with Jim's proposal; lately she had found herself growing closer to him, considering him a sound sort of fellow. She couldn't quite say the same about his wife, Jolene, whom she was ashamed to admit, she viewed as a competitor for Patrick's affection.

"And if I may," said member Fred Rumford, who was a professor at nearby Winchester College. "I suggest we have the town collector investigate and find out who, if anyone, actually owns the property. The town might very well be able to take it for uncollected taxes."

These proposals were generally met with approval, followed by a small voice. "I have some information. . . ."

"Ah, yes. The chair recognizes building inspector Fred Willets."

Fred, a very small man with thinning hair and a wispy mustache, stood up and consulted his clipboard. "As it happens, my office has recently received several inquiries from neighbors of the property in question at Sixty-Six School Street, and I conducted a thorough inspection yesterday. From the outside I have to agree that it looks to be in very poor shape, but that is merely surface. The structure itself is remarkably sound; those old folks sure knew how to build. Tax records show the house was constructed over a hundred years ago and I expect it to stand for another hundred."

"But what about the systems?" demanded Anna, smoothing her baby's silky head, which was tucked under her chin. "We all know about those gas explosions in Massachusetts. . . ."

"There's no gas in the house," said Fred. "The boiler is oil fired and was installed a few years ago. The wiring is up to code, and so is the plumbing. Someone could move in there tomorrow."

Frankie LaChance, who was the town's foremost real estate broker, as well as Lucy's friend and neighbor, was raising her hand.

"Ah, Ms. LaChance," said Roger, beaming as he recognized the attractive woman who was dressed as usual in business casual, wearing a quilted green jacket over her silky blouse. "Perhaps you have some information to share?"

"I do," said Frankie, tossing her auburn curls and smiling broadly. "I'm happy to say that Sixty-Six School Street is under agreement and the closing is imminent."

This news generated a certain excitement as everyone wondered who the buyers might be. Someone who already lived in town, or newcomers?

"They're a lovely young couple. Ty and Heather Moon. They are relocating from Portland where they lived in a tiny condo, and are very excited about the antique home's unique features and potential for a truly spectacular renovation, its generous square footage and the spacious yard, which is over an acre. I suspect they are thinking of starting a family."

The next question on everyone's mind, including Lucy's, was the price. Frankie wasn't about to reveal it, but she did offer a clue. "The owners . . . you may remember Hilda and Bob Edmiston? They moved into assisted living a few years ago, intending for their son to manage the property, but he got a job in California and moved out there. There was no one taking care of repairs and maintenance, which was unfortunate."

Lucy took this to mean that the Moons got a good deal.

"In the end, the Edmistons are very relieved that the house will be in good hands in the future," concluded Frankie.

Make that a very good deal, decided Lucy, making a note to follow up tomorrow with a call to Frankie. She noticed that the emotional temperature in the room had definitely cooled, and people were gathering up their belongings, chatting quietly as they made their way to the door. The room was soon back to normal, with Stan and Verity in their usual seats, as well as a handful of town officials who were there to advise the board members on agenda items.

"Item one," announced Roger, with a tap of his gavel. "Bandstand repairs. Fred, what's the situation?"

Lucy yawned, realizing the meeting was going to run late and trying to keep her mind on the much less interesting items that remained on the rather lengthy agenda. But instead, she found herself speculating about Verity's knitting, which it seemed she had been working on for a very long time. It was a horrible shade of green and there seemed to be a lot of it. Was it a sweater for a very large relative? An afghan for a hopefully color-blind friend? A camouflage cover for a tank? Whatever it was, she concluded, watching as Verity's needles clicked away, there seemed to be no end in sight.

Next morning, Lucy got to work later than usual. Phyllis, the receptionist at the *Pennysaver,* looked up from her spot behind the reception counter when the little bell on the door announced her arrival. "Late night?" asked Phyllis, peering at Lucy over her tiger-striped cheaters, which matched her bright orange sweater. Phyllis observed all the holidays, and this was one of her Halloween outfits.

"I didn't get home 'til after midnight," said Lucy, yawning as she hung up her fleece jacket. She then went straight for the coffeepot and filled her *#1 Mom* mug, looking up as the bell on the door jangled again, announcing the arrival of Ted Stillings. "Concerned citizens hijacked the agenda."

"What were the citizens concerned about?" asked Ted, who was the *Pennysaver*'s publisher, editor, and chief reporter. He'd inherited the paper, as well as his prized antique roll-top desk and the Regulator clock that hung on the wall above it, from his grandfather, a nationally renowned journalist.

"That old haunted house opposite the elementary school," said Lucy. "They're concerned it poses a danger to the kids."

"I suppose they have a point," conceded Ted, hanging his barn coat on the stand next to the little table containing the coffeepot. "What's the town going to do? Raze it?"

"Nope," said Lucy, taking a long drink of coffee. "It's under agreement. New people bought it."

"That old wreck?" asked Phyllis.

"The building inspector says it's not a wreck at all; it's structurally sound underneath all that peeling paint."

Ted filled his *Best Boss* mug with coffee and stirred in a couple of packets of sugar and a healthy dollop of fake cream, then took a sip. "That sounds like a good story, Lucy," he said, adding another packet of sugar. "Historic home saved from wrecking ball."

"Actually, I think the suggestion was to have the fire department do a controlled burn, for practice," said Lucy, furrowing her brow as she seated herself at her desk. "And if all that sugar doesn't kill you, that fake creamer will."

Ted added a bit more creamer and resumed stirring his coffee. "It'll be a great seasonal story," he continued, ignoring her objection. "We'll put a big photo of the house right on the front page, above the fold. Maybe jazz it up with a full moon and a bat, something like that. It's amazing what you can do with photos these days. A real Halloween haunted house."

"Whatever happened to journalistic integrity?" asked Lucy.

"An increase in the price of newsprint," said Ted, sighing and seating himself at his desk, where he fired up his computer. "That's what."

"Gotcha," said Lucy, flipping open her notebook and reviewing her notes, looking for a way to perk up her account of the meeting. She was just about to reach for her cell phone to call Frankie La Chance when it rang, and she began frantically digging into her jumbo purse, which was big enough to contain a couple of reporter's notebooks, countless pens, grocery coupons, wallet, keys, first-aid supplies, lunch, snacks, and finally, lurking in the bottom, her phone.

"Hi," she said, hoping the caller hadn't been sent to voice mail.

"Hi, Mom." She smiled, recognizing the voice of her son, Toby, calling from far-off Alaska. In Lucy's mind, Alaska was covered with snow year-round, was populated by polar bears, and everyone wore fur-lined parkas and lived in igloos.

"Hi, yourself," she said, absolutely delighted. Toby rarely called, relying instead on Facebook to keep in touch, and she was looking forward to a nice chat. Then that little niggle of anxiety wormed its way into her mind. "Is everything okay?"

"What? You only think I call because something's the matter?"

"Well . . ." began Lucy, not sure how to respond, because Toby most often called when there was some sort of problem.

"You're right, Mom, we are in a bit of trouble."

"Is it Patrick?" she asked, fearing the worst.

"No, he's fine. It's Molly."

Lucy was hugely relieved, then immediately guilt-stricken. She loved Molly, she really did, but she had to admit she sometimes found her a bit difficult. She hadn't approved of Molly's plan announced last Christmas to leave her husband and child for a year to study German language and folktales in Heidelberg, and had been much relieved when she decided instead to become a dog trainer after an unfortunate incident when Skittles bit her mother. As far as Lucy knew, Jolene was still struggling to recover full use of her leg. "Oh, no. What's happened?"

"One of the sled dogs she was working with bit her hand; she was training for the Iditarod, you know."

Lucy hadn't known of Molly's latest ambitious scheme. "That long dog sled race?" asked Lucy.

"Yeah, it was a dream of hers, but it's out of the question now."

Lucy thought of the extensive damage Skittles had inflicted on Jolene, a wound that stubbornly resisted healing as well as causing persisting pain and muscle damage, and was afraid Molly might lose her hand. "Will she be all right?"

"Eventually," said Toby, with a big sigh. "It's her right hand and she's going to need several surgeries and a lengthy rehab."

"I'm glad they can repair her hand," said Lucy. "But it's going to be a long haul, for you and Patrick, too."

"That's the problem, Mom. I've been asked to take part in a research cruise out of Woods Hole; you know, the Woods Hole Oceanographic Institute in Massachusetts. It's quite an honor, even though I'll be filling in for the first guy they asked; he actually needs chemo and won't be able to go. Anyway, it's a two-month commitment. . . ."

"But Molly needs you," said Lucy. She was trying to think how she could help, but she wasn't free to go to Alaska. She had plenty of responsibilities here at home. It was true that youngest daughter Zoe was spending her junior year abroad in France, where her older sister Elizabeth now lived, but there was still her husband, Bill, her middle daughter, Sara, and her job.

"Actually, Molly's okay with me going. She says it

will be easier for her if she can just concentrate on getting her hand fixed. The problem is Patrick. We need someone to take care of him."

"I'd love to help, but I can't just pick up and go to Alaska. I don't suppose Jolene . . ."

"She's gone to stay with her sister in Florida. There's a top wound-care clinic there, and she's hoping they can fix her leg. She's planning to stay for a couple of months," said Patrick. "And you won't have to come to Alaska. I could bring Patrick to you when I report to Woods Hole," said Toby. "Would that be okay? I know it's a lot to ask. . . ."

"Okay? It would be great," said Lucy, her heart leaping. Two months. Two months with Patrick. It was a grandmother's dream come true. "When are you coming?"

"In two weeks?"

"Super! I'll make cookies." Then, ashamed, she remembered poor Molly, who would be dealing with a painful recovery all alone. "Is there something I can send Molly?"

Chapter Two

Lucy gave the comforter on the bed in Toby's old room a tweak, and smoothed the freshly changed pillowcase, satisfied that everything was ready for Patrick and Toby's arrival sometime in the afternoon. Everything except the grocery shopping, which was the last thing on her list. Well, except for the peanut butter cookies that were Patrick's favorite, and she'd make them as soon as she got back from the store.

She had a big list, intending to stock up on all the foods she knew kids liked and that Patrick's mother didn't necessarily approve of, like Cocoa Puffs cereal. Molly had e-mailed her with a list of foods she wanted Lucy to provide for Patrick, things like kale and quinoa, and even a few that Lucy had never heard of, like faro and acai berries. Lucy had studied the list and decided it was probably a case of wishful thinking on Molly's part, and decided to spend her money on foods the child would actually eat. She'd seen plenty of pictures of Patrick on Facebook, and she was worried he looked much too thin. She was going to feed him up with good, old-fashioned mainstays like Cheerios, peanut butter and jelly sandwiches, and spaghetti and meatballs. After school, he would snack on homemade cookies and a big glass of full fat milk.

Lucy usually did her grocery shopping on Wednesdays, after the week's deadline when she had a free afternoon, and the IGA was not very busy. This week, she'd held off until Saturday morning, and the store was humming with shoppers getting ready for Halloween. Pumpkins and chrysanthemums were displayed outside the store and inside the produce section was brimful of winter squash, colorful gourds, tote bags of apples, and gallon bottles of cider. Lucy grabbed it all and her cart was nearly full, thanks to a very large pumpkin, when she headed on to the fish counter. Cod was on sale and she was planning to make chowder, which she figured was a surefire way to get Patrick to eat some fish. And since it was only going into chowder, she figured the cheap "previously frozen" fish from the grocery store would be just fine.

Franny Small was already there, buying a single swordfish steak. "That's much too big," she told the clerk, Carrie Bennett, who was weighing out the fish. "That's more than half a pound. I can't possibly eat that much."

"I can cut it in half," offered Carrie.

"If it's not too much trouble," said Franny.

"Not at all." Carrie removed the fish from the scale and sliced it in half, holding out one of the pieces for Franny's approval.

"Oh, that's much too small," said Franny.

"Let's try another piece," said Carrie, plopping another steak on the scale. "Six ounces. How's that?"

"You know, I don't really like swordfish all that much. I don't think I want any after all."

Carrie pressed her lips together, struggling to keep her temper. "Have a nice day," she told Franny, who was already headed off in the direction of the meat counter. She turned to Lucy. "What can I get for you?"

"Two pounds of cod," said Lucy, upping her order in an attempt to make up for Franny's annoying behavior.

Hearing her voice, Franny whirled around. "Oh, Lucy. I didn't see you there, behind me."

Lucy smiled. "Well, you don't have eyes in the back of your head."

"No, but the ones in front are perfectly fine," said Franny, eager to announce her big news. "Guess what? I think my new neighbors have moved in. The lawn has been mowed and there are lights on at night."

"So soon?" Lucy hadn't expected the sale to move so quickly. "It must be nice to finally have neighbors after the house was empty so long. I wonder if they're planning to remodel?" Lucy's husband, Bill, a restoration carpenter, was just finishing up his latest job and didn't have another lined up.

"I wouldn't know," said Franny, with a little jerk of her head. "I haven't actually spoken to them."

"But you've seen them?"

"Only briefly." Franny clearly did not approve of the situation. "I've had glimpses, the briefest of glimpses, when FedEx delivers a package and they open the door to grab it. Then it shuts, and they're out of sight."

Lucy suspected that Franny was keeping a close

watch on her new neighbors, perhaps even resorting to binoculars.

"Didn't you see them mowing the lawn? What
about when they moved in? Did they move themselves or did they hire a moving company?"

"Landscapers came one afternoon and did the
lawn," reported Franny. "That was my first clue that
something was up." Then she lowered her voice
and stepped closer to Lucy. "I think they must
have moved in after dark. Under cover of night."

"That's weird," said Carrie, handing Lucy the
wrapped package of fish. "Of course, the days are
getting shorter. It's dark at five in the afternoon."

"That's true," said Lucy. "And daylight savings
will end soon, too, and then it's dark at four."

"It happens every year; it shouldn't come as a
surprise to anyone," said Franny, raising her eyebrows. "If you ask me, I think they planned to
move in after dark so no one would see them."

"Why would they do that?" asked Lucy, placing
the wrapped fish in her cart.

"Maybe they're in the witness protection program or something," teased Carrie.

"You can make fun," said Franny, narrowing her
eyes, "but mark my words: Those Moon people are
hiding something. They're not behaving like normal people." With that, Franny switched her plastic basket from one arm to the other, turned on
her heel, and marched off in the direction of the
frozen foods.

"She's a card, isn't she?" observed Carrie, with a
chuckle.

"For sure," said Lucy, but as she headed for the
cereal aisle she wondered if Franny was on to

something. She was no dummy; she'd built her costume jewelry company from the ground up, combining nuts and bolts into unique designs when she was a salesclerk at Slack's Hardware Store. Slack's was long gone, replaced by a national chain, but Franny had become a self-made millionaire.

Back at the house on Red Top Road, Lucy got busy mixing up cookie dough, and assembling the chowder. The cookies were cooling on wire racks and she had just set the completed chowder on a low heat to simmer when she heard a jubilant series of honks. Toby and Patrick had arrived!

She was the first to greet them, getting a big hug from Toby. His size, at nearly six feet, always amazed her. How had that happened? She remembered him as a kid, but now here was Patrick, looking an awful lot like Toby did when he was a boy. She got a nice hug from Patrick, too, and then Bill and Sara flew out the door and there were more hugs and exclamations of welcome. Libby, the family's black Lab, tried to join in but was somewhat hampered by arthritis and had to limit her participation to wagging her tail.

"How was the traffic? You made good time," said Bill, eyeing the shiny new rental car. "How do you like the car? Keyless ignition, right?"

"How's Molly?" asked Sara. "What about the dog? They didn't put it down, did they?" She was a big animal lover, and it wasn't clear whether she was more worried about Molly's condition or the dog's situation.

"Let them come in and get settled," chided Lucy, noticing Patrick's drooping eyes. "They've had a long trip."

Once in the house Bill and Toby were supplied with beers, Lucy brewed some tea for herself and provided glasses of cider for Sara and Patrick. They all gathered at the big golden oak table in the kitchen, munching on Lucy's still-warm home-made peanut butter cookies and catching up on the news. It was just like old times, thought Lucy, beaming at the sight of her son and grandson within arm's reach. Too bad for Jolene, she thought, who would miss Patrick's visit.

"My goodness, you've grown so much since I last saw you," she told Patrick, who was busy on his third, or perhaps fourth, cookie.

"So, Toby, what's this project you're going to be working on?" asked Bill.

"They're studying how climate change is affect-ing patterns of predation, and my focus is going to be on salmon," explained Toby.

"That sounds interesting," said Sara, who was also a scientist, currently working on a graduate degree in geology.

"Yeah, it's a great opportunity," said Toby, reach-ing for another cookie. "It's just hard that the tim-ing's so bad. But Patrick's excited about being here with you guys. Right, Patrick?"

Patrick didn't look terribly excited; Lucy thought he actually looked rather unhappy. She suspected he already missed his mother and home and was anxious about going to a new school. "So tell me, Patrick," she began, "what's your favorite subject?"

"Science, I guess. We've been learning about

volcanoes and how the earth's center is made of hot, melted rocks."

"Cool!" exclaimed Sara. "Don't you love it? How the earth has changed over millions of years?"

"It's okay," said Patrick, with a shrug and a sigh.

"So what do you like to do after school?" asked Lucy.

Now Patrick brightened up. "Soccer!"

"Patrick plays after school and his team is having a great season," said Toby. "He's one of the best players and they're going to miss him."

"What position do you play?" asked Bill.

"Sometimes I'm goalie, but I also play center."

"We have a soccer program, I'll call Janet Nowicki and see if you can join a team," offered Lucy.

"Cool," said Patrick. "Do you have a ball? I'd like to kick it around now."

"Sure thing," said Sara, popping up. "I'll play, too. I could sure use some exercise."

The house had been much too quiet lately, thought Lucy, enjoying the thwack of feet on the soccer ball and the cries of the two players as she cleared the table and loaded the dishwasher. Bill and Toby were unloading the car, thumping suitcases up the back stairs, and grunting. Even Libby was involved, greeting them every time the door opened and escorting them through the kitchen, her nails clicking on the wooden floor. Lucy's almost empty nest was once again full, if only temporarily, and she was going to enjoy it while it lasted.

On Monday, Lucy took Patrick to school, enrolling him in the third grade. The principal took

them on a quick tour and then it was time for
Patrick to report to his class and for Lucy to leave.
He knew his father was already on his way to
Woods Hole, and now he was going to be on his
own, facing a new teacher and new kids. "You'll be
fine," said Lucy, giving him a quick peck and
watching as he walked through the door. She felt a
bit as if she was watching him go before a judge,
maybe even a firing squad, and knew it was ridiculous because he would be riding home on the
school bus in a few hours.

Nevertheless, she was glad when she met Janet
Nowicki, who was coming into the school as she
was leaving, carrying a big mesh bag filled with
soccer balls.

"Hi, Lucy," said Janet, with a big smile. "Great
story about that selectmen's meeting—the one
about the haunted house. You really nailed it."

"It was a lot more interesting than most of those
board meetings, that's for sure," said Lucy. "But I
guess the problem's been solved. I hear the new
people have moved in to the old house."

"They haven't done much, though," said Janet,
with a sniff. "The grass has been cut but there's no
sign of any renovations or repairs."

"I'm on the case," said Lucy. "I'm going to stop
by with one of Bill's fancy new brochures. His current project is ending and he doesn't have anything else lined up until spring."

"If they've got any sense, they'll grab him. He's
not often free, is he?"

"Not often. And I gotta tell you, I'm a bit nervous about our finances. It's going to be a long,
cold winter and I've got an extra mouth to feed,
too."

"You do?"

"Yeah, my eight-year-old grandson is staying with us for a few months."

"That's great. You must be thrilled, especially with Halloween coming so soon."

"Yeah," agreed Lucy. "It's going to be a lot of fun. But I think he's going to be a bit homesick. He says he loves to play soccer. . . ."

"Well, sign him up!" exclaimed Janet. "Practice is right here Tuesdays and Thursdays after school, games are on Saturday morning."

"Thanks," said Lucy, with a little wave, pushing open the door.

"Thank you," said Janet. "We can always use another player."

The elementary school was positioned so that the parking lot was behind the building, approached from Oak Street, which intersected with School Street. That meant that Lucy hadn't passed the Moon house at 66 School Street when she brought Patrick, even though it was actually located opposite the school. Since it was so close, she left her car in the lot, to walk over. Pausing at the curb, she took a moment to study the house.

It was early days, of course, as the Moons had just moved in, but apart from the newly mowed lawn there was little evidence that the house was now occupied. Lucy wouldn't have expected a new roof to magically sprout, or a fresh coat of paint to bloom on the weathered clapboard, but she thought most newcomers would have announced their arrival by setting a pot of chrysanthemums or a pumpkin on the porch steps. And they might have put up new curtains or set a lamp in a window. At the very least, she thought, crossing the street and stepping onto the porch, she would have expected a new doormat. Perhaps one that said *Welcome*. But there was no sign of the new homeowners, and the doorbell didn't work when she pressed it. So she knocked, and waited, and knocked again. There was a car in the driveway, which usually signified that someone was home, but nobody was answering the door.

Perhaps she should try the back door. She'd gone to the front because she had approached from the street, and because she felt it was a bit more polite since she didn't know the Moons. Most people in Tinker's Cove came and went through their back doors; front doors were mostly for show. In fact, a lot of people never actually opened their front doors and filled their unused entrance vestibules with golf bags, fishing rods, croquet sets, and out-of-season coats and boots, using the space as a sort of extra closet.

She made her way around the house, where she perched on a rickety set of unsteady steps and banged at the kitchen door. The door had a window, covered with a rather grimy bit of gingham curtain, and after she'd banged a second time she saw the curtain twitch, and a face appeared. A rather handsome face, with a beard and wire-rimmed glasses.

The door opened a crack. "Yes?" said the owner of the beard and eyeglasses, who appeared to be a well-built man in his mid-thirties, dressed in jeans and a black turtleneck sweater.

"Hi!" said Lucy, realizing she sounded awfully enthusiastic. Toning it down, she continued. "I'm a neighbor here in town and I just wanted to introduce myself. I'm Lucy Stone and my husband, Bill, is a restoration carpenter. We thought you might be considering some renovations, so I have some information for you. . . ." She produced the colorful brochure Bill was so proud of, offering it to the man, whom she believed must be Ty Moon.

"Not interested," he said, stepping back and starting to shut the door.

Lucy wasn't a reporter for nothing; she'd picked up a few tricks of the trade. "Oh, my," she moaned, putting her hand to her head.

As she'd hoped, the door opened a bit wider. "Are you all right?"

"I'm a bit dizzy. Perhaps if I could sit down?" She was looking past him, at the glossy black high-top table and stools that seemed out of place in the shabby old kitchen.

"I can call nine-one-one," he offered.

Behind him, Lucy saw a woman standing in the kitchen doorway. She had long, almost white hair and seemed to be wearing some kind of nightgown. Was this Heather? And why was she wearing a nightgown when it was almost lunchtime?

"Ty, is something the matter?" she asked, in a soft voice that was little more than a whisper.

"It's under control," he snapped.

"If you say so," she replied, vanishing so quickly that Lucy wondered if she'd actually seen her, or if she was only some sort of ghostly apparition.

"Well, do you want me to call the rescue squad or not?" demanded Ty, sounding as if he was losing patience.

"No, no. I'm feeling better," said Lucy. "Thanks anyway."

He shut the door in her face and, somewhat shocked, she stepped down carefully, holding on to the splintery wooden railing, and headed back to the street. She glanced at the windows on the side of the house, but the shades were all down even though it was a bright, sunny day. Who does that? she wondered. Closed shades were definitely a worrisome sign in Tinker's Cove. What were they hiding? Reaching the sidewalk, she tucked the brochure in the brand-new rural mailbox that had been installed by the road, snapped the little door shut, and crossed the street.

That was pretty weird, she thought, as she started her car and pulled out onto Oak Street. Stopping at the corner of School Street, she took one last look at the house before turning right and heading toward the *Pennysaver* office on Main Street. She might be wrong, she admitted to herself, but it didn't seem as if the Moons had any community spirit and weren't the least bit interested in getting to know their neighbors. And as for Ty Moon's handsome features, she was reminded of her mother's frequently voiced reminder that "handsome is as handsome does." Judging by that standard, Ty wasn't good-looking at all.

Chapter Three

As Janet Nowicki had pointed out at the select-men's meeting, the Tinker's Cove school department budget didn't run to a late bus, so Lucy had to pick Patrick up after soccer practice on Tuesdays and Thursdays. This first Tuesday was a bright, crisp fall day and she was enjoying the sunshine and the colorful yellow and orange trees that surrounded the field. Patrick seemed to be having fun, chasing the ball and getting a few kicks in, which was a relief, since she'd been worried about whether he'd fit in with the kids in the new school. That didn't seem to be a problem, she decided, watching as the other kids high-fived him when the practice was over.

Spotting his jacket and backpack lying on the ground, she picked them up and approached the little knot of players, who were deep in some sort of discussion. As she drew closer, she realized they weren't talking about the practice, but were instead debating whether a witch actually lived in the haunted house across the street.

"I saw her; she has a hooked nose and a big wart

on her chin," declared one boy, who she thought might be one of Dottie Halmstad's grandkids. He had that very blond, almost white hair that was a Halmstad trait.

"When I walked by the house I heard groans and weird noises," offered a little girl with quite a few missing teeth.

"And I saw a black cat over there," added a slightly chubby kid, whose shirt didn't quite reach his soccer shorts and showed some bare belly. "And the house number is sixty-six. That's a sign of the devil."

"Nah, it's got to be three sixes," said the blond kid.

"Maybe one fell off," suggested the chubby kid.

Patrick was taking it all in, looking a bit scared. "Hi, Grandma," he said, sounding relieved to see her.

"That's all a lot of nonsense," she told the group. "That house isn't haunted; it just needs some paint. The people who moved in aren't witches or monsters; they're just regular people. I've even met them."

"My mom says they're stuck up," offered the chubby kid. "She took them some muffins she made and they said they didn't want them because they were too gluey or something."

"Maybe they only eat gluten-free foods," said Lucy, not the least bit surprised at the idea.

"Yeah, my sister's gone gluten-free," said the little girl with missing teeth. "My mom says it's ridic'lous."

"My mom says they can go eat worms," said the chubby kid, spotting the arrival of a very large SUV. "That's her now. I gotta go."

"Well, my mom said I shouldn't go trick-or-treating at that house," said the young Halmstad boy. "She said it wasn't a good idea."

"Not everybody likes Halloween. You should listen to your mom." Lucy handed Patrick his jacket and together they started walking to the car.

"Grandma?"

"What's on your mind, Patrick?"

"Do you think that house really is haunted?"

"No."

"Does a witch live there?"

"No. There's a man and a woman—their names are Ty and Heather Moon. I Googled them and he works in screen arts and she's an interior designer." Lucy didn't mention that she hadn't the faintest idea what "screen arts" actually were, but supposed it had something to do with creating silk-screen designs for T-shirts. She also didn't mention her surprise that the Moons hadn't eagerly accepted Bill's brochure, if Heather was planning to use her interior design skills on the old house. Of course, she admitted to herself, as a design professional Heather might already have developed relationships with contractors she preferred to work with. Contractors who weren't local and, whom Lucy smugly assumed, would charge an arm and a leg, and probably do inferior work.

"Are they nice?"

For a moment, remembering her encounter with Ty Moon, Lucy wasn't sure how to answer. Those Moons had seemed pretty odd, and Ty was positively unfriendly. Then she remembered her mother saying you couldn't understand anyone until you'd walked a mile in their shoes, and she bent down, looking Patrick straight in the eyes.

"I'm sure they are," she said. "I'm sure they're very good people."

When they got home, Lucy got Patrick settled at the kitchen table with his homework, and some milk and cookies. Not homemade—those were long gone—and she'd resorted to giving him Oreo cookies. They were on sale this week and she'd bought the allowed limit, stocking up. Libby stationed herself next to Patrick, ever hopeful that a bit of Oreo might come her way.

Lucy was humming to herself as she unpacked the groceries and unloaded the dishwasher, preparing to start cooking dinner. Patrick, she noticed, seemed to be making a lot more headway on his snack than on his homework, which was a sheet of math problems.

Setting the last glass in the cabinet, she went over and took a look at the paper, which was a series of addition problems with fractions. "Confused?" she asked.

"Yeah. I don't get it."

Remembering a trick she'd used with her kids, Lucy got out her measuring cups and lined them up by size on the table. "Here we've got a whole cup. That's one. This cup is a half. It takes two half cups to make one cup."

"But two is more than one," said Patrick.

"That's true," said Lucy, scratching her head. "Okay, let's try this." She filled a pitcher with water and used it to fill the half cup and had Patrick pour it into the one-cup measure. "That's one-half, see?"

Patrick nodded, and she filled the half cup a second time. "Now pour it into the cup."

"It's full," he said.

"Do you see? Two one-halves make a whole one. It's the same for four quarters. Four make one."

"Okay. But what's this one here, three over two?"

Lucy sighed. It was going to be a long afternoon. She was still soldiering on, trying to help Patrick with his homework, when Sara came home, dropping an armful of books on the table by the kitchen door and shrugging out of her puffy jacket, which she hung on a hook. She then kicked off her Ugg boots, leaving them where they landed in the middle of the kitchen floor.

"Do you mind?" asked Lucy, giving her a look.

"It's all right if Patrick leaves things everywhere, but not me?" She pointed to Patrick's jacket, which was lying on the floor in the corner, where he'd tossed it.

Lucy rolled her eyes. "Patrick is eight. You're not."

"Mom," began Sara, in an aggrieved tone, "I've got to prepare for my orals and I can't get any work done here because he's always playing those noisy video games. It's wham, bang, crash, all the time and I need quiet to concentrate. . . ."

"It's quiet now," said Lucy. "Why don't you study now?"

"Oh, Mom. You don't understand anything. I can't study now!"

"Why not?"

"I'm exhausted, that's why." Sara let out a huge sigh. "I had to teach two undergrad chem labs, if you can imagine it. Two! One right after the other. They treat us teaching assistants like scum. And believe me, it's a miracle those idiots didn't blow up the building." She gave a little shudder. "Ugh. I need a shower."

"We'll work it out," said Lucy, reaching for Patrick's social studies book. "Hey, since you can't study, after your shower, would you mind peeling some potatoes? I'm helping Patrick with his homework."

Sara paused at the bottom of the stairs, her hand on her hip, and gave a toss of her shoulder-length blond hair. "I'm not a slave, you know." Then she turned and thumped her way up the stairs.

"Okay, Patrick," said Lucy, checking off Patrick's completed homework assignments. "Just one left. A paragraph about what costume you're going to wear on Halloween and why."

"I don't know yet," said Patrick.

"Really?" inquired Lucy, somewhat concerned. These days you couldn't wait until the last minute to get a costume; they went fast. She'd noticed that the display in the drugstore was already pretty depleted.

"No. I couldn't decide what to be."

"Any ideas now?"

"Well, Mom had this idea about these two guys, Dr. Jackal and Mr. Wide. . . ."

"You mean Dr. Jekyll and Mr. Hyde?" prompted Lucy.

"Maybe. It was going to be two-sided. I'd be this doctor on the front and the other guy on the back. . . ."

Lucy sighed. That sounded just like something Molly would come up with. Something terribly ambitious and absolutely impossible for her to manage. Executive action was definitely called for. "First things first. You've got to write a paragraph about a costume. We don't have a costume yet, so why don't you write about something you'd like to be? Say a pirate. That's definitely doable, even if we can't find a costume. We can make one."

Patrick's face was set in a stubborn expression. "I don't want to be a pirate."

"Then write what you want to be," said Lucy, slapping her hands into her lap with exasperation and standing up. "I've got to get the potatoes started."

When Lucy had gotten the potatoes peeled, and simmering on the stove, along with the pot of beef stew she was reheating, she took a look at Patrick's essay. "I decided werewolf was good, 'cause it's real scary," he said.

"Looks good," said Lucy, smiling at Patrick's large, childish handwriting and the occasional mis-spelling. She nodded with approval as she tucked the paper into his folder, hoping that Patrick wouldn't insist on a *wharewolf* costume.

The next morning, she stopped at the drug-store on her way to work and discovered that they were completely out of werewolf costumes. Also pi-rates, zombies, and superheroes. All that was left was Casper the Ghost and Lucy knew that would definitely not fly with Patrick. She'd have to take him shopping after school at the nearest big box store, which happened to be some ways along Route 1 in South Williston.

So as soon as he got off the bus she bundled him into the car and off they went, in search of a costume. It was a bit of a drive to South Williston, but the weather was bright and the roads were clear and they made good time. The store was brand-new, and Lucy had mixed feelings as she parked the car and helped Patrick out of his seat belt, which had gotten stuck. It was certainly convenient to have the gigantic store, which sold everything under the sun at very good prices, but it didn't seem very Maine somehow, squatting alongside the road in the middle of a huge parking lot. "What did we do before we had it?" people asked, but it seemed to Lucy that people had managed pretty well. Instead of the cheap imported work boots that the big box store sold, people bought more expensive, but better made work boots from Country Cousins, which lasted forever and could even be repaired. And as for Halloween costumes, well, people improvised and got creative, making them from scratch.

"Do you think they'll have werewolf costumes?" asked Patrick, interrupting her thoughts.

"I hope so," she said, as they crossed the immense parking lot and approached the huge brick monolith. Stepping through the doors, which opened automatically, Lucy felt for a moment as if she were being swallowed up.

Dazzled by the bright lights inside, Lucy took Patrick's hand and headed for the area where seasonal merchandise was displayed. There, amazingly, they found one lonely werewolf costume, in Patrick's size.

Nearby, she noticed a display of laundry detergent, her brand, at a fabulous price. And beyond that, some rather attractive sweaters, amazingly cheap. "Okay," she said, grabbing a couple of jugs of detergent, "we're going to need a cart."

Lucy and Patrick had no trouble at all filling the cart, topping it off with a large pumpkin, planning to add it to the one she'd already bought at the

IGA. This one was half the price that she'd paid for the first, and a fraction of the price out at Mac-Donald's farm stand, where you had to pick your own. Lucy was terribly pleased with her shopping when she got in line at the checkout. She expected a hefty bill, but she was getting excellent value, and wouldn't need to buy detergent, or coffee, or toilet paper anytime soon.

She was checking the balance in her checking account when there was a fuss at the next checkout lane. She turned to see what the matter was and saw that someone had fainted, collapsed on the industrial tile floor.

The store manager was already there, bending over the woman, who was protesting in a weak voice that she was really all right.

"Take your time, there's no rush," advised the manager, a young guy wearing the company's ugly yellow polo shirt.

"Really, if you'll just give me a hand . . ."

The manager took her hand, and also her elbow, and gently helped her to her feet, where she supported herself by grabbing the handle of her shopping cart and hanging on for dear life. "I'm fine," she said.

Lucy was quite sure the stricken woman was Heather Moon, whom she'd glimpsed the other day, and she sure didn't look fine. She was ashen faced, and terribly thin, with long, stringy hair that was prematurely gray, and dressed in baggy washed-out pants and shirt that looked like pajamas. Her hands, which were gripping the cart handle, were red and chapped looking, and as she stepped forward in the line she seemed to be in pain. The manager watched for a moment, then went to answer the flashing light at checkout number thirteen.

"Perhaps you remember me," said Lucy, speaking to her. "I stopped by your house the other day and spoke to your husband."

"Yes?" Heather looked at her blankly.

"Well, I'm from Tinker's Cove and if you need a ride home, or some help . . ."

"Thank you," she said, pushing the cart forward with a little jerk. "But I'll be fine. My husband is waiting for me outside."

"Okay," said Lucy, as Patrick began unloading their cart onto the conveyor belt. "But if you need anything, well, that's what neighbors are for."

Heather didn't answer, but reached for a gallon jug of cider and struggled to lift it. "Here, let me help," said the man in line behind her, taking it and setting it on the checkout counter.

Lucy's attention was taken by her own order, and when she'd finished paying and gotten her receipt, Heather was already gone. Maybe she'd see her in the parking lot, she thought, concerned for the frail woman's welfare, but when they stepped outside there was no sign of Heather, or Ty Moon.

"Who was that lady?" asked Patrick, as they headed for the car.

"She lives in the house by the school, the one the kids think is haunted."

"I guess she's a ghost then," said Patrick. "She sure looked like one."

"She didn't look well," said Lucy, opening the rear hatch. "I hope she's okay."

Chapter Four

On Saturday morning Lucy dropped Patrick off at the field at nine o'clock for his first soccer game. She was supposed to take some photos of Halloween decorations for the paper and had a couple of errands she had to do, planning to tick them off her list as quickly as possible in order to catch as much of the game as she could. She was organizing her route in her mind, first the bank, then the hardware store and finally, the post office, when she braked at the corner of School Street. The Moon house loomed opposite, as dilapidated as ever, which she had to admit kind of worked for the season. Why bother with Halloween decorations when you already had a very scary, spooky-looking haunted house?

A couple of maple trees on the street had turned and were bright spots of color, yellow and red, which contrasted sharply with the Moon house's weathered gray clapboards. Next door, Franny Small's neat little ranch sported window boxes loaded with bronze chrysanthemums, a huge pumpkin sat on the stoop, and a decorative scarecrow hung on the door. The other neighbor had gone big-time, with a huge inflatable pumpkin that had a little ghost that popped in and out. And as if that wasn't enough, they also had a large inflated dragon and a skeleton that dangled from an upstairs window.

As she drove through town she noticed almost every house had some sort of seasonal decoration, and some people went all out, constructing fake graveyards populated with ghoulish figures in the front yards. One display featured a zombie bride and groom, which Lucy decided was definitely newsworthy, so she parked the car and snapped a photo for the paper. Continuing down the street on foot she took a few more pictures, capturing a witch peering out a window, a pair of pumpkin-headed harvest figures seated on a porch, and another porch boasting a huge spider's web with a truly hideous, extremely large spider lurking in its middle. That one made her cringe and she deleted it, fearful that Ted would put it right on the front page, terrifying any readers who were afraid of spiders.

Checking that task off her to-do list, she hurried back to the car and headed for Main Street, where she quickly accomplished the rest of her errands. Back at the field she learned the second half had just started and neither Patrick's Coastal Collision team, nor their opponents, Marzetti's IGA, had scored.

"It's funny watching them play. I'm not sure they know the rules of the game," confided her informant, a perky young mom in workout pants. "I'm Karen Halmstad," she said, introducing herself. "I know you're Lucy Stone. I saw you at the selectmen's meeting."

"Nice to meet you. I think my grandson, Patrick, is friends with your son."

"Henry. He's friends with everybody," said Karen.

"Do you know Lori? Lori Johnson?" she asked, introducing another mom Lucy recognized from the meeting. "Her daughter Caitlin is in the goal."

Lucy nodded, smiling broadly. "Hi." It was a bit weird, and she experienced a certain sense of déjà vu, recalling all the games she had watched her kids play along with her friends, Sue, Pam, and Rachel, all gathered together on the sidelines. Now she was the grandmother, chatting with the young moms.

"Patrick is quite a good player," said Lori, when Patrick blocked an opponent's kick and passed the ball to a teammate. "Most of these kids don't have a clue about passing; they just want to get the ball and head for the goal themselves."

"Mostly they just want to get the ball," agreed Karen, as Janet Nowicki blew her whistle and explained the offsides rule to the players.

"Good luck with that," laughed Lori, as play resumed. "All they can think about is Halloween. Henry's been practicing his Transylvanian accent for weeks."

"Caitlin's going to be a princess. Her father suspects she thinks she really is a princess who belongs in a castle but was somehow cursed and ended up with us. Kind of like Snow White with the dwarves, and we're the dwarves."

"Or Cinderella," offered Lucy, who had experienced a similar situation with Elizabeth. "Especially when it comes to doing the dishes."

"Especially then," agreed Lori.

"Henry's fascinated with the haunted house," said Karen, casting a glance toward the Moon house. "I've told him to stay away, but I'm afraid he's going to get himself into trouble."

"Have you met the Moons?" asked Lucy.

"Briefly," snorted Karen. "I tried to do the good neighbor thing, baked an apple cake for them, and introduced myself. They pretty much shut the door in my face."

"They didn't want your apple cake? The one with sour cream?" asked Lori, incredulous.

"Nope. They're on diets."

"I don't think she needs a diet," said Lucy, remembering how thin Heather looked at the big box store. "I saw her in South Williston the other day. She looked awful."

"I've got my suspicions about him," said Karen. "He comes and goes, but she hardly ever comes out of the house." She paused. "I can't imagine what she does in there all day. The windows are as filthy as ever, she hasn't touched the curtains, and they keep the raggedy old things closed all the time."

"Do you think he's abusive?" asked Lori.

"I don't know," Karen said with a shrug, as a cry went up from the gathered parents. "Look! Patrick's got the ball!"

Lucy watched, amazed, as Patrick deftly maneuvered the ball down the field and whacked it right into the goal. "Way to go!" she yelled, excited for him, and joining the other cries of approval. His teammates were gathered around, high-fiving him, and Janet was blowing her whistle, startling a huge flock of starlings that had roosted in the trees around the field. They rose up in a huge cloud and flew off. It was then that Lucy noticed the clouds that were moving in, dimming the bright morning sun.

"I don't like those birds," said Lori, with a shudder. "They remind me of that movie."

"*The Birds?* Yeah," agreed Karen. "And that house, it's right out of *Psycho.*"

"And it looks like we're in for some rain," said Lucy, casting her eyes skyward. "I hope we get the game in."

The sky darkened steadily as the game progressed, and the wind picked up, catching the fallen leaves and blowing them every which way. When Janet blew the final whistle, the score remained one-nil and the Coastal Collision team had won their first game. There was no time for congratulations, however, as the rain started to fall in sheets and everyone dashed for cover. Lucy and Patrick were soaked and chilled when they reached the car.

"Whew! That was crazy," she exclaimed, turning on the ignition and firing up the heater.

"I got a goal!" exulted Patrick. "I can't wait to tell Dad."

"It was a great game, Patrick. Did you have fun?"

"Yeah. It was super." He was silent for a moment, then spoke up. "I'm really hungry."

"I bet you are," laughed Lucy. "We'll have lunch as soon as we get home. Sara promised to make her famous sloppy joes."

She released the brake and backed out of her parking spot, joining the line of SUVs and pickups exiting the lot. The rain was coming down in buckets, the wind was tossing the trees, sending the falling leaves whirling every which way, and there were occasional bursts of thunder and lightning. Lucy was feeling uneasy about falling branches on the ride home, and wishing they were already safe at home, when she finally reached the stop sign. She merely tapped the brakes—the road was clear and she wanted to keep moving—when a flash of light caught her eyes.

It wasn't lightning, she realized; it was coming from the Moon house. As she watched, it happened again, a burst of light from the window at the top of the tower.

"Did you see that?"

"What?" asked Patrick.

The driver behind her honked, and she turned onto the road. "Nothing, I guess," she said, wondering if she'd really seen what she thought she'd seen. "Let's get home!"

The car wasn't heating up as quickly as she would have liked, and Lucy was worried about Patrick, sitting there on the back seat. He was only wearing his soccer uniform, shorts and a T-shirt, having refused to wear a jacket or sweatshirt. "I'll get too hot," he'd insisted, and she hadn't wanted to press the issue. Fortunately, it was a short trip home and a nice, hot lunch was waiting for them in the cozy old farmhouse.

"I'm cold," complained Patrick. "Can you turn the heat up?"

"It's up as far as it will go," said Lucy, tempted to remind him he could have worn his sweatshirt, or even a water-repellent fleece jacket. "We'll be home soon and the sloppy joes will warm you right up."

It was a bit of a disappointment when they made the mad dash through the rain into the house and discovered the kitchen was dark and there were no sloppy joes. No delicious spicy tomato and beef aroma, no toasty buns, nothing but a cold stove. Lucy switched on the light, sent Patrick upstairs to change into warm clothes, and went in search of Sara. She found her daughter lying on the sofa in the family room, watching *The Handmaid's Tale.*

"What happened to lunch?" asked Lucy.

"Oh, sorry, Mom. I got caught up in the show. This is scary stuff."

"I thought you had a lot of work to do preparing for orals. Shouldn't you be studying?"

Sara's tone was defensive. "Look, I can't spend every minute of my life studying, can I? I need some time for myself, right?"

Lucy didn't want the argument to escalate, so she decided on a tactical retreat. "Well, sure, but you could have made the sloppy joes. Cooking is relaxing and creative, too. Meditative even."

"Maybe if you're doing some fancy Julia Child dish, but sloppy joes? Come on, Mom. That's not creative; that's following directions on a foil packet."

Lucy's good intentions were weakening. "It would have been a big help to me, especially since you knew I was going to be out all morning. And now, because of the rain, Patrick and I are cold and wet and hungry."

"So what's the big deal?" She flicked off the TV and stood up. "I'll make your sloppy joes for you. Will that make you happy?"

"It'll be a start," said Lucy, with a sigh. "Patrick and I are going to put on some dry clothes."

The sloppy joes weren't ready when Lucy and Patrick had changed into warm clothes; Sara hadn't noticed the thawed package of hamburger meat in the refrigerator and was instead cooking up a frozen block of ground beef, to which she'd added chopped onions. The meat was only half cooked and the onions were burning.

"Oh, my word," exclaimed Lucy, angrily grabbing the pan and dumping the stinky mess into the trash.

"What can I eat?" asked Patrick, looking on with a stricken expression.

"I'll make grilled cheese and tomato soup. How about that? And in the meantime, you can have a glass of milk and some cookies. Dessert first."

"Well, I know when I'm not appreciated," griped Sara. "I think I'll grab something to eat on my way to the library."

Lucy knew she should try to smooth Sara's ruffled feathers, but somehow she couldn't muster the will to do it. "Good idea," she snapped, pouring a glass of milk for Patrick.

Sara put on her rain slicker, grabbed her book bag and umbrella, yanked the door open, and marched out, giving it a good slam behind her.

"What's the matter with Sara?" asked Patrick, prying apart the two halves of an Oreo.

"I suspect it's a guilty conscience," said Lucy, snapping the lid off a can of tomato soup and dumping the contents into a pan.

After lunch, Patrick settled down with his Legos and Lucy loaded the washer with their wet clothes. The rain was still coming down hard, much too hard to even contemplate any outdoor activities, so Lucy settled herself on the sofa and looked for a free movie. *Gaslight* was just starting, so she settled in to watch one of her favorite films.

Golly gee, Ingrid Bergman was gorgeous, her skin luminescent and glowing even in black and white. Charles Boyer, who played her husband, was charming and suave, but always with that little touch of menace. Not someone you could trust, thought Lucy, as she was caught up yet again in the unfolding story of an innocent young wife whose husband attempts to drive her mad.

Lucy found herself holding her breath as the gaslights in the house dimmed and brightened, terrifying poor Ingrid Bergman when she was alone in the house. Was it really happening? Was she imagining it? Was she truly going out of her mind? Thank goodness for Joseph Cotten, the Scotland Yard inspector who saves Ingrid in the end.

Clicking off the TV, Lucy noticed that the rain had stopped, but it was still cloudy, wet, and windy outside. She went upstairs to check on Patrick, finding him happily occupied installing Batman in his newly constructed Lego bat cave.

Returning to the kitchen, she went downstairs to the cellar to put the washed clothes in the dryer. She was just heading upstairs when the ceiling light went out, plunging the cellar into darkness and giving her a momentary fright. Simply a blown light bulb, she told herself, intending to ask Bill to change it.

She made her way carefully up the darkened stairs, amused by the coincidence. Here she'd been watching *Gaslight* and what should happen? The cellar light went out. It would make a cute story to tell Bill at dinner.

Which reminded her, she really needed to get dinner started.

She was scrubbing potatoes when she remembered that odd flashing light she'd seen in the tower of the Moon house. It wasn't like a light going on and off; it was much brighter than that. More like a strobe, or a flash from some sort of explosion.

She thought of Heather Moon, who seemed so frail and helpless, actually in much worse shape than poor Ingrid Bergman in the movie. Was that what was happening? she wondered. Was Ty Moon engaged in a diabolical plan to destroy his wife's health, or sanity? The more she thought about it, the more likely it seemed. He'd been so curt and abrupt when she'd dropped by that it had been impossible for her to talk to Heather. And when she had encountered Heather at the store, the poor thing had seemed terribly frightened. What was she afraid of?

"Grandma, I'm hungry." A little voice broke into Lucy's thoughts. Patrick had come downstairs and was eyeing the cookie jar, which Lucy knew was empty.

"How about popcorn and a movie?" she suggested.

"With butter?"

"With lots of butter!"

Chapter Five

Somehow Lucy had forgotten how challenging it was to combine child care with a job, even one as flexible as her part-time position at the *Pennysaver*. These days, as she struggled to make Patrick's lunch every morning, spent hours helping him with homework, and shouldered the constant task of chauffeuring him to soccer practices and games, she wondered how she'd ever managed with four kids. She felt as if she was under a curfew, having to be home by three-thirty to meet the school bus. And then there were all the extras: baking something for the youth soccer bake sale, collecting box tops, selling wrapping paper to the neighbors. Of course, she reminded herself, she'd been much younger then and had a lot more energy.

As the clock ticked by on Tuesday afternoon, and facing a noon deadline on Wednesday, Lucy was faced with a mountain of work. Work that she'd put off in order to meet Patrick's needs. That was the big drawback with part-time work, she decided, as she tackled the backlog. It was easy to put things off. She was supposed to manage her thirty hours; Ted wasn't looking over her shoulder advising her to write that story as soon as the meeting ended or the interview was completed. And even worse, she still had to interview Officer Sally Kirwan for a feature story Ted wanted about domestic abuse. In fact, she hadn't even called Sally to request an interview, or to schedule it.

Reaching for the phone, she crossed her fingers hoping that Sally was available. The police officers worked shifts to provide twenty-four-hour coverage, and for all she knew Sally might be working nights this week. Her luck held however when the dispatcher put her call through and Sally answered her phone in person.

"Boy, I feel like I've won the lottery," said Lucy. "I was sure I'd get voice mail."

"Close. I was just on my way out," said Sally.

"Oh, gosh. Any chance I can interview you today? It's for a series on domestic abuse."

"Today? I'm on call until three, when my shift ends. Does that work for you?"

Lucy hesitated; she knew soccer practice had been called off since the field was still too wet for play, and Patrick would be coming home on the school bus.

"I'll make it work," said Lucy, intending to have Bill or Sara meet the bus. Perhaps Bill could leave work a bit early, or Sara could study at home since she had no classes on Tuesday afternoon.

Ending the call, Lucy first tried Bill, who was in the final stages of enlarging a Craftsman-style bungalow for a young banker and his growing family. "Gosh, Lucy, I can't leave today. They're installing the kitchen cabinets and I have to make sure they're the right ones and that they go in the right places."

"I understand," said Lucy. She had an old-fashioned notion that a wife wasn't supposed to interfere with her husband's career, and she found it hard to shake. Her job wasn't as important, she didn't make as much money as Bill, so it usually fell to her to juggle her schedule. Which hadn't actually been much of a problem until Patrick came to stay.

That left Sara. Not her first choice, considering how difficult she'd been lately. This time, when she called, she did get voice mail. No problem, she told herself. Sara always had Tuesday afternoons free. She was probably just in a noisy place, like the student union, and didn't hear her phone. Sara was obsessive about checking her messages, so it would be okay to leave one.

"Hi, Sara. I need to ask a big favor. I've got an interview at three o'clock so could you please be home by three-thirty to meet Patrick's school bus. I don't want him left alone, so if you can't make it, send me a text, okay. Thanks."

Somewhat uneasy, Lucy buckled down and wrote up an account of the selectmen's meeting, and another including the finance committee's projected town budget. At ten to three she checked her phone and found no message from Sara, so she packed up and left the office to go to the police station across the street.

Sally met her in the anteroom, where the dispatcher sat behind a solid sheet of thick plexiglass and communicated to visitors through a speaker system.

"I thought I'd greet you myself," said Sally. "The station isn't very welcoming."

"Better safe than sorry," said Lucy, giving the dispatcher a smile and a wave. It was Jodie Kirwan, a young member of the Kirwan clan that filled most of the jobs in the town's fire and police departments. Lucy had seen Jodie at the soccer field, cheering on her son Angus, who was on Patrick's team.

Sally led her into a conference room, where they took seats at the end of the long table. Lucy was quick to thank Sally for making time to see her.

"No problem, Lucy. I'm glad you're doing this story. Family violence is on the uptick; families are under so much pressure these days. Wage stagnation's a big part of it; a lot of folks are working two or three jobs and they're not quite making enough to pay all the bills. All it takes is a broken-down car or an emergency room visit, and they're thrown into a tailspin. Then you throw in opioid addiction and mental health issues, it's a toxic mess, and it's usually the wife or the kids who pay the price."

"So what's the department doing? What services are available?" asked Lucy.

"First of all is education. I spend a lot of time speaking at the high school, and for all sorts of groups: schools, church groups, clubs, organizations. A lot of people, kids especially, don't recognize abuse for what it is. They think it's okay if Dad loses his temper once in a while, or a young woman thinks it's a sign of affection when her boyfriend wants to keep her all to himself and discourages outside relationships. There's a misconception that it's only abuse if the victim is physically injured, but there's also emotional abuse that's every bit as damaging.

"Secondly, I'm working with the other officers in the department to set up protocols for dealing with victims and abusers. There's been a lot of focus on supporting victims of rape, and that's important, but other victims need support, too. We're developing ways of intervening in domestic situations that de-escalate the event, we're starting to rethink some of our approaches to the accused abusers, too.

"And finally, we're partnering with other towns in the county to establish a shelter for victims of abuse. Up 'til now the best we've been able to do is advise victims to get restraining orders or to move in with relatives, which sometimes only makes things worse. This shelter will provide protection for abuse victims, provide meals and comfortable accommodations for women and their children, and will offer counseling and legal assistance. We hope to have it up and running by the new year."

"That sounds great," said Lucy. "One last question: What should a person do if they suspect someone, a neighbor or relative perhaps, is being abused? Should they report it to the police?"

"That's a tough one," replied Sally, as Lucy felt her phone vibrating in her pocket, announcing an incoming text. "Making a police report about someone, whether it's a neighbor or relative, is really a last resort. It's preferable to reach out to the victim in an unthreatening, non-confrontational way to let them know that help is available. And they need to know that this is a process; it can be very difficult for a victim to overcome denial and recognize what's really going on. It's important to remember that victims may love their abusers, in spite of the abuse, and they may not want to get the abuser in trouble."

"Wow, I hadn't thought of that," said Lucy, pulling her phone out and discovering that Sara had sent her a text. **Sorry, I've got a meeting.**

Lucy checked her watch: three twenty-five. "Oh, gosh, I've got to run. School bus."

"Give me a minute. I've got some information for you, I've just got to pull it out."

"Can't," said Lucy, her heart beating furiously. "My daughter let me down and I've got to get home to meet the school bus."

"No problem. I'll drop it at the *Pennysaver* on my way home," said Sally.

Lucy was overcome with gratitude. "Thanks a million," she yelled over her shoulder. Then she was through the door, down the hall, out to the sidewalk, and dashing across the street to her car. "Please, please, be late today," she prayed, as she slapped on the turn signal and pulled out onto Main Street.

She was lucky and just hit the town's single traffic light on orange, sailing beneath as it switched to red. Then seeing that the highway was clear she merely tapped the brakes at the stop sign and zoomed ahead, cruising along at ten miles above the speed limit. Ten was okay, right? She wouldn't get stopped for ten; people did it all the time. And she knew all the cops; they'd understand that she was in a hurry to get home for Patrick.

It was three thirty-five when she reached the cutoff for Red Top Road, but that was only minutes from the house. She whizzed round the curve, braking as little as possible, until she spotted the huge dump truck that was laboring up the hill and slammed them on, causing the SUV to shimmy. This was going to take forever, she realized, noticing that the dump truck was only going eight miles per hour. Could she pass? She pulled out to get a peek and was almost creamed by a pickup truck; passing was clearly not an option on the winding, hilly road.

She was growing frantic at the slow pace, hoping against hope that the school bus was late today. There was a new policy requiring that all students under ten years of age be met by an approved adult at the bus stop, or the driver was not to let them off. They would be returned to the school until an approved adult could pick them up, and the incident would be reported to the child welfare authorities for review.

She could just imagine Molly's reaction if that happened. And of course it would have to be included in the weekly police report that was the *Pennysaver*'s most popular feature. "Spare me," moaned Lucy, as the truck finally made it over the hump at the top of Red Top Road. From there Lucy had a clear view of her house, and the school bus that was approaching from the opposite side of the road. The yellow lights were flashing; it was almost at her driveway. They switched to red, and Lucy pulled into the oncoming lane and approached it, with her own hazard lights on. Reaching her driveway she pulled in, braked, and got out of the SUV.

The doors of the bus opened, and Patrick stepped out. "Close call," said the driver, Nancy Sullivan, with an amused smile.

"I was terrified you wouldn't let him off," she said, taking Patrick's backpack.

"How long have I been driving this route?" asked Nancy.

"Like forever," said Lucy, remembering Toby's first day of school, and how anxious she'd been when he boarded the big yellow bus.

"I know there's a reason for that new policy, but I intend to use my judgment. I knew you'd be home soon. And Patrick's a good kid; he wouldn't get himself into trouble."

For the second time that day Lucy felt a surge of gratitude. "Thanks. Thanks for trusting me."

"No problem." The doors closed, and the bus went on its way.

"So, Patrick, how was school?"

"Okay," he said, as they walked to the house. "And I have a project. It's for the whole family to do. We're supposed to make up a Halloween board game. That'll be fun, won't it?"

"Tons," said Lucy, who didn't think it would be fun at all.

Chapter Six

"So when is this project due?" asked Lucy, as they climbed the porch steps.

"For the class Halloween party, on Halloween, of course." Patrick's tone implied she really ought to be aware of this bit of information.

Lucy wasn't about to defend herself to an eight-year-old. "Do you have any ideas for this game?" she asked, opening the kitchen door.

"Oh, yeah!" he replied, shrugging out of his jacket and dropping it on the floor, and then kicking off his shoes. "There'll be monsters and witches and vampires."

"Sounds great," said Lucy, pointing to the jacket and shoes.

"Oh, sorry," he said, quickly scooping them up. He dropped the shoes in the basket on the floor by the door and hung his jacket on one of the low coat hooks, which Bill had installed at child height years ago for their own brood.

He sat at the kitchen table, waiting for his snack, while Lucy flipped through the papers in his folder. She found several worksheets for homework, and an orange-colored sheet enthusiastically announcing the game contest as a "fun family project." What exactly did that mean? she wondered. So, all of a sudden, was it okay for parents to help with projects? Was it expected?

She poured a glass of milk, filled a plate with several chocolate-chip cookies, and sat down opposite him. "How about something based on Chutes and Ladders?" she suggested.

Patrick took a cookie. "That's boring."

"You could make it three-dimensional, with pop-up stairs. . . ." Despite her initial resistance, she was becoming somewhat interested in the project.

"And hidden rooms!" he added, giving her a clear view of his chocolate-chip-filled mouth.

"We'll work on it later," she said, presenting him with the math sheet. "But first, fractions."

Patrick took a big swallow of milk, and took another cookie, fortifying himself for the ordeal.

Lucy was watching her weight, but halfway through the sheet of math problems she found herself nibbling on a cookie. It was frustrating, and boring, to try to help Patrick understand the concepts that seemed so obvious to her. It seemed ridiculous to have to keep explaining about halves and quarters and thirds over and over. Why couldn't he remember?

And while part of her brain was occupied with fractions, another part was fretting about Heather Moon. Officer Sally had given her good advice about reaching out in a friendly, non-threatening way, but it was hard to see exactly how she could do that. Visitors certainly weren't encouraged at the house, and whenever she had encountered Heather she hadn't seemed eager to chat. In fact, thought Lucy, the couple had resisted any and all neighborly efforts to welcome them.

Patrick was done with homework and was watching TV when Bill came home. Lucy was bent over double, plucking silverware from the little slots in the dishwasher's silverware rack, and he grabbed her by her hips and pressed himself against her bottom. She responded by twisting around and waving a serving spoon in his face.

"Is that any way to greet a man when he comes home from a hard day's work?" he grumbled, opening the fridge and grabbing a beer.

"You took me by surprise when you grabbed me from behind," she said, glaring at him. "Is that any way to treat a person? I'm not just here for your pleasure, you know."

"I sure do know," said Bill, giving her a meaningful look. "There hasn't been much *pleasure* around here at all. You're always too tired, or have a headache, or have to run a load of wash or pack a lunch for Patrick. . . ."

"Uh, yeah," said Lucy. "I do have to do all those things, and more, and it does make me tired and sometimes, most of the time, I've got a headache."

"Well, maybe you should see the doctor," suggested Bill, popping the tab on his beer.

"Well, I would, if I could find a spare minute, but I seem to spend an awful lot of time at the soccer field," countered Lucy, ripping open a package of pork chops. She grabbed a black cast-iron skillet from its hook and slammed it onto the stove, twisting the knob and lighting the burner. "It would be a big help to me if you could take over soccer duty, at least some of the time."

Bill took a long swallow of beer. "Gee, Lucy, I

wish I could, but I'm really stretched to the limit finishing up this addition by Thanksgiving."

Lucy sighed. "Well, Patrick has to make a Halloween board game for a school project; it's supposed to be a family fun project. Maybe you could help him with it? Sort of a spooky three-D version of Chutes and Ladders. You're clever with your hands, and I really don't want him using a box cutter without supervision."

"No can do, Lucy. I've got to work on some plans tonight and call some subs, and the Celtics are playing the Nuggets. . . ."

Lucy considered pointing out that he could DVR the basketball game to watch later while she shook some Tater Tots onto a pan and shoved them into the oven, but decided it wasn't worth the fight. She needed to save her energy. She knew from past experience that she'd be wrestling with cardboard, folding construction paper into stairs, and cutting out ghosts and goblins late into the night.

"Rough night?" asked Phyllis by way of greeting when Lucy got to work on Wednesday morning.

"School project," said Lucy, yawning.

"Those are the worst," agreed Phyllis. While she and her husband, Wilf, had married late in life and didn't have any children of their own, the couple had recently taken in their niece Elfrida's brood when she had been wrongly accused of murder. Elfrida had eventually been cleared of all charges, but Wilf and Phyllis were still recovering emotionally from the experience of caring for five kids.

"Officer Sally dropped this off for you," said Phyllis, handing her a manila envelope. Opening it, Lucy found it contained the promised information about abusive relationships. Fueled by coffee, she quickly wrapped up that story and went on to recap a couple of meetings, wrote up the Town Hall News roundup, and came up with some clever headlines and captions for her Halloween photos.

"Good work, Lucy," said Ted, offering her a rare word of praise when he pressed send and shipped the paper off to the printer a few minutes shy of the noon deadline. "Your interview with Officer Sally was really fine. Her passion for her job really came through. She really wants to make a difference."

"The statistics were shocking," said Lucy. "I had no idea it was such a big problem because the police don't list domestic incidents in their weekly log for the paper. They say it's because of their policy to protect the victim's privacy."

"Maybe this will make more people aware of what's going on, and if they suspect a neighbor is being abused they will reach out," said Phyllis. "I know I wish I'd done more when Elfrida was with Angie's father. She only told me about it after he got killed in that motorcycle accident."

"It's hard to know what to do if all you've got is a feeling that something isn't quite right," agreed Lucy, thinking of Heather Moon.

"The neighbors even called and told me they were always fighting; there were raised voices and curses. . . ."

Lucy thought of the noises the neighborhood kids had reported hearing from the Moons' house, and how Heather seemed to be controlled by her husband. Impulsively, thinking she'd give it a shot, she called directory assistance and, much to her surprise since landlines were going the way of the dodo, was given a phone number for the Moons. Sensing that she might be on a roll, she dialed it, but only got voice mail. The voice inviting her to leave a message was the standard one that came with phone service; the Moons hadn't bothered to make their own personal recording.

Lucy was tired and had a small headache when she left the office, and considered using her free afternoon to take a nap. But if she went home, she knew she'd end up doing laundry and scrubbing the bathtub and most probably putting the finishing touches on Patrick's family fun project. Then there was grocery shopping; it seemed that even if she shopped every day she couldn't satisfy Patrick's enormous appetite. Come to think of appetites, she realized she was hungry. Really hungry, which was probably why she had that headache. She hadn't had time for breakfast; so far today she'd had nothing but black coffee, and lots of it.

Lunch, she decided, was what she needed. And why not treat herself to a quarter-pounder and a shake at McDonald's? Maybe even with fries. She really shouldn't, but she knew she was going to. She deserved a break, she thought to herself, looking forward to enjoying a guilty, high-calorie, pleasure. She was zipping along School Street, on her way to McDonald's when the Moon house loomed into sight.

Everything people said was true, she thought, slowing the car. No improvements had been attempted. If anything, the house looked worse than ever since it now had a pile of soggy moving cartons left in the driveway, as well as a few pieces of unwanted furniture: a broken chair, a bulky old TV, and a coffee table with a cracked glass top. There was also a pair of brand-new plastic garbage cans in front of the dilapidated old garage. Sometimes, she knew, it came as a surprise to newcomers to learn that the town did not provide trash pickup service. Residents were expected to take their trash to the disposal area themselves, and woe to those who didn't separate cans from glass bottles, or mixed magazines in with their newspapers. Someone ought to tell them that those cartons and bits of furniture would not be collected anytime soon.

Now that she thought about it, maybe she should be that someone. It would be a good excuse for stopping by the house, and maybe she could even drop off one of Officer Sally's pamphlets. Or even better, she thought, maybe she could invite Heather to join her for lunch at McDonald's.

By now she'd stopped the car and pulled up to the curb, a few feet from the Moons' driveway. Maybe it was kind of pathetic, inviting someone to lunch at McDonald's. The Moons had lived in Portland, known for its foodie scene, where every block had a trendy restaurant or a microbrewery. Maybe she should suggest the diner down the road, known far and wide for its walnut pie? Or maybe she should just feel out the situation and see what happened?

Lucy tucked a couple of Officer Sally's pamphlets into her purse, took a deep breath, and climbed out of the car. Once again faced with two doors, both facing the street, she wasn't sure which door to try. She decided to approach the back door, in the kitchen ell, because that's the door most townspeople used, and here she was, attempting to offer advice on local customs. Upon reaching the windowed door, and seeing once again the ratty old curtain, Lucy hesitated. This was probably a bad idea, but she plucked up her courage and knocked anyway.

The curtain twitched, and she caught a glimpse of Heather, peeking out at her. Lucy smiled and gave a friendly wave, but the door was not opened. She waited a moment or two, then turned to go. That was when she heard the door open and looked back to see Ty Moon standing there, glaring at her. "What do you want?" he demanded, angrily.

Talk about starting off on the wrong foot! Was this any way to treat a caller? Someone who simply wanted to be friendly? Her dander rose and she stood her ground; this time she wasn't going to scurry away.

"Well, I happened to be passing by, and I noticed you've got all this trash sitting out here."

"So what's it to you?" said Ty, beginning to close the door.

"Hold on a minute. I'm just trying to help," said Lucy, surprising herself with her authoritative tone. "I'm Lucy Stone and I work for the local paper. You're the Moons and you're new in town. Everybody knows, in fact, and they're all waiting to see what you do with this old place. But I want to let you know that you could get cited and even fined for that mess in your driveway. There's no trash pickup in this town."

Ty opened the door wide. "What?" he asked, a surprised expression on his face.

"No trash pickup. You have to take your stuff to the disposal area."

"I do?"

"Yeah. And you'll need a sticker or they won't take your trash."

Ty was puzzled. "Sticker?"

"Yeah. You put it on your car. Left front bumper."

"And where do you get one of these stickers?"

"Town hall." She paused. "Fifty dollars."

"The sticker costs fifty dollars?"

"Yeah. And there's rules. When you get the sticker they'll give you an information sheet about recycling. You have to separate newspapers, glass, and cans."

"So you're telling me I have to sort my garbage and take it to this disposal area myself and I have to pay for the privilege of doing it?"

"The sticker's good for a whole year," said Lucy. "Private pickup costs that much for one month."

"So there is private pickup?" Ty was interested.

"Sure. There's a couple of haulers; you see their trucks around town." She paused, deciding to plunge into the deep end. "Why don't you have lunch with me? Your wife, too. My treat. Then I could explain all about our town regulations."

Lucy had barely finished speaking when she realized she'd made a big mistake and gone too far. Ty's face hardened, he straightened his shoulders, and shook his head. "I don't know what your game is, but we're not interested."

"Game?" Lucy was quick to defend herself. "I'm just trying to be a good neighbor. Welcome the stranger."

"We just want to be left alone." Ty started to shut the door.

"Maybe you should let your wife speak for her-self," said Lucy.

Ty's face grew red and he started to yell, raising his clenched fist. "What's the matter with you? Stop pestering us! Get out of here. Get off my property!"

"Okay," said Lucy, with a shrug. "No problem. I was just trying to be helpful."

"You're just snooping around, you're a nosy busybody! Stay away and don't come back or I'll. I'll . . ." And with that, he slammed the door in her face.

Turning, she walked down the driveway to her car, and got in. Looking back, she saw the door was shut tight, but the curtain twitched and she knew he was watching, to make sure she left. She was tempted to slip a couple of the brochures into the mailbox, but figured he'd only come roaring out of the house and would grab them out of her hands and tear them up. Or even worse, she guessed, although he hadn't actually finished his threatening sentence.

She thought of Sally's advice, all those carefully crafted social work techniques designed to develop trust and offer the support that would enable an abuse victim to recognize the cycle of violence and the confidence to take action to end it. Well, it all sounded great, but what were you supposed to do when the suspected abuser wouldn't even let you speak to the victim?

Chapter Seven

Ty's insults were still ringing in Lucy's ears when she ordered her quarter-pounder with cheese, chocolate shake, and fries, and carried her zillion-calorie meal to a corner table. McDonald's wasn't very crowded, even though it was lunchtime, but there were a few moms with young preschoolers, and a handful of retirees. She unwrapped her meal, setting it all on the paper that had wrapped the hamburger, mindful of the possibility of hostile microbes. When had all this started, she wondered, this phobia about microscopic life forms? Her late mother had scoffed at the idea, frequently remarking that "You've got to eat a peck of dirt before you die." It turned out that she was right; it wasn't a microbe that killed her but Alzheimer's.

When Lucy bit into a fry, she didn't hear her mother; she heard Ty Moon yelling at her, calling her a snoop and a nosy busybody. Was that true? As she ate, she was uncomfortably aware that he was at least partially correct. One of the things she loved about working at the *Pennysaver* was the way it allowed her to get to know people by interviewing them, but she knew it went a bit further than that. The job sometimes entailed a bit of digging and investigating to find the truth, and that was the part she loved best. Like uncovering the fact that the chairman of the planning board wanted to change the zoning regulations so he could build an addition to his house that was closer than the current required twenty-foot setback. And then there was the member of the board of health who proposed an amendment to the town's wastewater regulations, arguing that the current rules were placing an undue burden on people living on limited incomes. That was certainly true, Lucy discovered, but she also learned that he planned to build a Laundromat on the town's well field.

It seemed, she concluded as she sipped on her delicious chocolate shake, that she was a snoop and a busybody, but maybe that wasn't such a bad thing after all. Things weren't always what they seemed, and people's motives weren't always pure. Maybe never, she thought, crumpling up a napkin. Even her own motives weren't always clear to her. Did she want to help Heather, because she appeared to be a victim of spousal abuse, or did she want a sensational story for the *Pennysaver?* She hoped it was the former, and not the latter, she thought as she shoved the empty cup and food wrappers into the trash bin.

Checking her watch, she decided she had plenty of time to get some groceries before she had to meet the school bus. Nowadays she was constantly aware of the time, mindful of Patrick's schedule, and she felt as if she was always in a hurry. The days when she could wander off for a long walk in the colorful autumn woods with the dog, taking as long as she liked, were over. Now she was on a strict timetable, and she had practically no time to herself. Instead of spending an evening curled up on the sofa with a book, or watching a TV movie, she had to help Patrick with his homework, make his lunch, lay out his clothes for the morning, and supervise bath and bedtime. It was exhausting and confining, but she was determined not to let it get her down. After all, she adored her grandson and this was a rare opportunity to spend time with him. She was going to enjoy every minute, if it killed her.

At the IGA, she noted with interest that Oreos were still on sale—yippee!—and so was beef stew meat. Grabbing a cart and passing through the floral department she spotted a huge bunch of mums, also on sale, and decided to splurge. Fresh flowers were a luxury, but she figured a few little indulgences were well worth the investment if they helped keep her spirits up. She had buried her nose in the flowers, inhaling their scent, when Franny Small joined her at the display, considering her choices.

"I like mums; they last a long time," observed Franny, pulling a maroon bunch out of the water-filled container.

"I'm going with yellow; they're nice and cheerful," said Lucy, dropping the bunch into a plastic bouquet bag.

"Yellow are cheerful," agreed Franny, "but I think these would look very nice in my copper vase."

"That would look great," said Lucy.

"Maybe I'll need two bunches; the vase is quite

large." She looked at Lucy, furrowing her brow. "Do you think that's too extravagant?"

"Not at all," said Lucy, well aware that Franny didn't need to count her pennies.

"I thought I saw you at my neighbors', the Moons, this morning," said Franny, bagging her flowers and laying them on her cart's kiddie seat.

Lucy didn't want to mention her suspicions about Ty to Franny, who was a notorious gossip, so she simply said she wanted to let them know the town didn't provide trash collection.

"I'll bet he was surprised," said Franny, with a smirk. "I saw him putting all that stuff out in the driveway. What a mess! I was considering telling him myself, but, well, when I took some cookies over, cookies I made myself, they didn't even answer the door. I had to leave them on the steps and, you know what, they never picked them up and they were eaten by raccoons. As for my plate, well, I guess that's gone forever."

"I hope it wasn't a good one," said Lucy, pulling out her shopping list and glancing at it, hoping to send a subtle hint to Franny that she couldn't stand here all day talking.

"No, thank goodness. I pick up pretty plates at estate sales and yard sales, so I don't have to worry that they'll be returned."

"Good idea," said Lucy, thinking she ought to do that, too, as she pushed her cart in the direction of the apples.

"I don't care about the plate," continued Franny, "but it sure made me wonder. You'd think they would have noticed the cookies, but they didn't. It seems as if they hardly ever leave the house. And now there are those flashing lights—have you seen them? From the tower?"

"I have," said Lucy, suddenly interested. "What do you think it is?"

"I haven't any idea," said Franny, raising her eyebrows, "but that's not all. There are terrible noises, too. Blood-curdling screams and cries. . . ."

"What do you think is happening?"

"I dread to think," said Franny, with a pious little nod of her head. "But it sounds absolutely terrible. And there's more. It isn't just those flashing lights; the lights in the whole house dim and grow bright. It's really weird. And it goes on late into the night. It's even awakened me, at one and two in the morning." She pursed her thin lips. "Awful screams, and I'm not sure they were human."

"Do they have animals in there?" asked Lucy.

Franny shrugged her thin shoulders. "I don't think so, but anything's possible. What I do know is that something awful is going on in there. Something diabolical." She turned, spying a pile of winter squash. "Well, it's been nice talking to you, Lucy. Have a nice day."

Diabolical, thought Lucy, making her way to the cereal aisle, and checking her coupon wallet in hopes of a bargain. Patrick seemed to eat a box a day, and the stuff was surprisingly expensive. But today, there was a special and she had coupons, too, so she filled her cart with ten boxes, the maximum allowed. Then she cruised through the store and picked up the other items that she needed, always with an eye for a bargain. When she had everything on her list, she headed for the checkout, where she discovered a bit of a line had formed thanks to Franny Small's insistence that chrysanthemum bunches were five ninety-nine, not six ninety-nine.

Lucy watched with amusement as Dot, the cashier who also happened to be the matriarch of the large Kirwan family, attempted to convince Franny that she was in error. Many had tried, thought Lucy, but few had succeeded, and in the end, Franny got her price.

"Wow. Talk about extortion," commented the person behind her, and Lucy recognized the voice of her friend, Officer Barney Culpepper. The two had become acquainted years ago, when they both served on the town's Cub Scout Pack Committee, and through the years Lucy had found Barney a reliable source on police department issues.

"That's Franny for you," said Lucy, laughing. "She didn't get rich by throwing her money around."

"I bet she's got every cent she ever earned." Barney grinned. "So how are you? I haven't seen you in a while."

"Great. My grandson, Patrick, is staying with us for a few months," said Lucy, pushing her cart ahead.

"I guess that's why you've got ten boxes of cereal in your cart."

"Guilty as charged," said Lucy. "He eats a ton. I guess I forgot how much boys can eat."

"So, is he adjusting to the new school and all?"

"Yeah, but . . ." Lucy lowered her voice. "You know that old haunted-looking house across the street from the school?"

"Sure."

"Well, Franny tells me there's weird screams and flashing lights, all hours of the night, and the new people, the Moons, are really unfriendly. If you've seen the wife, Heather, she doesn't look at all well. It's as if she's being held prisoner by her husband. It's really worrisome since the house is so close to the school, you know. A lot of the moms are worried; they've warned their kids to stay away."

"Has this guy actually threatened anybody?" asked Barney, as Lucy started unloading her cart onto the conveyor.

"Me! He threatened me when I stopped by to let him know there's no trash pickup in town. And that's another thing." She paused, before setting a jar of pickles down. "The place is a mess; there's all sorts of cardboard boxes and old furniture just sitting out there, getting rained on."

Barney scratched his chin thoughtfully. "Well, you do have a bit of a reputation, Lucy," he said, "since you work for the paper."

"It's not just me. Poor Franny tried to give them cookies, but they wouldn't open the door. And she says the sounds she hears coming from the house are positively demonic."

Barney laughed. "Come on, Lucy. You know Franny is a bit old-fashioned. I bet they're just playing jazz."

Lucy was irritated by Barney's dismissive attitude, and plunked down the last item from her cart, a frozen turkey breast. "And what about the lights that dim and brighten?"

"They've probably loosened some light bulbs, from all that dancing to the music," he said.

"Aren't you going to do anything?" demanded Lucy.

"Not unless some laws are broken. Folks deserve their privacy and should be left in peace."

"You'll regret those words," predicted Lucy, as Dot announced her total.

"That'll be ninety-seven forty-two."

"Outrageous," said Lucy, unsure whether she was referring to her grocery bill or to Barney's refusal to take her worries about the Moons seriously. "Outrageous."

Lucy got home with time to spare before the school bus was due, so she got busy unloading the groceries. She had just finished when her phone rang, and she saw that it was Zoe, calling from Paris, and her heart gave a little leap. She hadn't heard from her in some time and was eager to learn how things were going.

"*Bonjour,*" she said, "*comment ça va?*" Lucy knew a little French and loved to use it.

"Awful," replied Zoe. "I hate it here."

Oh, dear, thought Lucy. The very fact that she was speaking English was a bad sign; when Elizabeth went to France she had jabbered away in French to her mother, not always correctly, but enthusiastically, whenever she called home. "So what's the problem?"

"Well, for one thing, they all speak French here, all the time."

"What did you expect?" asked Lucy.

"I hoped to improve my French, sure, but I thought they'd understand English. Doesn't everybody speak at least some English?"

"Not necessarily," said Lucy, "and French is their language. Why shouldn't they speak it?"

"Because it's rude, that's why. And when I speak French they correct me. Can you imagine?"

"Perhaps they're trying to be helpful," suggested Lucy.

"No, Mom. They're putting me down. Like the snotty little server in the café this morning, and when I asked for *plu* milk in my *café au lait* she practically snarled *plussss* at me. Like how am I supposed to know that even though they usually drop the ends of words, they don't always do it?"

"Maybe you could try listening to people," advised Lucy.

"I try, Mom, I do try, but it would be so much simpler if they just spoke English."

Lucy found it hard to argue with Zoe's point, so she changed the subject. "How's Elizabeth? Are you two getting along?" Zoe was actually staying with her older sister in her apartment while she was studying in Paris.

"Don't ask me. I hardly ever see her."

"Well, she does have a demanding job," suggested Lucy. Elizabeth was an assistant concierge at the tony Cavendish Hotel.

"It's not her job, Mom. She's got a new boyfriend, Jean-Claude, and she's always over at his place."

This was very interesting news. "Have you met him? What's he like?"

"Are you kidding? She isn't about to let me get a glimpse of him, or maybe it's him get a glimpse of me. She's keeping him all to herself."

Probably wise, thought Lucy, aware of how predatory sisters could be. Her aunt Helen had never forgiven Lucy's mother for supposedly stealing a boyfriend, and then adding insult to injury by marrying him.

"I suppose that means you've got a quiet place to study. How are your classes?"

"Boring, Mom, boring. You'd think a course about a revolution would be interesting, but it turns out it's actually a philosophy course: Voltaire and Descartes and a bunch of others nobody ever heard of. Even some English guys. Ever hear of Hume? The professor sounds as if he's sneezing every time he says his name; it took me forever to figure out he wasn't actually sneezing."

Lucy had a frightening thought. "You are taking these courses pass/fail, right? You don't want to blow your GPA."

"It's under control, Mom. I hadn't signed up for pass/fail but Elizabeth told me that I should."

"So she is taking care of you," said Lucy.

"One thing, Mom. She did one good thing and walked out the door. I'm on my own here."

Lucy heard the brakes on the school bus and looked at the window, where she saw the big yellow bus at the end of her driveway. "You'll be fine," she said. "It will all work out. Meanwhile, I've got a bus to meet. They won't let Patrick off if there's no adult at the stop."

"You're as bad as Elizabeth, Mom. I know I don't rate . . ."

Lucy didn't have time for this. Nancy was already tapping the horn. "Sorry, gotta go, sweetie," she said, ending the call and running down the driveway to meet Patrick.

Patrick was sitting at the kitchen table, eating his after-school snack when Sara came home, full of news. "It looks like I got the research job," she announced, as she took off her jacket and hung it up. "It's pretty exciting, I'm going to be analyzing some deep-sea rocks from those underwater vents. It's hands-on, which is pretty exciting. I won't just be taking notes."

"Congratulations," crowed Lucy. "That's wonderful. Good work."

"You should tell my dad," said Patrick, reaching once again into the cookie jar. "He'll be interested."

"Good idea, Patrick," said Sara, which Lucy thought might be the first nice thing she'd said to Patrick since he'd arrived at the house.

Lucy joined Patrick at the table and took a bite of a cookie. "Zoe called, from Paris."

"So what's up with her?" asked Sara, an edge in her voice.

"She's miserable," said Lucy. "She says everybody there speaks French. . . ."

"Uh, yeah," offered Sara, rolling her eyes.

"And Elizabeth is never home because she's always out with a new boyfriend."

"That's Elizabeth for you."

"And her coursework is more demanding than she expected."

"Poor baby," cooed Sara, bouncing up the stairs with a smile on her face.

Chapter Eight

Dinner was remarkably pleasant, as Sara was much too pleased with herself to bother picking on Patrick. Halloween was fast approaching and Patrick was looking forward excitedly to the big day, reporting on the various costumes his classmates were planning to wear. He was convinced that his was the coolest, by far.

"All the girls are going to be princesses," he said, sounding disgusted. "Henry's going as a vampire, that's pretty neat, and Jack is going as Spiderman because his brother was Spiderman last year and his mom didn't want to buy a new costume."

"Isn't Spiderman cool?" asked Sara.

"It's okay, but it's not scary," explained Patrick.

"So you think the best costumes are scary?" asked Bill.

"Absolutely," said Patrick.

"But what if people are too scared to give candy?" mused Lucy. "What if they scream and slam the door shut?"

"Not gonna happen," insisted Patrick, with the certainty of a trick-or-treat veteran.

Lucy was replaying the dinner conversation in her head while she loaded the dishwasher, smiling at the pleasant memory, when her phone rang. Glancing at the screen she saw that her best friend, Sue Finch, was calling.

"Hi, Sue," she sang. "What's up?"

"I'm calling to ask a favor. . . ."

"Oh, no," moaned Lucy, dramatically. "I'm flat-out, taking care of Patrick. Honestly, I don't know how we did it with our kids. There's soccer practice and homework and making lunches and tooth brushing and I don't know what all."

"Well, we were younger, for one thing," said Sue.

"Don't remind me," moaned Lucy. "This kid is wearing me out. I'm exhausted most of the time."

"Now that you mention it, I think we were exhausted back then. I know I felt about twenty years younger when Sidra went off to college. I remember feeling somewhat ashamed that I wasn't sadder to see my little chick fly out of the nest."

"I'm looking forward to that day," admitted Lucy, who still had Sara home full-time, Zoe part-time, and Patrick, too. "So what is this favor you're asking me to do?"

"It's for the Hat and Mitten Fund Halloween party for the kids on Friday." Lucy and several other friends had started the fund years ago to supply warm winter clothes for the town's less fortunate kids. It had grown over the years and now also provided back-to-school supplies and summer camp scholarships.

"I'll be there, no problem," said Lucy, who was planning to bring Patrick to the party, which was an annual affair.

"Great. So can you help put up the decorations

tomorrow afternoon? We really need help since Chris broke her arm. . . ."

Lucy knew that Chris, Sue's partner in the Little Prodigies Child Care Center, had pretty much put up last year's spectacular decorations single-handedly. Sue now focused on the center's business end and no longer taught there, but filled in occasionally when needed. "She did? How'd that happen?"

"She fell, hanging up new curtains in the twins' room."

"That's why I never change the curtains," said Lucy, noticing that the gingham-checked cafe curtains in the kitchen were decidedly dingy. "Or wash them, for that matter."

"No washing is involved in the party decorations, which Chris has organized for us," said Sue. "She's written out directions so all we have to do is put them up."

Lucy bit her lip, trying to decide what to do. She wanted to help, but Patrick had soccer practice and she knew she couldn't be in two places at once. "I wish I could but Patrick's got soccer. . . ."

"So what's the problem? The practice is at the school, right? You can keep an eye on him from the gym."

"Not exactly," protested Lucy. "The gym doesn't have windows. I wouldn't be able to see outside."

"Do you have to watch him every minute?"

"Things have changed a lot since our kids were kids. Now they can't be alone for a minute. I have to meet the school bus or they won't let him off. And all the moms go to the practices, and if they can't go because they have jobs or something, Grandma or Grandpa goes. It seems that you can't let them wander off in the woods or go for a bike ride like our kids used to do." Lucy sighed. "It's really exhausting."

"I bet," said Sue. "I've heard of helicopter parenting, but I thought it was a big-city sort of thing."

"Nope. It's here. And I gotta say, my arms are getting pretty tired of all this flapping to stay aloft."

Sue laughed. "Maybe Bill, or Sara, could fill in for you at the game? What about Jolene?"

"Bill and Sara are too busy, and Jolene's visiting her sister in Florida."

"Well, I don't know what to do, Lucy. You're the last one on my list and we really need at least four people."

"What if you reschedule and we do it this evening?" suggested Lucy.

"No way. There are all these new rules since the school shootings began, and once they lock up, the school stays locked until morning."

"It's a brave new world. . . ."

"You said it. Well, I guess we'll just have to simplify the plan. No streamers."

Lucy felt conflicted. She wanted the party to be every bit as wonderful as it always was; she was tired of all the *shoulds* she'd encountered since Patrick's arrival, and her natural rebellious streak took over. "I'll do it," she said. "Patrick will be fine. If he needs me I'll make sure he'll know where to find me. The field is just outside the gym and there will be plenty of parents at the practice."

On Thursday afternoon Lucy arrived at the soccer field a few minutes before dismissal. Spotting Karen and Lori chatting with coach Janet Nowicki,

Lucy approached them, intending to let them know she would be inside the school during the practice and asking them to keep an eye on Patrick. As soon as she joined the group, however, she realized they were discussing a team member they considered to be a problem.

"He's too rough," complained Lori. "He ran right over Caitlin the other day and knocked her to the ground."

"It wouldn't be so bad if he was running over the other team, but most of the time it's members of his own team," said Karen. "Henry's got a big bruise on his elbow, thanks to Jared."

"I know, I know," agreed Janet. "He's just big and clumsy; he's not a bad kid."

"Right, right, there are no bad kids," said Lori. "They're misunderstood, or there's trouble at home. There's always excuses. But if you ask me, he really shouldn't be on the team if he can't be a team player."

"It's unacceptable behavior; he's always hogging the ball," said Karen.

"What do you think, Lucy?" asked Janet, turning to her.

Lucy didn't know how to answer. Sure, she'd noticed Jared's rough play, but she'd figured it was the way soccer was played. The whole point of the game was to score, and Jared was playing hard to do that. She'd simply thought he was more committed to the game than some of the others, who didn't seem to quite understand what soccer was all about. "It's supposed to be fun, right? Maybe you could remind the whole team about good sportsmanship," she suggested.

Janet nodded, looking relieved, but Lori and Karen weren't pleased.

"At the very least you ought to have a one-on-one talk with Jared," insisted Lori.

"I'll try the team pep talk first," said Janet. "I understand your concern, but I have to think about all the kids and what's best for them. But if the problem continues, I will talk to Jared." Noticing that the kids were streaming out of the school, she squared her shoulders and blew her whistle. "And I really do appreciate your concern," she said, before running off to round up the team.

"Typical," snorted Karen, watching her go. "I bet she thinks we're just overprotective."

"I know," agreed Lori. "Coaches and administrators always stick up for the troublemakers."

Lucy thought they had a point, but she also knew from experience that the day might come when their own perfect angels got in trouble and they would appreciate a tolerant and understanding approach. It had sure happened to her, when she learned the hard way that her own kids were not quite as well-behaved as she had thought.

The kids were lining up for some drills when she remembered she was supposed to be inside the gym, helping with the party decorations. "Oh, gosh, I almost forgot. I promised I'd help with the Hat and Mitten Fund party preparations. Would you mind keeping an eye on Patrick for me? I'll be right inside. . . ."

Lori and Karen exchanged a look, seeming to imply that Lucy was shirking her responsibility to the team. "The party is for everyone; all the kids are welcome," she added, hopefully.

"Oh, no problem," said Lori.

"You can count on us," said Karen.

Somewhat relieved, Lucy hurried into the gym where she found Sue, along with her friends Rachel and Pam, busy sorting through a couple of big boxes of Halloween decorations. Lucy was especially happy to see her old friends since she hadn't been able to make their weekly Thursday morning breakfasts at Jake's Donut Shack since Patrick's arrival. Seeing her, the others greeted her with smiles and hugs.

"Long time, no see," said Pam, who was married to Lucy's boss, Ted Stillings. She still wore her hair in the ponytail she'd had as a college cheerleader, and had also retained that gung-ho spirit.

"How's it going with Patrick?" asked Rachel, who was married to Bob Goodman, who had a busy legal practice in town. "Is he adjusting to all the changes?" Rachel had majored in psychology in college and had never gotten over it.

"He's actually doing pretty well," said Lucy. "He loves soccer; it's been a godsend. He's out there now, practicing."

"Physical activity; that's the key to keeping kids happy," said Sue. "Those little bodies have got to move." As always, Sue was dressed to the nines, wearing slim black slacks and a nubby gray tunic. Her husband, Sid, had a custom closet business which he claimed he'd had to start in self-defense, because of his wife's love of fashion.

"Okay, ladies," began Sue, "you know the drill. Crepe paper streamers from the lights, pinups on the walls, black cloths for the treat tables."

"I've got the fortune-telling tent in the car," said Rachel, who always played Madame Fortuna for the party. "I'll need a hand getting it out."

"No problem," said Pam. "I'll help you set it up. And we need a table near the electric outlet for the DJ. And don't forget the whirly light machines."

"Right," said Sue. "Let's get the tables up first and get the heavy lifting out of the way. You guys can do that while I check with the office about getting some ladders. I also want to make sure the janitor will be on hand for the party. We'll have to pay overtime for him, you know."

"Typical," observed Pam, as Sue hurried off to the school office. "Leaving us with the heavy lifting."

"She has a bad back," said Rachel, who was terribly kindhearted. "And she's put in a lot of work organizing things."

"And I'm going to have a bad back, when we're done," said Lucy, getting a laugh.

The three had just finished setting up the tables and were taking a brief rest to catch their breath, when Sue returned. "You know," she said, "I did try to save us all this work. I had a sudden inspiration and called those new people, the Moons, and asked ever so politely if we could use their house for the party. It's an old wreck anyway and I figured they'd be renovating, so why not have the party in a real haunted house? But I didn't get anywhere. . . ."

"Not surprising," observed Pam, wryly, "if you called their house an old wreck."

"I said it tactfully," insisted Sue. "I thought it would be fun for them. They're young and new in town; it would be a great way to meet some people their own age. They don't have kids, but they're probably planning to. . . . I was really surprised at their negative reaction. Well, his reaction. I didn't get to talk to her."

"She doesn't talk to anybody," said Lucy. "He doesn't let her."

"That sounds like classic controlling behavior by an abuser," said Rachel. "They isolate their victims, don't allow them to have friends, and block contact from family members."

"I know," said Lucy. "I interviewed Officer Sally for a story and she gave me some ideas, but when I tried to reach out to Heather—that's her name—Ty answered the door and told me to get lost. He was very insulting, actually kind of threatening. He's not a nice guy; he gave me the creeps. And I can tell you that a lot of the moms are really uneasy about him living so close to the school. They've warned the kids not to go near the place."

"Oh, my goodness, Lucy. That was very brave of you to try to help Heather. I think those moms are right about him," confessed Pam. "I was walking my neighbor's dog, you know the Franklins; they're away in Hawaii for a second honeymoon. Anyway, Boomer's one of those active dogs, an Australian sheepdog or something, so he needs a nice, long walk, and I was passing by the Moons' house when I heard some awful, blood-curdling screams. The dog bolted; it was all I could do to hang on to him." She paused, shuddering at the memory. "It was absolutely terrifying."

"What's going on in there?" wondered Sue.

"Plenty," said Lucy, going on to tell about the flashing lights she'd seen, and Franny's reports of electric lights that dimmed and brightened. And then there were the weird noises that accompanied the light show, the noises that Barney had suggested were simply jazz music.

"That doesn't sound like jazz to me," said Pam, who had done some modern dance in college, along with cheerleading.

"I wonder if he's gaslighting the poor woman, trying to drive her insane," suggested Rachel.

"I wouldn't be surprised at all," said Lucy, remembering the insults Ty had hurled at her. "She's in bad shape; that I can tell you. She looks malnourished, she's positively wraithlike. I wish there was some way to help her."

"Well, although all this is fascinating, it's not getting the gym ready for the party," said Sue. "First things first. Let's get through Halloween, and afterward we can have a brainstorming session and come up with some ways to help poor Heather Moon. In the meantime, we have work to do."

So they all got busy with their various tasks and when they'd finished, they decided it was all worth it, back aches and all. The gym had been completely transformed with spidery lace curtains hanging across the entrance door, orange and black crepe paper streamers hanging overhead, and pinups of witches and pumpkins and black cats on the walls, highlighted by Rachel's swirly lights. Madame Fortuna's tent was ready and waiting in one corner, and the DJ's table was in the other, near an electric outlet. All that was missing were the kids.

"Good work, ladies," said Sue, flicking all the switches on the light panel and ushering them out, closing the doors behind them. "See you tomorrow night."

Chapter Nine

Leaving the gym, Lucy's mind wasn't on the coming party but instead was wondering why some men seemed driven to mistreat the women they professed to love. One man in particular, she thought, turning her head and glancing across the street at the looming shape of the Moons' house. It was the familiar Halloween motif of a haunted house standing right there on School Street, and she had a set of seasonal dish towels decorated with a similar design, with the playful addition of a ghost floating out of the chimney. A puff of smoke from the Moon chimney startled her, giving her a momentary fright as she said her somewhat distracted good-byes to her friends.

Daylight savings was still in effect, but the sun was low in the sky and would soon set, plunging the town into darkness. Furthermore, soccer practice, which was usually a noisy affair with screams from the players and blasts of Coach Janet's whistle, seemed unusually quiet today. The playing fields were behind the school, hidden from view when Lucy exited through the side door, and she figured Coach Janet was probably wrapping up, giving the kids a pep talk. When she glanced at her watch, she realized with a shock that it was almost five, which meant that soccer practice had been over for almost half an hour. Why didn't anyone come to tell her? What about Lori's and Karen's promise to keep an eye out for her? They were busy, sure, but it would only have taken a moment to stop in at the gym to let her know they were leaving. And even more troubling, why didn't Patrick himself follow her careful instructions and report to her when the practice ended?

No reason to panic, she told herself as she gave her friends a quick wave and hurried away on the path that ran alongside the school. She knew that some of the neighborhood kids stayed on after practice to kick a ball around, and she figured Patrick had joined them. He much preferred playing soccer to doing homework, and this was a rare opportunity to hang with his new friends. So when she rounded the corner and she saw a handful of players on the field, she was relieved.

It was only when she drew closer and began to recognize the individual kids that she realized Patrick wasn't among them. There was the notorious Jared, and the two kids who lived on School Street near the school, Caitlin and Henry, along with several others she didn't know by name, but no Patrick.

That couldn't be right, she thought, taking a closer look. Patrick must be with the group. Kids all looked pretty much alike, she thought, watching as they ran around and trying to remember what Patrick was wearing this morning. A blue jacket, that was it. But none of the kids were wearing blue jackets, or jackets at all for that matter. What color was his shirt? she wondered, wracking her brain. Then it came to her: a black and white plaid flannel shirt, seemingly brand-new, she remembered, thinking he looked pretty sharp when he sat down at the breakfast table. But none of the kids was wearing a snazzy black and white plaid shirt. There were five in total, two girls and three boys, and Patrick was not among them.

"Hey!" she yelled, wishing she had Coach Janet's whistle. "I need to talk to you."

The kids ignored her, running down the field after the ball.

"Hey! Stop!" she yelled, trying again.

Henry had miraculously snagged the ball and was kicking it back in her direction, followed by the others. He wasn't very fast, however, and Jared quickly stole the ball and headed back downfield. Lucy sighed. There was only one way to handle this, so she dropped her bag and coat on the ground and took off after the pack. She hadn't been running in quite a while, but her legs were longer and her adrenaline was kicking in, so she was able to keep up with the kids. Seeing her chance to get the ball she scooped it up in her hands.

"No fair! You can't use hands," protested Jared.

"Yeah!" added Henry, red-faced and panting.

"I'll give the ball back in a minute. I need to talk to you guys. Where's Patrick?"

Jared screwed up his face. "Who?"

"You know," said Caitlin. "The new kid."

"From Alaska," added Henry.

"Oh, him," said one of the kids Lucy didn't recognize.

"Yeah, him," said Lucy. "When did you last see him?"

"Dunno," said Jared with a shrug. "Can we have the ball back now?"

"No. I need to know what's happened to Patrick. Did one of the moms give him a ride home?"

The kids exchanged glances but didn't answer.

"Was he playing soccer with you or not?" she demanded, losing patience and fighting down a growing sense of panic.

Again, the kids remained silent, until Jared spoke up. "No, he wasn't here."

Well, that was progress, thought Lucy. If he hadn't stayed to play, somebody must have given him a ride home. Not time to panic, yet, she told herself. Tinker's Cove was a safe town, where everyone knew each other. There was no way some horrible predator could have snatched Patrick. There had probably been some sort of miscommunication and he'd been picked up by Bill, or even Sara.

"Okay, thanks," she said, turning and heading toward her car. As she walked she pulled out her cell phone and called Bill.

"Just checking with you," she began. "Did you pick up Patrick after soccer practice?"

"Nope. Was I supposed to?"

"No. I was decorating the gym and I've lost track of him. . . ."

Bill's voice was abrupt, almost accusatory. "What? Have you lost him?"

"Well, he isn't where I thought he'd be, but he's probably perfectly fine somewhere else," she replied, resting her hips against the car and wishing her heart would stop pounding quite so hard in her chest. "Maybe he's already home. I'll check with Sara."

"Well, let me know as soon as you find him, okay?"

"Okay." But Lucy didn't feel as if everything was going to be okay. This was no time for hysterics, she told herself as she quickly called Sara.

"Hi, it's me. Are you home?" she asked, her voice sharp.

"Yeah, Mom, I'm home," replied Sara, defensively. "Have you got a problem with that?"

"No. No problem. I'm glad actually." She took a deep breath and crossed her fingers. "Is Patrick there with you?"

"No, Mom. Just me and the smelly dog."

"Are you sure?" asked Lucy, pinning her hope on the slight chance that Sara hadn't realized her nephew was home. "Would you just check around the house for me?"

"What's going on, Mom?"

"Well, I was decorating the gym for the Halloween party and he was supposed to come find me when soccer practice was over but now there's no sign of him here at the school."

"Golly. I hope he's okay."

"Yeah. I'm sure he is. He probably went home with one of the other kids or something. I'll make a few calls. Meanwhile, if he does show up, give me a call."

"I will, Mom. I'll search the house right away."

While she waited for Sara to call back, Lucy flipped through her contacts and found no soccer moms. She was of a different generation; her kids had graduated from elementary school years ago and she hadn't developed a fresh network of contacts. She didn't even have Lori's and Karen's numbers. She did, however, have one for Coach Janet and she dialed it.

"Hey, Lucy, Patrick had a great practice," said Janet, having seen Lucy's name pop up on her phone.

"That's great," said Lucy. "But I've got a bit of a problem. I'm here at the field and I can't find Patrick."

"Probably went home with somebody," said Janet.

"I was in the gym, getting ready for the Halloween party, and he was supposed to come and find me when practice was over."

"You know how kids are, in one ear and out the other. Something better probably came along."

"I hope that's the case," said Lucy. "Just tell me, did you see him when practice ended?"

"I can't say I did, Lucy. Sorry. It's so busy then, you know. There's always a few moms with schedule conflicts and the kids are all over the place. . . ."

Her phone was signaling an incoming call, so Lucy quickly went to call waiting, expecting to hear Sara's voice. "Yeah?" she barked, fingers crossed, hoping that Sara had found Patrick upstairs, playing quietly in his room.

"Lucy?" It wasn't Sara, it was Molly on the other end.

"Oh, hi, Molly," said Lucy, trying to sound upbeat. "How are you feeling?"

"Pretty good, actually. I'm between operations so I decided to come and spend some time with Patrick. I really miss my little guy. I hope it's not too much of an inconvenience. . . ."

"Oh, no, not at all. Patrick will be so happy, I think he's been missing you."

Molly was right on it. "Has he been homesick?"

"No, no. Nothing like that. Sometimes he's a bit wistful, that's all," said Lucy. "So when will you be coming?"

"Didn't I say? I'm actually in New Hampshire; my flight to Boston got diverted. I figured I'd rent a car and drive myself. It'll be quicker than waiting for the airline to sort things out. I can be there in three hours or so."

Lucy swallowed hard. "Three hours?"

"Well, probably a bit longer because I haven't got the car yet, and I'm going to try to get some sort of refund from the airline, at least get them to cover the car rental."

"Right," said Lucy. Three hours, she told herself. Three hours to find Patrick before his mother arrived. Three hours and she didn't know where to start. What if she hadn't simply miscommunicated, or misplaced the boy? What if some sicko had lured him into a car and carried him off? What if they never found him?

"Lucy, is everything okay? You sound a little funny."

"Just a bit short of breath," admitted Lucy, who couldn't seem to get any air into her lungs at all. "I was chasing a ball."

"Is Patrick there?" Molly's voice was excited and eager. "Can I talk to him? Give him the good news?"

"Sorry," replied Lucy, desperately trying to think of a reason why Patrick couldn't come to the phone. Any reason except the real one. "Wouldn't you know. He's in the bathroom."

"No matter." Molly was disappointed. "I'll be seeing him in a little while anyway."

"Yup, that's right," said Lucy, praying it would be so.

"And the sooner I get that car, the sooner I'll be there. Thanks for everything, Lucy."

"See you soon," said Lucy, ending the call and wishing desperately that Patrick would suddenly materialize, walking around the corner of the school building, or popping out from behind a tree or a bush. She took a few deep breaths, trying to decide what to do next, when she spotted a lumpy shape beneath one of the benches that lined the soccer field.

Lucy was running back to the field when her phone rang again. This time it was Sara, reporting there was no sign of Patrick in the house. "Your line was tied up. I couldn't get through."

Lucy had been so involved with Molly's call that she had ignored the beeps from call waiting. "Molly called; she's on her way here."

"Molly's coming?"

"Yeah. She's between surgeries and she misses Patrick. She'll be here in three hours."

"Talk about bad timing," said Sara. "We've got to find Patrick. Fast."

"I found his backpack," she said, stooping down and retrieving the bag. It was definitely Patrick's; it had his initials embroidered on the flap.

"You should call the police," said Sara.

Lucy scanned the field and saw the five kids huddled in a little group, across the street from the Moon house.

"Not yet. There are some kids here and I think they know something."

"Keep me posted, Mom," said Sara, her voice breaking.

"Will do," replied Lucy, fighting back her own tears. Not now, she told herself, straightening her shoulders and marching across the field. Now was not the time for tears, it was time for action. She pulled out her notebook and pen and confronted the little group.

"First of all, I want names," she said. "I know you, Henry, and you, Caitlin. Jared, what's your last name?"

"What's it to you?"

Lucy narrowed her eyes. "I want to send you a birthday party invitation, okay? What's your last name?"

"It's Winston," he admitted. "Really? A party?"

Lucy ignored the question. "And you?" She pointed to the girl she didn't know. "Who are you?"

"I'm Lily Lennart, and my address is One Forty-Five Front St. I love parties and cake."

"Great," said Lucy, jotting down her name and address.

"And you?" she demanded, turning to the last kid.

"Jackson Keilly," he admitted, looking at his shoes.

"Okay, Jackson," said Lucy, sensing a weak link in the group. "What happened to Patrick?"

"Nothing, nothing happened," answered Jackson, resorting to a typical juvenile answer when pressed by an adult. "He wasn't even here."

Lucy had heard it all before and wasn't impressed. "Well, Jackson, I know you're lying because I just found his backpack. Patrick was here. I've got the proof."

"That doesn't prove anything," claimed Jared. "Maybe he left it yesterday."

"No, Jared. He had it this morning when he left home." She glared at each of the kids, one by one, watching them squirm. "There's something you're not telling me, something you're hiding, and if you don't tell me right away, this instant, I'm going to call your parents." She let her threat sink in. "I don't think they'll be very happy to learn that you wouldn't help me find your missing friend."

"We didn't do anything wrong!" declared Jackson.

"Okay," said Lucy, swiping her phone and asking for directory assistance. "It's up to you."

The two little girls were holding hands and looking worried, so Lucy asked for the number for Lennart on 145 Front Street. She activated the speaker app and soon the sound of a ringing phone could be heard, and with each ring Lily's face grew paler. On the fifth ring, she broke.

"Jared dared him to knock on the door of the haunted house. That's what happened," she said, bursting into tears.

"And what happened then?" asked Lucy.

"The door opened and he went inside," whispered Caitlin. "He's in there. We've been waiting for him to come out."

Chapter Ten

This time Lucy didn't hesitate. She immediately dialed 9-1-1 and reported that her grandson had entered the house at 66 School Street and had not come out.

"That's the Moon house, right?" asked the dispatcher, Jodie Kirwan. "The house everybody calls the haunted house?"

"Yes."

"Well, Lucy, why don't you knock on the door and ask for him? This doesn't seem like a police matter."

"I'm afraid it is. I have a history with the husband. He's violent, he's threatened me. I'm truly afraid for my grandson's safety."

"Why did he go into the house? Was he abducted?"

"Possibly." Lucy glared at the little group of kids. "He went there on a dare."

"I see," said Jenny. "I'll send a car over right away."

"Thanks."

It was only a matter of minutes before a squad car turned the corner and sped down School Street with its lights flashing and halted in front of the Moon house. Lucy hurried over, followed by the pack of kids, reaching the car just as Officer Barney Culpepper was hauling himself out. Barney was a big man, approaching retirement, and getting out of the department's aged squad car was a bit of a challenge for him. When he was finally free of the low-slung sedan, he shook himself, adjusted his heavy belt, and settled his cap on his crew cut head.

"So you say your grandson is inside that house?" he asked, as Officer Sally Kirwan came around from the passenger side of the car and joined them.

"What's the problem?" asked Officer Sally. "An abduction?"

"Not exactly. The kids say they dared Patrick to knock on the door, and when he did, the door opened and he disappeared inside. I'm worried, because, well"—Lucy lowered her voice, aware of the kids' big ears—"I suspect Ty Moon is an abuser."

Officer Sally stepped close to Lucy and spoke quietly, mindful of the group of kids. "I think you mentioned this particular situation to me, is that right?"

Lucy nodded.

"We need some facts here," said Barney. "Name and age?"

"Patrick Stone, my grandson. He's eight."

"Right." Barney turned to the kids. "Is this true? You dared him to knock on the door?"

There were solemn nods all around.

"But what happened then? Was he grabbed? Or did he just walk in?"

"I don't believe he would have walked in," protested Lucy. "He must've been grabbed."

"Is that true?" asked Officer Sally, speaking to the kids.

"He walked in," said Lily. "He wasn't grabbed."

"You can tell me the truth," said Officer Sally. "You guys aren't in trouble. We just want to know what happened."

"He walked in," said Jared, and the others all nodded in agreement.

"That doesn't make sense," said Lucy. "He knows better. He wouldn't do that."

"Calm down, Lucy," said Barney. "Maybe he was offered candy or something, a chance to pet a dog; could be anything that would get a kid to forget everything he ever learned about stranger danger. Happens all the time." He paused, thinking. "The question is, is this a hostage situation or what?"

"We need more info before we go in," said Officer Sally. "Do you have any clothes, anything that Patrick was wearing?"

Lucy held up the backpack and unzipped it, producing a hooded sweatshirt. "He wore it this morning."

"Let's get the K-9 unit over here," said Sally, taking the sweatshirt. "That way we'll know for sure if Patrick's inside."

Lucy's heart sank at this delay; at this rate Molly would be walking into a terrible situation. "Couldn't you just knock on the door?" she asked.

"Sorry, Lucy. Department policy," said Barney,

as Officer Sally got on the radio to request the K-9 unit and backup. "Times have changed. Everybody's got guns for one thing. These days we never know what's on the other side of the door."

It was then that the rat-a-tat-tat of an automatic weapon was heard, and everyone hit the ground. Then there was a sharp, piercing scream and the lights in the house began to dim and brighten.

"What the hell," exclaimed Barney, ducking behind the squad car and talking into the personal radio fastened on his shoulder. "Shots fired," he reported, as Lucy and Sally quickly shepherded the children to safety behind the school. Lucy was ordered to stay with them while Sally ran back to join Barney, staying low and with her gun drawn.

It seemed to take forever before Lucy could hear the wail of sirens, signaling that reinforcements were on the way. She knew that the Tinker's Cove police department only had a couple of cruisers, so she assumed mutual aid had been called in from neighboring towns, and probably the state police, too.

Desperate to know what was happening, Lucy peeked around the corner of the school building. First on the scene was the K-9 unit, Scratch, and his handler, Officer Todd Kirwan. Todd consulted briefly with his cousin, Sally, apparently discussing whether it was safe for the dog to approach the house. No additional shots had been fired, so after a few minutes the dog was allowed to sniff Patrick's sweatshirt, and ran right up to the front door.

"What's going on?" asked Jackson, tugging on her sleeve.

"They sent the dog, he went on the porch," re-

ported Lucy, as Todd whistled and Scratch obedi-
ently turned around and returned to safety behind the K-9 unit's SUV.

"Is Scratch okay?" asked Lily. "He was at the
school, for a special assembly, and I got to pet him."

"He's okay," said Lucy, who was struck with the
surreal aspect of the situation, which seemed to be
spinning out of control as the arriving squad cars
began to fill the street. Or maybe, she thought, as
another volley of shots rang out, maybe it really
was a hostage situation, and her Patrick was the
hostage. A SWAT team, dressed in black, was taking up positions, holding big black shields in front
of themselves. Lucy watched in horror as a couple
of snipers with long-range weapons positioned
themselves, ensuring they had clear shots at the
house.

Then there was the cackle of a loudspeaker and
a voice announced, "This is the police. Come out
with your hands up."

Nothing happened; the front door remained
closed. A burst of light, as if from a strobe, illuminated the tower, and an unearthly scream was
heard.

"You are surrounded."

Lucy noticed a tightening of ranks among the
SWAT team, and the snipers raised their weapons,
ready to shoot.

"Come out with your hands up."

Something crashed inside the house, followed
by an explosion.

"This is not a drill."

Now the flashing lights were quicker, and a
drumbeat could be heard. What was going on in
there? wondered Lucy.

"We are initiating extraction. Any resistance will be met with force."

The SWAT team began advancing in formation behind their shields.

"I'm scared," moaned Lily, collapsing on the ground and curling up in a ball.

"Me, too," admitted Jared, who looked as if he was going to faint, or vomit.

"It will be all right," said Lucy, wishing she believed her reassuring words. How was she ever going to explain this to Molly? How did she let this happen? Why didn't she keep better track of Patrick?

The SWAT team had reached the porch steps when the front door opened and Ty Moon stood there, in a T-shirt, arms above his head. "What's going on?" he asked, looking puzzled.

"Step forward," ordered the voice on the microphone.

Ty obeyed and was immediately tackled, thrown to the ground facedown with his hands cuffed behind his back.

"Who else is inside? Any guns? Bombs?" demanded one of the SWAT officers.

Ty shook his head. Behind him, in the doorway, stood Heather and Patrick. As soon as she saw them, Lucy started running across the school lawn to the street, where she was stopped by Barney. "Hold on, Lucy. We've got this under control."

"Wow, this is cool," she heard Patrick exclaiming, as he took in the scene outside the house. "Is this part of the movie?"

"No, Patrick," said Heather, who was holding him by the hand. "This is what grown-ups call a cock-up."

Meanwhile, the SWAT team rushed past them into the house, where they began a systematic search. Ty remained facedown on the porch. Patrick was handed over to Lucy, and Heather asked for a chair. "I'm not well," she said, in a thready voice. "I'm getting chemo for Hodgkin's Lymphoma."

She was sitting on the porch steps, wrapped in a blanket, when the SWAT team returned from searching the house. "No guns, no explosives, lots of computer equipment," reported the leader.

"I'm creating special effects for a movie," said Ty, raising his head. "That's what I do. I'm an FX designer."

"Oh," said Lucy, somewhat embarrassed. "I guess that explains everything," she added, giving Patrick a big hug.

"I'm going to need a statement," said Barney, releasing Ty from his handcuffs and helping him get to his feet. "Let's go inside, where it's warm."

Then, almost as quickly as they arrived, the dozens of squad cars and scores of officers disappeared, driving off into the night. The kids were collected by their parents, and the little crowd of neighbors who had gathered at a safe distance also went on home. Lucy went inside the Moon house, along with Officer Sally and Barney, where they all gathered around the Moons' artfully distressed refectory-style table in their shabby, not-yet-renovated, dining room.

"Let's begin at the beginning," said Barney, activating the video app on his cell phone.

"This kid knocked on the door," began Ty.

"Who answered?"

"It was me," said Heather. "Ty was working at

the console, there." She pointed at a large piece of electronic equipment that occupied most of the dining room.

"I asked what he was doing," said Patrick, "and he invited me to come and see."

"Patrick! What were you thinking? You know better than that, to go into a stranger's house," protested Lucy.

"I know, Grandma. But it looked so interesting, like the stuff in the lab where Dad takes me sometimes, only this isn't for counting fish, it's for making movies, right?"

"So that explains all the screams and wails and lights going on and off?" asked Lucy.

"The lightning, too," said Ty. "I do that in the tower. It's perfect for this movie. But I guess I didn't realize that people would wonder what was going on."

"You can say that again," said Officer Sally, giving Lucy a look. "Some people were quite worried about your wife's condition; they suspected there was some sort of abuse going on."

"It's abuse, all right," said Heather, with a wan smile. "Chemo is terrible. The doctors tell me I've got a good chance of a complete recovery, but it's going to take some time."

"Do you want to see what all the excitement's been about," invited Ty, with a nod toward the big computer console. "I can show you part of the movie."

So they all trooped into the living room and gathered behind Ty, who was seated at the keyboard. "First I'll show you the scene as it was filmed," he said, running a clip picturing a group of attractive teens entering a derelict, deserted house. For no reason at all, it seemed, they were terribly frightened, screaming, and hugging each other. "What do you think?" he asked.

"Kind of confusing," said Sally. "Why are they so frightened?"

"All will be explained when I add the special effects," said Ty, running the scene again.

This time, there was spooky music as the kids approached the house, a bolt of lightning split the sky, making them jump. The music intensified as they entered the cobwebby hallway, and an ear-splitting scream was heard, making them scream in fright and hug each other.

"That's some difference," said Barney, scratching his chin. "So this is what you've been doing all this time."

"Yeah. I didn't realize it was noticeable outside the house. And I've been under a lot of deadline pressure. I've been so focused on this project, and Heather's illness, that I guess I haven't been very friendly. No wonder people have been giving me weird looks."

"Yeah," agreed Heather. "We've been so wrapped up in our problems that we haven't been very good neighbors."

"Well, now that everybody knows what's going on, I think you can expect a lot of support from the community," said Lucy, pulling Patrick close to her and hugging his shoulders.

"We'd better get you home," she told him. "There's going to be a surprise for you."

"A good surprise?" asked Patrick, sounding rather worried.

"You'll have to wait and see," said Lucy. "Otherwise it won't be a surprise."

Patrick was on tenterhooks for the ride home, and all through dinner and bath, stories and bedtime snack. "What's the surprise?" he kept asking. "Is there really a surprise or are you teasing me?"

"Be patient, Patrick. There's really a surprise," Lucy reassured him, spotting headlights pulling into the driveway.

"In fact, I think the surprise has arrived," said Bill, opening the kitchen door.

Lucy and Patrick joined him there, watching as the car door opened and Molly stepped out.

"Mom!" screamed Patrick, flying down the porch steps and into his mother's arms.

"Careful, careful," she said, holding out her bandaged hand. "My goodness, I think you've grown while you've been here." She wrapped her good arm around him and together they walked into the house. "So, Patrick, tell me all about what you've been doing. Anything interesting?"

Lucy and Bill waited nervously for his answer. Knowing Molly, they didn't think she would appreciate the fact that her child had been the focus of a police action.

"Yeah, Mom. I'm going to be a werewolf for Halloween."

Together, Bill and Lucy let out big sighs of relief. Tomorrow there would be time to fill Molly in on the whole story, before she read about it in the *Pennysaver*. But for now, there was a little boy to tuck into bed.

DEATH BY
HAUNTED HOUSE

Lee Hollis

Chapter One

October 29, 2009

Hayley Powell loved everything about Halloween. It was her favorite holiday, except for the fact that it wasn't officially a national holiday, so she had to still work. She was the office manager at the *Island Times* newspaper in Bar Harbor, Maine. Hayley had been lucky to get the job. Her husband, Danny, was out of work again, and taking his time finding a new gig that he deemed "the right fit." So at least she had a steady paycheck coming in to cover the household bills. She had tried pressuring Danny to look for something part-time that would bring in some extra income while he searched for something more permanent. With an aggravated sigh, Danny had recently been hired at the Big Apple convenience store as a cashier for the graveyard shift. He grumbled and complained about the horrible hours, but he knew his family needed the cash, so he shuffled out the door every night at 10 PM and tried to keep his whining to a minimum.

The only upside in Danny's mind was that he was at home during the day when the kids got home from school, which allowed him to hang out with them, watching TV or playing video games, or teaching their new puppy, Leroy, how to fetch a ball. Hayley had gently suggested he help them with their homework too, but he just sort of chuckled at the idea, and quickly moved on. Danny had never been a good student, so he felt if he tried to guide them in their assignments, their grades might actually suffer. Hayley finally accepted this logic and stopped hounding him.

Danny was especially excited as they barreled toward October 31 on the calendar because he could help the kids carve pumpkins and find the perfect Halloween costume. He loved Halloween just as much as Hayley did and she knew at the end of the day that she had married a big kid at heart.

Danny had been calling Hayley at the office several times a day, once to ask where she kept the scissors to adjust Dustin's Jack Sparrow outfit. Then, just a few minutes later, he called from a yard sale to excitedly inform Hayley that he had found the perfect blond wig for her Marilyn Monroe costume. Later, when Hayley was on the phone with a local restaurant owner trying to place an ad for his business, Danny blew into the office with an armful of pumpkins, hoping she would sign off on the two best ones he could use to carve into Batman and Harry Potter, Dustin and Gemma's traditional choices for what kind of pumpkins they wanted lit up on the front porch. When Danny wasn't working, he seemed to forget that there were other people in the world, including his wife, who actually had jobs to do.

At four minutes to five, Hayley's quitting time, her phone rang and she scooped up the receiver as she reached under her desk to grab her bag. "*Island Times,* this is Hayley speaking."

"You are never going to guess where I am," Danny said breathlessly.

"Danny, I'm really trying to get out of here. Can't this wait until we both get home?"

He didn't seem interested in answering her question. "Al Foley's house."

Al Foley was one of Danny's buddies from high school. They used to get into a lot of trouble together, which included a two-week suspension after releasing a live skunk into the chemistry lab of the teacher who failed both of them their junior year.

"Well, say hello for me. I'm heading home now."

"Wait! You have to hear this! You know Al is a Blue Knight, right?"

The Blue Knights was an international motorcycle club for law enforcement officers.

Hayley sighed. There was no way she was going to get out of this conversation. "No, I didn't. I thought you had to be a police officer to be in the Blue Knights."

Al was a garbage collector.

"You do," Danny answered. "But Al's brother Del is a cop and kind of fibbed and sponsored Al by telling them he was a reserve officer here in town."

"Lying to a gang of cops doesn't seem like the smartest idea to me," Hayley said.

"That doesn't matter!" Danny yelled. "That's not the most important part of the story."

"Then why are you telling me all this?"

He ignored her. "Anyway, Al's little girl Samantha is old enough to ride on the back of his bike and for her birthday last summer he had this adorable helmet custom made for her. It's pink and white!"

"I'm so happy for her," Hayley quipped, rolling her eyes and making a confused face even though there was no one in the office to see it.

"Don't you *get* it? A pink and white helmet! It's perfect for Gemma's Power Rangers costume!"

The point of all this was slowly coming into focus.

"Al said we can borrow it for Halloween! Gemma is going to freak out! It will look so good with the matching bodysuit I found at Kmart!"

Danny really needed to find a full-time job.

"That's great! Tell Al I sure appreciate him lending it to us," Hayley said. "Now I'm going to stop by the Shop 'n Save and pick up some Halloween candy, and then I will meet you at home for dinner. I've got a stew in the Crock—Pot that's nearly done so don't be late."

Before Danny could talk her ear off some more, she hung up. As office manager, she was in charge of locking up the building at the end of the workday, which meant making sure all the reporters and photographers were gone before she left and accidentally locked one of them inside for the night. She breezed through the bullpen, scanning the row of empty offices, including her boss Sal's corner office and crime reporter Bruce Linney's office, which was located right next to it. Those were the only two who tended to hang around past five o'clock. On her way back, she happened to see Hattie Jenkins still sitting behind her desk.

Hattie was well into her eighties and had been the *Island Times* cooking columnist since the 1960s, long before Hayley was even born. Hattie was a staple at the news-paper and everyone in town diligently copied all her recipes, handed down for generations in her family, dating as far back as the ones who had endured the first *Mayflower* crossing.

Hayley popped her head in and noticed that Hattie's head was slumped over on her chest and her eyes were closed.

"Hattie, it's time to go home," Hayley whispered.

Hattie didn't respond.

"Hattie?" she said a little louder.

Hayley's heart jumped into her throat. She feared Hattie might have died sometime during the afternoon after eating her hard-boiled egg for lunch that she reliably put every morning in the office refrigerator along with a stern note that warned, DO NOT EAT! THIS EGG BELONGS TO HATTIE!

Hayley moved slowly into the office, and gently shook Hattie's shoulder.

Still nothing.

The tip of Hattie's glasses hung precariously over the bridge of her nose.

Hayley shook her again, this time harder. "Hattie, are you okay?"

Suddenly Hattie let out a loud grunt. Her eyes popped open and she sat straight up in her chair and let out a scream at the sight of Hayley, who stumbled back.

"Hayley, what are you doing sneaking in here like that! You nearly gave me a heart attack!"

"I am so sorry, Hattie. It's five o'clock. I need to lock up. You were asleep at your desk."

"I most certainly was not."

"Yes, your eyes were closed and—"

"I was thinking. That's what writers do. We think about how we are going to compose our next sentence before we actually write it."

Hayley glanced at Hattie's desktop computer screen. She had fallen asleep watching a cat video.

"I'm sorry, I didn't mean to interrupt your creative process."

"Now you made me lose my train of thought," Hattie said, shutting down her computer. "I might as well call it a day."

In her mind, Hattie had saved face. She didn't like admitting she was getting old.

After helping Hattie on with her coat and finally sending her on her way, Hayley was finally able to lock up the office, swing into the supermarket to pick up some candy, and head home for the day. When she arrived, she walked through the back door that led into the kitchen and found twelve-year-old Gemma already modeling her Power Rangers helmet for her father. He stood against the stove, beaming proudly. One of Hayley's best friends, Mona Barnes, who was married with four or five kids—Hayley could never keep track of the actual number—and who was also the owner of a very successful lobster business, was gulping down a bowl of Hayley's beef stew.

Hayley stared at the Crock-Pot. "Mona, that's not going to be fully cooked for another forty-five minutes."

"I couldn't wait," Mona said, slurping the broth

off a large spoon. "What can I say? I'm seven months pregnant. I get hungry."

"Mom, look! I'm the Pink Power Ranger!" Gemma squealed.

Hayley turned to her daughter who was jumping around the kitchen striking superhero poses. "You look awesome, sweetheart!"

Mona suddenly set the empty bowl on the counter and snatched the brown paper sack out of Hayley's hands. "What's in here?"

She rummaged around in the bag and her face lit up. "Candy!"

"That's for the trick-or-treaters, Mona," Hayley admonished.

Mona was already tearing open a bite-size Snickers bar. "That's two whole days away. I'll replace whatever I eat. I'm eating for two, you know!"

"Shouldn't you be eating something a little more healthy, for the baby's sake?" Hayley quietly suggested.

Mona gave her a dirty look, and in an act of defiance, popped the Snickers into her mouth whole, and then began unwrapping a Three Musketeers bar.

Hayley decided that the best course of action was to just let Mona do what she wanted. She turned to Gemma. "Where's your brother?"

"Upstairs playing video games," Gemma said, pulling the helmet off her head. "Dad says we can watch an old scary movie tonight."

"What kind of scary movie?" Hayley asked suspiciously.

"*Psycho!*" Gemma shouted before her father could stop her.

Hayley spun around to Danny, who had guilt written all over his face. "Are you *kidding* me?"

"It's a film classic," Danny argued, unconvincingly.

"It's also entirely inappropriate for children their ages," Hayley said.

"It's in black and white. I mean come on, how scary can it be?" Mona said, reaching into the bag for another piece of candy.

Hayley snatched the bag out of Mona's hand. "No more candy until you take my side."

Mona got the message. "I got that Lindsay Lohan Disney movie, *Herbie: Fully Loaded,* at home on DVD you can borrow."

"It's Halloween!" Danny groused.

Hayley shook her head and turned back to Mona. "He does this every year. He gets the kids all hepped up on scary movies, and then right before they go to bed, he tells them how the last owner of the house next door deserted it because he was frightened off by evil spirits! And then they can't get to sleep because he's got them so terror-stricken! That's *not* responsible parenting!"

"It's true! They say he ran screaming out of the house in the middle of the night a few years back and never returned and no one has seen him since!" Gemma bellowed. "I know because Daddy said so!"

"It's not true, Gemma. He just moved away, that's all," Hayley said firmly.

"Then why has no one ever bought the house since? I'll tell you why. It's because . . ." Danny said, before taking Gemma by the hand and smiling at her. "Say it with me . . ."

Danny and Gemma both screamed, "It's *haunted!*"

"Help me out here, Mona, please," Hayley said.

Mona made sure she had her tiny box of Milk Duds open and in her mouth before she responded. "I heard the same thing."

"You're all impossible!" Hayley said. She whipped open her cupboards and removed four dinner plates to set the table, passing by Danny. "When they're seeing ghosts in their rooms tonight, *you're* going to deal with it, not me!"

Hayley had always been the family skeptic when it came to creepy, spine-tingling ghost stories that supposedly had happened over the years in Bar Harbor, but she had no idea that this time, she might be the one proven wrong.

Dead wrong.

Chapter Two

The following morning as Hayley fed the kids breakfast before school, Danny slammed through the back door, having just finished his overnight shift at the Big Apple.

"You are not going to believe this one!" Danny bellowed before stopping at the counter and picking up a piece of bacon off a plate she was about to serve the kids, who sat at the kitchen table gorging on blueberry pancakes.

"Try me," Hayley said, pouring orange juice from a carton into two glasses and setting them down in front of Gemma and Dustin.

"Edna Poole stopped into the store around five this morning to buy a carton of cigarettes. . . ."

"She did?" Hayley gasped. "I heard she just beat lung cancer. Why on earth would she still be smoking?"

"That's not the big news, sweet pea." Danny sighed, slightly annoyed. "Edna told me she heard someone just bought the house next door."

Dustin shoveled a forkful of pancakes into his mouth, but still decided to speak despite Hayley's constant pleas to never talk with his mouth full. "You mean the *haunted* house?"

"Yep, that's the one," Danny confirmed.

"It's *not* haunted!" Hayley said sharply, glaring at Danny.

"Says you," Danny scoffed, peering out the kitchen window over at the house next door. "Man, I can't imagine why anyone would want to move into that House of Horrors!"

"Danny!" Hayley screamed.

"What if they bring in a priest to perform an exorcism and they get rid of the ghosts, but then the ghosts decide to come over here and move into *our* house?" Gemma wailed, suddenly frightened.

"How would you know anything about priests and exorcisms?" Hayley asked Gemma, who was now busy sucking down her juice.

Gemma didn't see her father pleading with his eyes for her not to expose him until it was too late. "He showed us the movie *The Exorcist* when you were down in Florida visiting Nana last month."

Hayley spun around to Danny, eyes blazing. "He did *what*?"

"That girl with the funny voice and spinning head who threw up that green stuff was awesome!" Dustin said excitedly.

Hayley shook her head. "Danny, how could you . . . ?"

He knew his defense was weak, but he valiantly stood his ground. "It's a classic."

"Is this what it's come to? I can't even leave you alone with the kids anymore?" Hayley said, shaking her head.

Danny decided it was best not to go there so he just skated past it and turned to Gemma. "Don't worry, baby girl, Daddy will protect you from any ghosts. You know why? Because I'm a bad-ass Ghostbuster!"

"Watch your language," Hayley scolded, before checking the clock on the stove. "Hurry up, you guys, the school bus is going to be here any minute."

Gemma and Dustin picked up their plates and set them in the sink as they were trained to do, and then grabbed their coats and knapsacks and headed out the front door to wait at the corner.

Danny, who was fully aware he was in the dog-house, grabbed another piece of bacon, and dashed down the hall for the stairs. "I'm beat, babe. I need some shut-eye after that long shift. I'll clean up after the kids later."

She knew he wouldn't, so she began scraping the remnants of the kids' breakfast off their plates and into the garbage can with a fork. When she went to put the carton of orange juice back in the refrigerator, she suddenly spotted Dustin's brown bag lunch that she had prepared the night before on the top shelf. Gemma always purchased her lunch through the school lunch program, but Dustin, who was a far pickier eater, preferred to know exactly what he was going to eat every day. Hayley had forgotten to give it to him when she rushed him out the door.

She snatched the sack and dashed out the door to the street where the kids were still waiting for the school bus. They weren't alone. A man in his late thirties, tall and lanky, with a receding hairline and a rather odd-shaped nose, almost more like a beak, and dark, almost coal black eyes, stood near-by with two children who were roughly Gemma's and Dustin's ages. The boy appeared to be about twelve or thirteen years old, pudgy, red-faced, with angry eyes, like he was having a perpetual tantrum, and the girl, a bit younger, perhaps around nine, was rail thin, with flat black hair and a pale, almost ghostly complexion. What added to her mystique was that she was dressed all in black, unlike most girls her age who usually gravitated toward bright colors.

"Dustin, you forgot your lunch," Hayley said, distracted by the strangers at the bus stop.

"Oh, thanks," Dustin said, grabbing the bag and ripping it open to inspect the items his mother had served him. "An apple, really?"

"I told you, I want you eating a piece of fruit at least four times a week, so don't you dare trade it for a chocolate bar. Do you hear me?" Hayley warned.

"Like anybody would take that deal," Dustin mumbled.

The man noticed her staring and looked away, but that didn't deter Hayley from bouncing over to him. "Hello, are you new to the neighborhood?"

Unable to avoid her any longer, the man gave her a gruff nod. "Yes."

The house next door.

A family had moved in.

"My goodness, we just heard someone had bought the house next to us, but when did you have time to move in? During the dead of night?"

Gemma chuckled and Hayley quickly realized her poor choice of words and quickly tried to correct herself. "I mean, I haven't seen any moving trucks."

He didn't answer her question. It was clear he had no interest in having a conversation, but that wasn't going to stop Hayley from trying again with his two children. "Hi, I'm Hayley, and this is my daughter, Gemma, and my son, Dustin. We're going to be your new neighbors. What are your names?"

The kids were slightly more responsive than their father.

The boy spoke for both of them with his high-pitched, grating voice that hopefully would be corrected when puberty hit. "I'm Casper and this is my sister, Carrie."

"Nice to meet you both," Hayley said, wishing her kids would do more than just stand there staring at these rather strange-acting kids.

Hayley put out her hand to the father. "Hayley Powell."

He was cornered and had no choice but to engage with her. "Damien. Damien Salinger."

"Damien, like the kid in that movie *The Omen!*" Dustin squealed.

Hayley was ready to kill Danny. *The Omen?* He showed the kids *The Omen,* too?

The father glowered at Dustin. "I never saw it."

"Well, let me be the first to welcome you all to the neighborhood!" Hayley chirped just as the school bus pulled up to the curb and all four kids piled in. "Have a good day! Nice to meet you, Casper and Carrie."

As the bus pulled away, Hayley turned back to chitchat with Damien, but he was already walking into his house, slamming the door hard behind him.

Hayley then hurried back to her own house and finished cleaning up the kitchen before driving to work. It was a busy day and there was a lot of news to cover, from a controversial new state regulation about the minimum size of wild oysters that could be harvested, to news that the heavily traveled Goose Cove Road in Trenton would be closed for a week for clean-up and repair work on the shoulders and drainage ditches. Hayley had briefly inquired about the family that had moved in next door to her, but her boss, Sal, and all the reporters working in the office that day had no clue about them. Despite the rather cold shoulder she had received from the patriarch, Damien, Hayley was determined to make an effort and befriend her new neighbors, so after work she stopped in the Shop 'n Save, picked up some ingredients, and went home to make the delicious-sounding Creamy Cheese Fall Vegetable Casserole that she had read about in one of Hattie Jenkins's columns.

When her oven timer rang announcing the casserole was fully cooked just after seven o'clock, she let it cool on the stovetop for about fifteen minutes before wrapping it in tinfoil and walking it next door. She knew that someone was home because a light downstairs was on even though the rest of the house was dark. She rang the bell and waited. After about a minute, she rang it again. Still no answer. She tried one more time and then turned around to go back to her house and write a note to leave with the casserole when the front door finally creaked open, and a rather striking woman in her early thirties, with lush blond hair, an hourglass figure, and perhaps a tad too much makeup, stood in the threshold. She wore a beautiful print sundress that was partially hidden by an apron that had a saying printed across it that read I'M A MOM. WHAT'S YOUR SUPERPOWER?

"Oh, that's cute." Hayley chuckled.

"What?" the woman asked, a bit confused.

"Your apron."

She woman stared down at it as if she was reading it for the first time, and then she looked back up at Hayley, and almost as an afterthought, remembered to plaster a warm smile on her face.

"Thank you for noticing."

The woman's behavior struck Hayley as a bit peculiar, but she decided to brush right past it and stick out her hand while balancing the casserole dish in the palm of her other hand with an oven mitt. "I'm Hayley Powell. I live next door. I met your husband and two children this morning while they were waiting for the school bus."

Hayley suddenly realized that she still had her hand out and the woman had yet to take it. She just stared at her blankly. Then, as the woman processed that she should probably do something to relieve the awkwardness, the woman took Hayley's hand and shook it limply before slowly, almost robotically, withdrawing it.

"I'm Rosemary," she said flatly.

She reminded Hayley of a Stepford Wife from another movie she was certain Danny had already shown the kids.

"What can I help you with, Hayley?"

"Well, I know you just moved in, and that it can be stressful unpacking boxes and pushing furniture around while feeding and caring for two young children, so I thought you might appreciate a casserole."

"We already ate," she said, eyeing the casserole like she had never seen one before.

"Oh, okay," Hayley said, grimacing slightly. "Well,

I can attest to the fact that this casserole tastes even better warmed up."

Rosemary still made no move to take the casserole from Hayley. "What kind of casserole is it?"

Now Hayley was on more solid ground. She loved talking about food. "It's a Creamy Cheese Fall Vegetable Casserole. My kids love it! Pretty much the only way I can get them to eat vegetables is when they're smothered in cheese! I put in carrots, sweet potato, butternut squash, celery . . ."

She didn't seem to care. "Is there any dairy?"

Hayley was deflated and stopped ticking off all the yummy vegetables in her casserole. "Uh, yes, the recipe requires some cream cheese, which is why it's called Creamy Cheese Fall Vegetable—"

Rosemary didn't let her finish. "What else?"

Hayley withdrew her friendly offering, knowing there was little chance at this point of this woman ever accepting her kind gesture. "Some shredded Parmesan and . . . three cups of milk."

"Casper is lactose intolerant."

"I see. Well, maybe your daughter will like it."

"She refuses to consume any dairy out of respect for her brother."

"That's very sweet . . . Maybe you and your husband might—?"

"We make it a habit of banning all dairy in our house."

"Okay, then, I will just take this home with me then," Hayley said. "You have a good evening."

Rosemary, who seemed to be two steps behind in the conversation, finally had the awareness to part with a curt "Thank you."

And then she slammed the door in Hayley's face.

Hayley looked down at her rejected casserole and decided that since she had already prepared the kids a spaghetti pie, there was only one thing left for her to do: Drop her scrumptious Creamy Cheese Fall Vegetable Casserole off at Mona's house where it would be properly appreciated.

Of course Mona was elated over Hayley's casserole and declared she was going to hide it from her deadbeat husband, Dennis, and her greedy, marauding kids. She more than made up for the chilly reception Hayley had received from Rosemary Salinger.

And when Danny heard about Hayley's two run-ins with the new neighbors, he came to the simple yet appropriate conclusion that the Addams Family had just moved in next door.

Chapter Three

The Powell family candy haul for Halloween 2009 was particularly successful. Mostly because, in Danny's opinion, he and Hayley had dressed up too to escort their kids door to door to all the houses in the neighborhood. It was something about an entire family decked out in costumes that nudged people to give away more of their stash. Maybe it was the above and beyond effort put into the trick-or-treating tradition. Most parents would just throw on a coat and simply chaperone their children. But not Danny Powell. No, this was as much fun for him as it was for the kids. His Russell Crowe-inspired gladiator costume was impressive, and Hayley had to admit to herself that it was also kind of sexy. A lot of the mothers who opened the door after Dustin rang the bell were flabbergasted and a bit flustered at the sight of Danny's muscled arms and sturdy legs. Danny's body armor and leather tunic were a bit itchy, however, and he had to keep scratching himself with his plastic sword. It was a bit colder than had been forecast so Hayley had to wear an overcoat over her white Marilyn Monroe dress that she had tailored specifically to look like the one Marilyn wore in *The Seven Year Itch* in that famous scene where she stands over a subway grate and the skirt blows up as a train shoots by below. The wind in Bar Harbor was also gusty on this Halloween night, and more than once Hayley had to hold her blond wig down tight so it didn't fly away. Gemma and Dustin both looked adorable in their Power Ranger and Jack Sparrow costumes respectively, and at this point, with only a few houses to go, their plastic orange pumpkins were overflowing with candy as was Danny's. Hayley had tried to talk him out of participating in the actual trick-or-treating, but Danny insisted that if they went to the trouble of dressing up, they should be rewarded for it. Hayley finally was too tired to argue the point further, and so Danny beamed excitedly as they hit their last house on Ledgelawn Avenue, and he got not one, not two, but three packages of Reese's Peanut Butter Cups.

Hayley checked her watch. "It's almost nine o'clock. I think it's time we wrap this up."

"We still haven't hit School Street yet," Danny cried.

"You guys don't have room for any more candy in your pumpkins," Hayley said, laughing.

"I figured this might happen given how awesome we all look, so I bought extra pumpkins for us earlier today! We can drop the full ones off at the house and pick up the empty ones and do another round!"

"That just sounds greedy, Danny," Hayley said.

"Halloween comes around just once a year. Why not take full advantage of it?"

"Mommy, my feet are tired," Dustin whined, tugging on the bottom half of her white dress.

Hayley turned to her husband. "We're done, Danny. Let's just go home."

Danny shuffled his feet, and bowed his head, moping, but did what he was told. The family turned onto Glenmary Road and walked en masse down the sidewalk toward their house.

"Can I have a Jolly Rancher when we get home?" Gemma asked.

"Just one. I don't need you on a sugar high before bedtime," Hayley said.

As they approached the Powell family home, Hayley noticed two people standing in the driveway of the house next door to them. It was dark, but Hayley could make out a man and a woman, and they appeared to be in the middle of an argument. The porch light from the Powell house was bright enough to illuminate the man's face so she could identify him. It was Damien Salinger. He was clutching a sharp ax in one hand, moving it around menacingly, as if he was coiled and ready to strike at any moment. The woman's back was to them, but Hayley instantly knew it wasn't Mrs. Salinger because this woman was about a foot shorter and rather stout and had auburn hair.

"Look, it's Gomez Addams," Danny sneered.

"Shhhh, he'll hear you," Hayley scolded.

"Mommy, is Mr. Salinger going to hit that lady with his ax?" Dustin practically yelled.

"Let's hope not, dear," Hayley whispered.

They were finally close enough to hear what Damien and the woman were saying.

"If you think this is over, you're wrong," Damien seethed. "Not by a long shot. You're tangling with the wrong man, I promise you that," Damien retorted.

"You don't scare me with your threatening tone. I've dealt with a lot worse than you," the woman spit out, not the least bit intimidated by the weird man brandishing an ax.

"Get off my property," Damien warned.

"Listen, Salinger, I'm not some submissive housewife you can boss around, like your own wife!"

At the mention of his wife, Rosemary, Damien gripped the ax tighter and then, without warning, raised it in the air. The woman, startled, stumbled back a few steps, almost tripping over her own two feet.

Hayley opened her mouth to scream, but Danny beat her to it by shouting, "Good evening!"

Damien suddenly noticed the entire Powell family, Gladiator Dad, Marilyn Mom, and the two kids, Pink Power Ranger and Jack Sparrow, all frozen on the sidewalk, gaping at him with an ax raised over his head.

This had discombobulated the woman enough that she had her hands up in front of her face to protect herself. "You're crazy! Do you hear me, crazy!"

When she spun around, Hayley instantly recognized her. It was Wendi Jo Willis, a local Realtor, and if she was being honest, a big pain in the butt. Wendi Jo was abrasive, conniving, and willing to do just about anything to sell a house. Whenever her name came up in conversation, either at work or at their favorite watering hole in town, Drinks Like a Fish, people would easily refer to her as that "loudmouth" or "annoying harpy" or "she-devil," just to name a few choice descriptors.

As Wendi Jo hustled past the Powells, she screamed so loud she scared the kids, "You're living next to a crazy person!"

And then she was gone.

Danny stood protectively in front of his family as Damien, as if almost in a trance, still had the ax raised over his head. "Dude, what the hell do you think you're doing?"

Damien stood there, gazing after Wendi Jo as she got into her car parked across the street and sped off. "She was trespassing."

"So what? You were going to settle the matter with *that?*" he hollered, pointing to the ax.

Damien finally seemed to snap out of it. He looked at the ax he was holding above his head and slowly lowered it. "No . . ." He then gestured to the side of the house where a stack of chopped wood was piled up. "I was chopping wood. We've got a fire going inside."

Hayley didn't believe him for a moment. She had seen the wild look in his eye, as if he was unable to control his rage. In her gut, she knew he was fully capable of using that ax as a weapon.

Without another word, Damien tossed the ax over by the pile of wood and stalked back inside his house.

Dustin called after him, raising his plastic pumpkin, "Trick or treat!"

Danny covered Dustin's mouth with his hand. "I don't think you want any tricks or treats from that guy, champ."

Hayley had been disappointed that the new family next door wasn't friendly, but now she was worried that it might be more than that after what they had just witnessed. Damien Salinger struck her as unhinged and possibly dangerous.

Chapter Four

Hayley reached over and pinched Danny's nose in an attempt to stop his incessant snoring. He had been particularly amorous when they went to bed just a few minutes earlier, but after whispering some sweet nothings in her ear as he wrapped her in his arms, he drifted off to sleep. He had taken the night off from the store but was still exhausted from escorting the kids around the entire neighborhood trick-or-treating. Five minutes later, as if on cue, Danny's mouth opened like a drawbridge and he was off to the races, snoring as loud as a jackhammer.

Hayley always wondered why, when it came to married couples, the one who snores always falls asleep first. She tried her usual tactics first, nudging him and gently telling him to stop, as if that had any chance of working. Then she rolled him over on his side, and he stopped for a bit, but as soon as she turned over he started up again. And now she was cutting off air to his nose, and got ready to duck when he would inevitably start thrashing around and waving his arms. She let go just as he stirred awake and she quickly closed her eyes, pretending to be asleep. He looked around and then settled back down again, mumbling something to himself that she couldn't make out.

Two minutes later he was at it again. Hayley reached over to the bedside table and picked up her iPod and earplugs and began listening to some Enya songs hoping they would lull her to sleep. It seemed to be working. Her eyes got heavy and were slowly closing when suddenly she felt something wet on her face. She tried to brush it away, but it was relentless, like a sloppy tongue lapping up salt on her skin. When she realized this wasn't some kind of strange dream and there was something on her face, she jolted up in bed and yanked the buds out of her ears.

She squinted at a little fur ball sitting in her lap and relaxed as she could make out in the dark the happy, panting face of the new family puppy, Leroy. She reached down and patted him gently on the head and then glanced up to see two figures standing at the foot of the bed. Hayley let out a scream and pulled the covers up to her neck as if that would help. Leroy bounced off her lap and almost flew off the side of the bed. Hayley quickly reached over and snapped on the light to see the large blinking eyes of Gemma and Dustin in their pajamas, looking terrified.

"What? What is it?" Hayley gasped.

"Mommy, we're scared!"

Danny was still snoring and Hayley decided she wasn't going to deal with this matter alone since he was the one responsible, so she shook him, harder this time, and when that still didn't work, she slapped his face until he groggily opened his eyes.

"What's happening? What time is it?" he sputtered.

"It's time for you to deal with what you've done!"

"What are talking about?" He moaned as he sat up, rubbed his eyes, and yawned.

Hayley pointed at the two children, who were now climbing up on the bed with them.

"What are you guys still doing up?" Danny asked as Gemma scurried over and hugged her father while Dustin did the same with his mother.

"I'll tell you what they're still doing up," Hayley said, exasperated. "You frightened them with all your scary movies and ghost stories and now they can't sleep!"

"Aw, come on. You guys know none of that is real, don't you?"

"They're nine and twelve, Danny. They're very impressionable," Hayley scolded.

Danny looked at them curiously. "So which one kept you both up?"

Gemma shook her head. "It wasn't a movie or one of your stories, Dad . . ."

Hayley looked at Gemma, confused. "Then what?"

Gemma exchanged a look with Dustin, as if they were afraid to speak because they might get into trouble.

"Tell me . . ." Hayley warned.

Dustin was the first one to break. "We snuck downstairs to eat some of our Halloween candy! It was Gemma's idea!"

"Tattletale!" Gemma screamed.

"Okay, so you ate too much and you had a bad dream!"

"It wasn't a dream! It was real!" Dustin declared.

"We saw him . . ." Gemma said quietly.

"Who?" Danny asked.

Gemma shivered slightly. "That mean man who just moved in next door . . ."

"Mr. Salinger?" Hayley asked.

Gemma nodded, fear in her eyes.

Danny was now captivated by where this was going. "Where did you see him?"

Gemma spoke slowly, making sure to remember all the details. "We were in the dining room picking out candy and we saw him out the window in his yard and he was dragging something across the lawn. It was rolled up in one of those thingies . . ."

"A rug?" Hayley asked.

"No . . . That thing Aunt Mona uses to cover the back of her pickup truck sometimes," Gemma said.

"A tarp!" Hayley guessed.

"Did you see what was in the tarp?" Danny asked.

Gemma nodded again. She looked to her brother, who had his whole face buried in the crook of Hayley's arm, like he didn't want to relive it.

Danny held Gemma tighter and looked down at her cute but anxious face. "Well, what was it, sweetheart?"

"It was dark, but then as he passed by the garage, the light outside came on, like it does whenever a deer comes out of the woods and gets too close, and we could see one end of it and it looked like . . ." Gemma stopped and scrunched up her nose at the memory.

"A lady's head!" Dustin interjected.

"What?" Hayley yelled.

"A body?" Danny bellowed.

"Yes! We could see her hair and part of her face and she wasn't moving!" Gemma shouted.

Hayley might have suspected the kids were playing a trick on their father, trying to get back at him for scaring them with his spooky stories, but neither of her kids was that good of an actor, and so she took them at their word. They had seen *something*.

Danny shot out of bed. "Show me!"

The kids dutifully hopped down off the bed and followed him as he bolted down the stairs.

Hayley sighed and crawled out of bed. She threw on a robe and trudged downstairs, where she found Danny and the kids staring out the dining room window. Leroy was with them, tail wagging.

"He was right there!" Dustin said, pushing his index finger against the glass and smudging it.

"He's gone now," Danny said, sounding disappointed. "You think he might have followed that real estate lady Wendi Jo Willis after we went inside and whacked her in the head with his ax and was getting rid of the body?"

"Danny! Not in front of the kids!" Hayley screamed.

"I'm sorry, but I've gotten nothing but creepy vibes from Salinger ever since he moved in a few days ago!" Danny said.

"I don't believe any of this nonsense!" Hayley said. "Now one of you give Leroy a treat and then we'll all go to bed."

"Can we sleep with you tonight?" Dustin asked, shaken.

Danny patted him on the head. "Of course you can, champ."

Hayley was halfway up the stairs at this point, resigned to the fact that she would be overtired tomorrow at work because she was about to be kept up by a snoring husband and two squirming kids who would be bumping into her all night.

Chapter Five

Hayley was exhausted at work the following morning, having gotten very little sleep after her impromptu slumber party with the kids. She had downed two extra cups of coffee to try and stay awake at her desk. It was unseasonably warm outside and so the office was stuffy and hot and empty since all the reporters were out covering stories. The peaceful quiet threatened to lull her into falling asleep. Her eyes were drooping and a heavy yawn relaxed her to the point where her shoulders sagged as she tapped the keys on her computer. Suddenly the door to the front office blew open and Hattie Jenkins hustled inside at a remarkable speed for a nearly ninety-year-old.

"Good morning, Hattie," Hayley said, shaking her head to wake herself up while suppressing another yawn.

"I don't have time for small talk, Hayley," Hattie barked. "We have an emergency."

"We do?" Hayley asked, looking around at the empty office.

"Yes, I just got a call from Dottie Willis on my car phone as I was driving here."

Car phone? What was this, the 1970s?

Hattie didn't even pretend to be caught up in all the latest technology nonsense like cell phones. She said she didn't have time. She had a life to live.

"Did something happen to Dottie?" Hayley asked, concerned.

"No, why?" Hattie said, puzzled.

"You said there was an emergency."

"Dottie's fine. Where is everybody?"

"There's a meeting at the Town Hall about seasonal worker housing, and a volleyball game at the high school, and a barrel of bait fell out of the back of a fisherman's truck on Main Street, so it is pretty slippery and stinky. The reporters have a lot to cover . . ."

"Where's Sal?"

"Good-bye breakfast for Razor Rick. He's closing his barber shop after fifty-some years."

"Why wasn't I invited to that? I am a good friend of Razor Rick. We even dated for a bit when we were younger. I bet it's because of his wife, Cecile, why I was left off the guest list. She never liked me, probably because Razor Rick still carries a torch for me even after all these years. I was never in the habit of dating much younger men back in the day, but I just couldn't say no when he first asked me out in 1967. How could I possibly resist that beautiful smile of his? It still warms the cockles—"

"Hattie, I don't mean to interrupt, but when you walked in here you mentioned something about an emergency," Hayley said gently.

"I did?" Hattie asked, confused. Suddenly it came back to her. "That's right! I did! Dottie Willis called me!"

"And you said she's fine," Hayley said, trying to be helpful.

"She is, but her daughter's missing! The crazy one that nobody likes!"

"Wendi Jo?"

"Yes! Wendi Jo! She was supposed to have dinner with Dottie last night but she never showed up."

"She didn't call?"

"No, and Dottie says they talk on the phone at least three times a day, although I don't know how Dottie can stand it. Have you heard that grating, annoying voice of hers?"

"Well, I guess she puts up with it because Wendi Jo is her daughter, after all."

"I couldn't do it. Anyway, Dottie is extremely worried. She must have left a dozen messages on Wendi Jo's voice mail, but she still hasn't heard from her."

"That is rather odd," Hayley remarked, her mind racing.

"Dottie called that new chief of police, you know the one I'm talking about," Hattie said, lowering her voice to a whisper. "The one who is light in the loafers, if you know what I mean."

"You mean gay," Hayley sighed. "I do know because he's dating my brother."

Hattie scrunched up her nose. "Oh, that's right. I forgot. Well, Chief what's-his-name . . ."

"Chief Alvares," Hayley said tightly. "Sergio Alvares."

"Yes, Chief Aloe Vera. He said he can't file a missing person report until Wendi Jo is gone at least twenty-four hours."

"When did Dottie last speak to Wendi Jo?"

"Yesterday around two o'clock, she said."

"So he can officially open a case in about three hours."

"I just hope Dottie doesn't have a heart attack before then. She's worried sick. I'm going to go over and check on her during my lunch hour."

"Do you mind if I tag along?"

"I didn't know you two were friends."

"We're not really, more acquaintances. But I feel sorry for what she's going through, and would like to offer my help, if there is anything I can do."

"Not sure what you think you can do, but suit yourself."

Hattie ambled into the back bullpen toward her office.

Hayley watched her go, a wave of concern washing over her.

All she could think about was the fierce argument that she, Danny and the kids had witnessed between Wendi Jo Willis and Damien Salinger on Halloween night. Couple that with Gemma and Dustin swearing they saw Salinger dragging a tarp with what looked like the top of a woman's head sticking out if it, and Hayley felt there was now strong cause to be concerned. Her deepest fear was that Wendi Jo Willis wasn't just missing, she very well might be dead.

Chapter Six

"Wendi Jo would never just up and disappear like this," Dottie Willis wailed, tears streaming down her chubby cheeks as she twisted a finger through her overly bleached platinum blond hair. "Never, never, never . . ."

Beatrice Lumley, one of Dottie's closest friends, hugged Dottie, stretching her rail-thin arms around Dottie's plus-size figure as far as she could. "She'll show up, Dottie. She's alive and well. I can feel it in my bones. It's a strong feeling despite my osteoporosis."

"I just don't understand . . ." Dottie muttered, shaking her head. "This is so unlike Wendi Jo to scare me like this . . . unless she has been kidnapped and being held against her will somewhere!"

Ethel Morton, another friend, frantically waved her hands in front of her face. "Don't even let your mind go there, Dottie!"

Her third pal, who was there to comfort Dottie, Mildred Atkins, nodded in agreement. "We have to stay positive. Maybe she just left town to visit a friend and forgot to tell you."

"Wendi Jo tells me everything!" Dottie wailed before breaking down again. Beatrice got tired of holding her and finally let go and stepped back, leaving Dottie to stand in the middle of the room, basically hugging herself. "She would not leave town and not tell me! Something awful has happened to her! I just know it!"

Hattie hadn't expected to find three friends of Dottie's already on the scene when they came calling, but Dottie explained that she and the women played cards every Wednesday and had already scheduled a game at Dottie's house for that day, which they promptly cancelled after hearing the disturbing news about Wendi Jo's sudden disappearance.

Hayley stood off to the side of Dottie Willis's living room, next to Hattie, who kept her arms folded across her chest, supremely uncomfortable with all the heightened tension and emotion permeating the room.

"If someone did forcibly take Wendi Jo somewhere, do you have any idea who it could have been?" Hayley gently asked.

"No! I don't have a clue! Everyone loved Wendi Jo! She didn't have an enemy in the world!" Dottie cried.

Beatrice, Ethel, and Mildred all stared at the floor to avoid eye contact with each other. It was obvious they didn't agree with Dottie's assessment of her daughter's enduring popularity. Neither did Hayley, having witnessed the blistering altercation Wendi Jo had on the Salinger property with the man of the house.

The long pause in the conversation was excruciating, finally broken by Hattie erupting in a coughing fit.

"Excuse me . . ." Hattie said with a scratchy, weak voice when she finally finished hacking and choking.

"She would never go this long without coming to see me! She stops by here all the time!" Dottie wailed, starting her crying jag all over again. "I even leave a key to the house under the flowerpot out on the front porch so she can let herself in when I'm not here!"

Dottie's three friends rushed in for a group hug. The rotund Ethel nearly knocked the wispy Beatrice off her feet in order to get to Dottie first, and the tall, imposing Mildred came in last, drawing the whole group toward her with her long, outstretched arms. Dottie remained buried in the middle, sobbing.

Hattie, who appeared annoyed that there were so many women already here when they showed up to comfort Dottie, huffed, "Well, I can see you're in good hands, Dottie, so Hayley and I should probably get back to the paper."

"Thank you for stopping by, Hattie. It means the world to me. You too, Hayley . . ." Dottie sniffed from inside the crush of women around her.

"I'm sure she'll turn up soon with a perfectly reasonable explanation," Hayley said, although she wasn't sure she believed it. She had a sinking feeling in the pit of her stomach that just wouldn't go away.

Hayley noticed Mildred glaring at them, her eyes almost ordering them to leave. She was either being overly protective of Dottie or she didn't appreciate the competition for being the most supportive friend in a crisis.

As Hayley and Hattie made their way to the door,

Hayley heard Mildred take charge. "Ethel, you go put a pot of coffee on. I'm going to help Dottie to her room so she can lie down for a bit. Beatrice, you stay by the phone in case Chief Alvares calls."

Outside Dottie's modest house at the shady end of Hancock Street with its towering trees and gravel walkway to the Shore Path, Hayley and Hattie were almost to Hattie's car when they heard the front door open behind them. They turned around to see Beatrice, wrapping her Autumn Burgundy Liz Claiborne cardigan tightly around her as the chilly fall air caused her whole body to shake. She scurried down the walk to catch them before they got into the car. "Ladies, wait . . ."

Hattie clutched her car keys in her hand and sighed impatiently. "What is it, Bea? We have to get back to work."

"I don't want you two to worry about Wendi Jo. I'm certain she's just fine," Beatrice said.

"How do you know that?" Hayley asked.

"Because Dottie, God love her, is in total denial. All of us, me, Ethel, Mildred and yes, Dottie herself, know what really happened."

"Well, now you've got me curious," Hattie said. "Go on, Bea. Don't keep us in suspense. Get to the point before we catch a cold out here. At eighty-nine, I need to be careful."

"Dottie and Wendi Jo have been fighting for months over the fact that Wendi Jo has been seeing a new beau . . ."

"And Dottie doesn't approve?" Hayley guessed.

"Not in the least, because her new boyfriend happens to be married," Beatrice whispered.

"Do you know who it is?" Hattie asked, smelling a scoop.

Beatrice shook her head. "Dottie has kept mum about the man's identity mostly out of respect for his wife, who is clearly in the dark. You know what they say about the wife being the last to know. . . ."

"So what, you think Wendi Jo and the married guy ran off together?" Hattie asked.

"Yes! Wendi Jo has been threatening to do just that for months, but Dottie didn't believe her! She never thought the man would leave his wife and she just could not accept the fact that her daughter is a home wrecker, which is why she'd rather believe she's the victim of foul play!"

Hayley and Hattie exchanged a glance, neither quite ready to accept Beatrice's theory.

Beatrice sensed their trepidation and pressed further. "Trust me. We all know Wendi Jo doesn't have the personality God gave an eggplant. This married man is going to get bored with her very quickly and eventually go home to his wife, and then Wendi Jo will come crying to her mother. As for Dottie, well, I'm sure she will forgive her baby girl mostly because it will give her the opportunity to unleash an avalanche of 'I told you so's . . .' which is Dottie's favorite pasttime besides a good card game."

Hayley nodded. "Thanks for the info, Beatrice."

"I better get back inside and pretend to be worried," she chirped before turning around and bounding toward the house.

"Do you think she's right?" Hayley asked Hattie, who was unlocking the car door on the driver's side.

Hattie shrugged. "How the hell do I know? I don't trust any of them."

"Why not?"

"They never invited me to play cards."

Chapter Seven

Hayley clutched the phone to her ear. "So it's now officially a missing person case?"

"As of late this afternoon when Dottie still hadn't heard from her," Hayley's brother Randy answered. "Sergio also got Dottie to spill the beans on Wendi Jo's secret married boyfriend. Turns out it is Buster Higgins."

"No!" Hayley gasped. "Buster is so reliable and devoted to his wife, Kathy. He's like a loyal basset hound."

"Kind of looks like one, too," Randy said.

"I can't imagine him cheating on anyone," Hayley said, disappointed.

"Apparently, Wendi Jo hired Buster to do some repair work on one of her houses she was trying to sell, and one rainy afternoon, when the two of them were in the basement inspecting a leaky drain pipe, one thing led to another . . ."

"This is so disheartening. Buster, of all people . . . I mean, I can totally see Wendi Jo putting the moves on him in a basement. She's the epitome of *the other woman*."

"Sergio stopped by the Higgins house and found Buster at home having dinner with Kathy so that kind of blew a hole through Beatrice's theory of Buster and Wendi Jo running off together."

"Sergio didn't ask Buster about his affair with Wendi Jo in front of Kathy, did he?"

"Fortunately not. I mean, Sergio can be rather blunt when he's investigating a case, but I begged him to get Buster to come down to the station for questioning and not destroy a marriage before all the facts were in," Randy said.

"Poor Kathy . . ." Hayley said, her voice trailing off.

"I know. It's bad enough that your husband is having an affair behind your back, but then to find out it's with Wendi Jo Willis? I would kill myself."

"So the big question now is, if Wendi Jo didn't run off with her married boyfriend, then what did happen to her?" Hayley wondered.

Danny wandered into the kitchen and pointed out the window. "We know what happened! The answer is right next door!"

Hayley sighed. "Listen, I've got to go, Randy. Keep me posted."

"Will do," Randy said and hung up.

Hayley put down the phone. "Danny, you have to stop this. Our new neighbors are not the Manson Family."

"How do we really know that? We all saw Wendi Jo arguing with that weirdo Damien Salinger! And what about him dragging something in that tarp! The kids swear they saw it and we raised them to never lie!"

"That doesn't mean they saw a dead body rolled up in that tarp! It was dark outside! Maybe it was something that just looked like a body!"

"Come on, babe. I think we should poke around some more and get the real story on that creepy family. Something's just not right and you know it."

"We are not detectives, and this isn't some Alfred Hitchcock movie. I'm not going to spy on the neighbors. It would set a bad example for the kids. Let the police handle it."

"Sergio? He couldn't find a taco chip in a Mexican restaurant."

"Hey! That's my brother's boyfriend you're talking about and he is a fine chief of police, so you better stop bad-mouthing him right now!"

"Sergio's all right. But we have a distinct advantage. We're closer to the crime scene. It's right next door!"

"There is no crime scene, Danny! I'm warning you, do not keep talking about your suspicions in front of the kids. I don't want them exposed to all this dark subject matter. Do you hear me?"

"Yeah . . . Fine . . . whatever . . ." Danny sighed.

"Danny . . ."

"Okay, yes, I'll keep my mouth shut."

The doorbell rang, and after shooting Danny one last look of warning, Hayley spun around and marched down the hall to the front door and swung it open. Damien Salinger stood on the porch steps, with Gemma on one side of him and Dustin on the other. He gripped them both by the back of their necks and was boiling with anger. Both kids looked down at their shoes, avoiding eye contact with their mother at all costs.

"Hello, Damien," Hayley said warily as she eyed her two kids in his grip.

"I caught these rug rats peeking through my

windows while we were having dinner!" Damien said gruffly.

"W-What?" Hayley sputtered before glaring down at her two children, both of whom had guilt written all over their faces.

"I thought Rosemary was going to have a heart attack when she spotted them with their noses pressed to the glass! Gave her a good scare!"

The sound of Damien's voice drew Danny from the kitchen. "What's going on?"

Hayley folded her arms. "Damien—I mean Mr. Salinger—says Gemma and Dustin were spying on his family while they were trying to have dinner."

"Is that true?" Danny asked, mustering up as much of the disciplinarian dad persona as he possibly could.

Dustin kept his eyes fixed on the floor, but Gemma, who was on the verge of tears, bravely lifted her head and slowly nodded before squeaking out, "I'm sorry. . . ."

Danny practically swelled with pride. Hayley was so worried Damien would notice that she stepped in front of him to block his inappropriate reaction.

"Get in this house right now," Hayley barked to the kids.

Damien let go of them and they sprang forward, grateful to be free from his grasp, and disappeared into the living room.

"I am terribly sorry. This will not happen again, I assure you," Hayley said.

"It better not," Damien warned before doing an about-face and stalking off. Hayley shut the door and marched into the living room where Danny was already peppering the kids with questions. "So what did you see? Anything stand out as suspicious?"

"No! This ends right now! What you two did was wrong. You do not trespass onto our neighbors' property and disrespect their right to privacy!" Hayley shot Danny a look, who suddenly snapped to attention.

"Your mother is right. That's bad, what you did. Even if you saw something . . . which I'm sure if you did, you'd tell us, right?"

The kids were digging into their plastic pumpkins for candy.

Hayley snatched the pumpkins away from them. "No, you don't get to eat this candy. I'm confiscating it."

"But that's our candy from trick-or-treating!" Dustin wailed.

"Not anymore. I'm getting rid of it. I'm going to give it to Mona!" Hayley yelled.

"Mona! But she'll eat all of it!" Gemma cried.

"That's the idea. You need to be punished for what you did. Now go wash up for dinner and after you eat, you're both going straight to bed and no TV or video games. Do you hear me?"

Gemma and Dustin knew they were not going to win this one so they stomped upstairs. Hayley spun around to Danny. "And as for you, if you even mention the word *murder,* or tell another ghost story, or encourage the kids in any way to do something like this again, I promise you, Danny Powell, you will rue the day you ever married me! Do you understand?"

Danny nodded, a hangdog look on his face, like a puppy who just got caught chewing up the corner of a new throw rug.

Chapter Eight

Hayley knew the Wendi Jo Willis situation was getting more serious when Sal chose to run the headline POLICE STILL SEARCHING FOR LOCAL WOMAN MISSING TWO DAYS in tomorrow's issue of the *Island Times*. The paper's hotline had also been ringing off the hook with reports of Wendi Joe sightings all over the island, although none proved credible. Mostly the calls came from bored residents trying to stick their noses into the case in order to get in on the action and garner some attention. Dottie Willis had appeared on the local Fox affiliate begging for the safe return of her daughter. Chief Alvares was working with the credit card companies, but none of Wendi Jo's cards had been used anywhere since the day she disappeared.

After a long day at the office, Hayley needed to wind down, and so after calling Danny to look after the kids, she met with her other BFF besides Mona, local real estate agent and self-proclaimed fashionista Liddy Crawford. Liddy was already sitting at the bar of Randy's watering hole Drinks

Like a Fish when Hayley arrived after work, sipping her signature Cosmo and flirting with a couple of fishermen who flanked her on both sides, showering her with compliments about her hair and outfit. Liddy beamed and cooed breathless thank-yous, all the while feigning surprise and disbelief over the attention from these two handsome gentlemen, which she deemed unwarranted with the perfect dose of false modesty. The two fishermen didn't strike Hayley as "gentlemen," but more like two male dogs in heat sniffing around a coquettish Labradoodle.

"I'll take a Jack and Coke," Hayley yelled to Randy, who acknowledged her with a nod of the head while filling a mug of beer from the tap for another customer.

Liddy spun around on her stool, her face flushed from the attentiveness from her two gallant admirers, who in Hayley's opinion, both smelled of day-old trout. "How was your day, Hayley?"

"Crazy. We were inundated with tips on the whereabouts of Wendi Jo Willis, all of which we forwarded to the police, but not one seems to have panned out according to Sergio," Hayley said, climbing up on the stool next to Liddy.

"I cannot believe people are buying into that load of crap that Wendi Jo Willis has been abducted. I mean, let's face it, any kidnapper needs only to spend ten minutes with her before giving her back. Have you *met* the woman?"

"Liddy, that's not very nice," Hayley scolded.

"I'm sorry, but I refuse to believe this has anything to do with foul play," Liddy said as she sipped some more of her Cosmo. "We all know what really happened."

Hayley scrunched up her face, puzzled. "We do?"

"Of course. The poor woman has for years erroneously considered herself the premier real estate agent in Bar Harbor, and it was only a matter of time before she woke up to the fact that she will never be number one, and she will forever remain in my shadow. I am the number one agent on this island and that will never change!" Liddy declared as if she was standing behind a podium at a political rally, running for President of All Real Estate.

"That may be true, Liddy, but why would that have anything to do with her disappearance?" Hayley asked as Randy delivered her drink and she took a grateful gulp.

"She could no longer stand the intense competition so she left town to set up stakes somewhere else, and frankly I don't blame her. I wouldn't want to go up against me!"

"You're giving yourself a lot of credit," Hayley remarked.

"I deserve it! I sold nineteen houses last year. Six summer homes and thirteen year-round residences. That may be some kind of record."

Liddy could hardly contain her glee that her closest competitor, Wendi Jo Willis, was finally out of the picture, leaving the local real estate landscape all to herself. "There is no doubt in my mind she blew town of her own accord, right, Emmett?"

One of the fishermen, with wind-burned cheeks and a long brown beard speckled with gray, leaned in and bumped arms with Liddy. "Whatever you say, kitten. You got me under your spell."

Hayley couldn't help but roll her eyes.

The other fisherman, Cappy, more roly-poly and with a cheery scruffy face, downed his beer. "If you ask me, I think she joined some kind of cult. I heard there were a couple groups stockpiling weapons and supplies for when the Blackhawk government helicopters come to take away their guns."

"That's ridiculous, Cappy!" Liddy bellowed, shaking her head.

"Yeah," Emmett agreed, slipping an arm around Liddy's waist. "I heard she was up in Bangor at one of those Italian restaurants where the Boston mob sometimes frequents in order to bring their racketeering operations here to Maine and witnessed some kind of hit and now she's been put in the Witness Protection Program and is living in some cornfield in Iowa."

Liddy swiveled around to face her amorous fisherman. "Are you kidding me, Emmett? Is that honestly what you believe? That's just silly."

"It's no more silly than believing she got out of Dodge because she was afraid of you selling more houses than her," Emmett said, snickering.

Liddy arched her back and then pushed his arm down that encircled her waist. "Don't touch me."

Emmett bowed his head as it dawned on him that he had just ruined his chances of a make-out session with the glamorous and alluring Liddy Crawford.

"Go play darts or something. I need to talk to my best friend for a while," Liddy snapped.

Emmett and Cappy, resigned to rejection, picked up their beers and shuffled toward the back of the bar just as Liddy's mouth dropped open after turning back around and facing the front door of the bar.

"What is it?" Hayley asked, spinning around to see what had so suddenly gotten her attention.

She spotted Danny hustling toward them, his face a ghostly white.

"My God, Danny. What happened to you?" Hayley cried.

Danny reached out and grabbed her hands, squeezing them tight as he opened his mouth to speak, but no words came out.

Hayley shuddered. "What is it? Did something happen to the kids?"

Danny shook his head. "No . . . nothing like that . . ."

"Then *what*?" Hayley demanded to know.

Danny took a deep breath. "I was out in the yard raking leaves. . . ."

"That *is* shocking news," Liddy said. "Hayley says she can't get you to do *anything*. . . ."

Danny shot her an irritated look and then turned his attention back to Hayley. "I kept hearing this banging and then the sound of a power saw, and I couldn't tell where it was coming from at first so I followed the noise around the back of the Salinger house. It was coming from Damien's shed, the one I see him going into all the time where he spends hours . . ."

Hayley wrenched her hands out of his grip. "Danny, tell me you didn't . . ."

"I couldn't help it. I had to know. I snuck up and just took a quick look through the window. . . ."

"What did you see?" Liddy exclaimed, dying of curiosity.

"Please don't encourage him!" Hayley begged.

Danny swallowed hard. "The window was pretty dirty, and it was hard to get a good look, but I swear I saw him holding what looked like a woman's arm . . ."

Liddy screamed.

The entire bar fell silent except for Carrie Underwood's singing coming from the jukebox. After a moment, the bar patrons went back to their own conversations and Emmett and Cappy returned to their dart game.

"A woman's arm? Oh, come on, Danny!" Hayley snorted.

"I'm telling you, it looked to me like he was dismembering a body!"

Randy appeared, eyes wide. "What happened next?"

"Not you too, Randy!" Hayley cried.

"Nothing. I just got the hell out of there! I didn't want him to see me spying on him and then come after me with his chain saw!"

"Danny, I've had it up to here with your wild murder conspiracy stories!"

"I saw what I saw, Hayley!" Danny shouted.

"Then tell Sergio!" Hayley said, calling his bluff. "He's still at the office. You can go over there right now."

Danny hesitated.

"What's the matter? If you're one hundred percent certain you saw Damien Salinger cutting up Wendi Jo Willis's body, then what are you waiting for?"

Danny shifted uncomfortably, his mind racing. "Well, I'm pretty sure it was a woman's arm, but I can't be absolutely sure. Like I said, the window was smeared with dirt and it was kind of hard to see. . . ."

"Then that's that. If you're not confident enough to report it to the police, then that's the last I want to hear about it. Do you understand me, Danny?"

"But babe, just because I can't swear to it—"

Hayley was having none of it. "*Do you understand?*"

"Yes, babe," Danny whispered, defeated. "I need a beer."

"No, you need to go home right now and look after the kids while I enjoy some girl time with Liddy! It's Mommy's night off!"

"Yes, dear," Danny said sheepishly as he retreated out of the bar.

Chapter Nine

After walking home from Drinks Like a Fish about an hour later, Hayley instantly sensed something was wrong as she entered the house through the back door. Danny stood in the kitchen wearing a heavy plaid vest over his gray corduroy shirt, gripping a flashlight in his right hand. Gemma and Dustin hovered around him, both looking worried. Dustin's eyes were watery as if he had been crying.

Oh no, Hayley thought to herself. *What's happened now?*

Dustin ran to his mother and threw his small skinny arms around her waist. "Mommy, I'm sorry! Please don't hate me!"

Hayley hugged him and tried to comfort him. "I could never hate you, honey, no matter what."

"You haven't heard what he *did!*" Gemma sniffed, almost as upset as her brother.

Hayley eyed Danny for an explanation.

"He left the back door open when he got home and Leroy got out," Danny said quietly. "I've been around the block a few times already, calling to him, but so far there's been no sign of him."

"Well, he's got his tags on. I'm sure it's only a matter of time before someone finds him and calls us . . ." Hayley said before noticing the guilty look on Dustin's face.

"You told me to give him a bath and so I did, and I took the tags off first like you said, but I forgot to put them back on him after he was clean . . . !"

"Dustin, no . . ." Hayley gasped.

"See? You *hate* me!" Dustin wailed.

"No one hates you," Hayley tried assuring him.

"I do!" Gemma cried. "How could you be so stupid?"

Hayley whirled around and jabbed a finger at Gemma. "You stop that right now. It was an accident. Don't make your brother feel worse than he already does!"

"But Leroy's out there all alone! What if he can't find his way home? What if someone finds him and decides to keep him because they don't know who he belongs to! We may never see him again!" Gemma cried.

Dustin covered his ears with his hands to block out her voice.

Hayley kneeled down and kissed her son on the cheek. "Don't you worry, Dustin. We'll find him. We'll put an ad in the paper and blanket the town with pictures of him. Leroy will turn up. I'm sure of it." She gently took his hands and lowered them from his ears. "Okay?"

Dustin sniffed, wiped his nose with the back of his hand, and slowly nodded.

Hayley stood back up. "Now I want both of you to go upstairs and get your homework done before dinner. I've got some leftover spaghetti pie in the fridge. I'll warm it up when your father and I get back."

"Where are you going?" Gemma asked.

"We're going to go out and search some more. He may not have gone far," Hayley said.

"I've combed the neighborhood calling his name. He's not answering."

"What about the woods?" Hayley asked.

Danny didn't answer her. He didn't have to. She knew he had a fear of the woods after dark and it was almost pitch-black outside. The streetlights did little to illuminate the large pine and fir trees that swayed back and forth ominously in the fall night breeze.

"We'll be back soon," Hayley said, heading out the door.

"Maybe we should wait until morning to search the woods. It's awfully dark now . . ." Danny whispered warily.

"You can wait until it's light out. I'm going *now,*" Hayley said, snatching the flashlight out of his hand.

Danny only had to take one look at the expectant looks on his children's faces before he realized he had no choice. What kind of dad would he be if he stayed home while his wife ventured out into the night alone in search of the family's missing pooch?

"You heard your mother. Upstairs, now! Your homework's waiting!" Danny barked as Gemma and Dustin whipped around and scrambled up the stairs to their rooms.

Hayley marched out the door to the backyard. Across the way, she could see through the dining

room windows of the Salinger house, the whole
family seated at the table eating dinner in silence.
None of them looked the least bit happy. Danny
came up close behind Hayley and whispered in
her ear, "You think maybe they snatched Leroy?"

"Stop it, Danny," Hayley said, nudging him in
the stomach with her elbow. "Let's go."

With Danny close on her heels, Hayley hustled
toward the thicket of trees, which served as a gate-
way to the scary unknown of the woods. She could
sense Danny's rising panic as they trudged through
the leaves and dirt, deeper into the darkness. Hayley swung the flashlight back and forth, following
every sound, at one point revealing a mama deer
and two baby deer chewing on some plants, gawk-
ing at them, blinded by the light. They just stood
there, not making the slightest move to retreat until
Hayley moved the light off of them and onto a
squirrel scurrying up the bark of a tree. The tiny
critter froze for a brief moment as the light shined
on him and then continued on his way.

"We're never going to find him out here in the
dark," Danny moaned, wanting any excuse to return to the comfort and safety of their home.

Hayley ignored him. "Leroy! Here, boy! Leroy!"

She stopped and listened.

Nothing.

And then she continued on.

She heard Danny sighing behind her.

"Leroy!"

And that's when she heard it.

A faint yap.

She stopped dead in her tracks. "Did you hear
that?"

"Hear what?"

"I thought I heard a dog barking."

"I didn't hear anything."

She took a few more steps and heard it again. More yapping.

"*That!*"

This time they both stopped, not moving, waiting to hear the sound again.

Sure enough, another faint, almost inaudible bark, but it was loud enough for Danny to hear it this time. "That's Leroy!"

"It came from that direction," Hayley said, pointing east. They picked up their pace, but not so fast that they could run into a tree or trip over a fallen branch. They reached a small clearing, and as Hayley swept the flashlight over the area, she almost missed the puny-sized fur ball nearly buried in a pile of orange and yellow leaves. It was the sudden movement that caught her attention, and she pulled the light back until it hit the wiggling little four-legged body.

"Leroy!" Hayley called out.

But the puppy didn't answer. He was too preoccupied with something.

Hayley rushed forward. Danny stuck so close to her she could feel his hot breath on her neck. She was practically on top of Leroy now, still shining the light down on him. "Leroy, what in the world have you been up to?"

And then her eyes rested on something she couldn't quite make out at first. Leroy was busy digging something up from the soil. Hayley looked closer, not sure what it was, but as she crouched down to get a closer look, her eyes widened in horror.

Sticking up from the dirt was a fingernail painted

with pink nail polish. It was a woman's finger and Leroy was hard at work digging up the rest of the body that went with it.

"What'cha got there, boy?" Danny asked, kneeling down next to Hayley to inspect what was in the dirt, and then he shrieked louder than Jamie Lee Curtis in the final scenes of the original *Halloween* movie.

Bar Harbor Cooking
by
Hattie Jenkins

Now as you all know, I am never one to complain about things, but I really wish someone in this town could enlighten me as to why all the folks around here have such a crazy obsession for the Halloween holiday. Because frankly, if you ask me, allowing children to dress up in costumes from a small age well into their teens and go around the neighborhoods begging for candy is just asking for trouble. Why would anyone in their right mind honestly think that is a good idea?

And another thing while I'm on the subject. Why would anyone with a clear head promote an entire night of mischief and mayhem? I have personally borne witness with my own eyes to all the destruction resulting from this gruesome annual tradition, including egg-splattered windows, shaving cream sprayed all over cars and mailboxes, and Lord, don't forget all those smashed pumpkin carcasses strewn across the roads.

Now as you also know, I never engage in gossip, BUT I am sure many of you remember the Robinson twins, Gabe and Abe, who used to live here in town about ten years ago.

Well, let me tell you, those boys were a

handful for their momma and daddy. Those ruffians were running around the streets from the time they were five years old, and always up to no good! Lordy, every time a helpful neighbor brought them home after catching them lighting matches on the front lawn or calling to complain to the boys' parents that they were chasing a poor cat, Dick and Joan Robinson would just laugh and say, "Boys will be boys!" Apparently, discipline was not a part of their vocabulary.

Well, as you all know, I would bite my tongue before I told someone else how to raise their kids, but those boys needed a good swat on their behinds from a very young age, if you ask me! But Dick and Joan Robinson didn't ask me, so they continued to allow their evil spawn to continue running around the streets unsupervised.

So it came as no surprise to me that when they got older they became the leaders of a gang of wild and unruly troublemakers who wreaked havoc on many Halloween nights. Those boys kept the local police very busy, and it was a rare occurrence when you didn't see the twins solemnly riding in the back of the police cruiser after getting caught breaking the law with one of their latest escapades.

Seems to me the final straw was Halloween night around 1996 when the Robinson twins were fourteen years old and they, along with their pack of faithful followers, were in the middle of town egging and smearing shaving cream all over the windows of the fire station when a young police officer, just out of training, pulled up in his cruiser and hopped out of his vehicle to put a stop to the hooligans' destruction of public property. The boys took off running down the alley next to the drugstore with the young officer in hot pursuit. As the story goes, the officer caught up with a couple of the boys, but the twins managed to give him the slip. They doubled back and jumped into the police cruiser to play with the sirens and lights. Unfortunately, the inexperienced officer had left his key in the ignition. Unable to resist, Gabe and Abe took the cruiser for a joy ride, racing straight down Main Street, and then left on Cottage Street, blue lights flashing and sirens blaring. They were going like a bat out of hell when all of a sudden a group of young trick-or-treaters began crossing the street in front of them. Gabe, who was driving, panicked and yanked the steering wheel hard to the right. According to the parents who were accompanying their kids and nearly got mowed down by the police cruiser, it was like watching a scene from a movie with the speeding car jumping the sidewalk curb and then launching into the air, landing halfway up the Bar Harbor Post Office's front steps with a horrendous crash. Eyewitnesses confirmed that the sirens were still blaring and the lights were still flashing as the twins howled loudly in the front seat, terrified, tears streaming down their faces. Serves them right, if you ask me.

Well, Dick and Joan Robinson finally decided they needed a fresh start since their twins now had a hardened reputation, so they packed up and moved the boys to another town in Maine. I heard a while later that the family had relocated to Thomaston, which ironically is where the Maine State Prison is located. I wondered to myself if it might not have been out of convenience for when the boys turned eighteen and could move right in, but as you all know, I'm not one to gossip.

A co-worker here at the *Island Times* recently told me that she made my delicious Creamy Cheese Fall Vegetable Casserole, and how much her family had enjoyed it! She said she was thinking about trying to make one for a friend's birthday potluck, but then she had heard her friend had a dairy allergy. Well, I've never heard of anything more ridiculous because back in my day, you ate what was served to you, and you didn't worry about such a thing as allergies! But I'll save that discussion for another day. So for you non-finicky eaters, be sure to try my special fall recipe!

Hattie's Creamy Cheese Fall Vegetable Casserole

Ingredients:

3 cups milk
2 carrots, peeled and diced
2 sweet potatoes, peeled and diced
2 parsnips, peeled and diced
2 stalks celery, diced
1 small onion, peeled and diced
1 small butternut squash, peeled and diced
1 8-ounce package cream cheese, cubed
1 cup shredded Parmesan cheese
Salt and pepper, to taste
1 cup seasoned panko or seasoned bread crumbs
2 tablespoons melted butter

Preheat your oven to 375 degrees.

Grease a 3-quart casserole dish and set aside.

Place your milk, carrots, sweet potatoes, parsnips, celery, onion, and squash in a large saucepan and bring to a boil. Reduce heat and simmer, stirring occasionally until vegetables are tender.

Stir in the cream cheese and mix until melted. Now stir in your Parmesan and season with the salt and pepper to taste. Pour the mixture into the prepared casserole dish.

Stir the panko or bread crumbs with the melted butter and top casserole with the crumb mixture.

Bake covered in the oven for 25 minutes or until hot and bubbly. Remove cover and bake for another 5 minutes to brown topping on casserole.

Let your casserole rest for a few minutes, then serve and enjoy!

Chapter Ten

Hayley immediately scooped up Leroy. The curious puppy wiggled in her arms for a few moments before settling into the crook of her arm and trying to reach up to lick her face. "Danny, call 911!"

"I don't have my phone with me! I left it back at the house!"

"Well, I didn't bring mine either! You go, and I'll stay here with the body," Hayley offered, although the idea of keeping an eye on a mostly buried corpse was unsettling.

Danny dashed off toward the house. Hayley nuzzled Leroy and rocked him gently like a baby to calm him down. She glanced over at the finger with the pink nail still disturbingly pointing up from underneath the dirt, and it sent another shiver down her spine. She stepped away from it, trying to keep her distance, half expecting a whole hand to shoot up and grab her ankle or arm like in that final shocking gravesite scene in the movie *Carrie*.

She was huddling with Leroy near a tree when she suddenly noticed a shiny object on the ground next to her feet that was illuminated by a stream of moonlight through the thick trees. Holding Leroy in one arm, she leaned down to examine it more closely. It was a heart-shaped silver locket. Did it belong to the woman who was buried a few feet away, or did someone else drop it?

Hayley stood back up, and nervously eyed the pointing finger with the chipped pink nail polish, waiting for it to move, but mercifully it never did. She shivered again and asked herself why she didn't make Danny stay with the body so she could have been the one to run back to her warm and safe house. Finally, she heard sirens in the distance and within a few minutes she was surrounded by police officers and crime scene investigators. As they set up some lights and worked to dig up the corpse to see who it was, Hayley pulled Sergio aside and pointed him toward the tree near where she had spotted the piece of jewelry. "I found a locket over there, which might be important. Don't worry, I didn't touch it."

"Thanks," Sergio said, heading over to inspect the clue.

Danny returned, out of breath, and stood next to Hayley, watching as the team of county CSI guys unearthed enough of the body to get a good look at the face. Hayley had to lean to one side to peek through the space between two of the investigators, but she finally managed to get a glimpse of the dead woman.

"It's her . . ." Hayley gasped.

"Wendi Jo?" Danny asked.

Hayley nodded solemnly. Leroy suddenly shot out of Hayley's arms and scampered over toward the crime scene. "Leroy, come back here!"

She raced to intercept him, but he was too fast for her and ran over and started sniffing around Wendi Jo's body. Hayley pushed her way through the crowd of investigators surrounding the corpse. "Leroy!"

"Ma'am, please get your dog and step back, please," one of the CSI guys admonished.

"I am so sorry! Leroy! Get over here!"

Leroy was too curious to listen, so Hayley had to awkwardly step over the corpse, being careful not to bump into anything or disturb any evidence, before she managed to get her hands around Leroy's little body and carry him off. As she backed away, gripping a squirming Leroy as tightly as she could, she caught sight of the dirt-smudged pink blouse that Wendi Jo was wearing. She noticed that it matched her nail polish. It was also covered in blood. She overheard one of the investigators remark as he lifted the blouse, "Looks like she's been shot twice."

Hayley walked back to Danny, carrying Leroy. "Let's go home."

"No, I want to stick around until we find out what happened to her," Danny said.

"I know what happened to her. Someone shot her twice and then dragged her body out here to bury it so it would never be found."

Danny gulped as he took this in, and then, with steely-determination in his eyes said firmly, "And we both know who did it."

"No, we don't, Danny."

"Come on! Look how close we are to their house! You know the Salingers had something to do with this!"

"We know nothing, Danny, and I do not want you getting involved. Do you hear me?"

Danny didn't answer her, and that worried Hayley, because when Danny remained silent, which was exceedingly rare, that always meant he was about to stir up trouble.

Chapter Eleven

The following morning as Hayley scurried down the stairs and into the kitchen to grab her bag on the kitchen table and head off to work, she found Danny standing by the sink, staring out the window.

She fished around inside her bag for her car keys. "What's got you so curious?"

"She's gardening," Danny said in a somber tone.

"Who?"

"Morticia Addams."

Hayley sighed as she grabbed her keys and threw the leather strap of her bag around her shoulder. "I don't have time for this. I'm going to be late for work. Make sure the kids don't miss the school bus."

Hayley brushed past Danny and out the back door. At first she didn't notice him following right behind her, but by the time she had reached her car, she realized he was practically on top of her. "Are you coming with me? Is it Bring Your Husband to Work Day?"

Danny kept his eyes trained on Rosemary

Salinger who wore a gray floppy hat and sunglasses while shoveling dirt with a spade in her small flower bed that was mostly weeds. "Who tends a garden in November?"

"Maybe she's planting bulbs for next spring," Hayley said before waving at Rosemary. "Good morning!"

Rosemary looked up, startled. She lowered her sunglasses and stared blankly at Hayley and Danny before realizing she should say something. She instantly plastered on her fake Stepford Wife smile and waved back.

"Why is she wearing sunglasses?" Danny wondered. "It's cloudy and gray out."

"Would you please just leave it alone, Danny?"

But Hayley knew he wasn't about to listen to her. Danny bounded over to Rosemary's garden, his hands thrust in the pockets of his sweatpants, and hovered over her. "You haven't seen Leroy digging around here, have you?"

Rosemary gave him a puzzled look. "Leroy?"

"Our new puppy," Danny answered. "Shih Tzu. Nosy little guy. Likes to go around digging things up. I just wanted to make sure he didn't disturb your beautiful garden."

Hayley shook her head. She knew exactly what Danny was up to and she didn't like it.

Rosemary stared at the weeds. "No, I haven't seen him anywhere near here."

"Happy to hear it," Danny said.

Hayley lamely tried to put a stop to the conversation. "Danny, the school bus will be here any minute! You need to nudge the kids along or they're going to miss it!"

"Got it, babe," Danny called back to her, never

taking his eyes off Rosemary. "Once he smells a bone or something buried in the ground, there's no stopping him from digging and digging until he finds it, which is why the police have him to thank for finding Wendi Jo Willis."

Hayley noticed Rosemary gripping her spade, stabbing it into the dirt faster and faster. She looked as if she was hoping that if she just kept at it and ignored Danny, he would finally stop talking and go away. But Hayley knew her husband would never take the hint.

"I'm sure you heard about Wendi Jo," Danny said, looking down at her, the gray floppy hat hiding most of her face.

"Danny . . ." Hayley said, mouth clenched.

"In a minute, babe . . ." he said, waving her off.

Hayley thought about just getting in her car and driving away, but she didn't want to leave Danny on his own in case she had to intervene and put a muzzle on her chattering husband, who clearly was not welcome on their neighbors' property.

"Who?" Rosemary asked, never taking her eyes off the weeds in her garden.

"Wendi Jo Willis. Her body was found not too far from here," Danny said, not quite accusingly but pretty close.

"I'm sorry, I don't know who that is," Rosemary said evenly.

Danny raised an eyebrow. "You don't? That's odd. She's all anybody's been talking about in town the last few days. You didn't hear she had gone missing?"

"No," Rosemary said as she climbed to her feet, realizing the only way to escape this conversation was to stop gardening and go inside her house.

"It's strange you don't know her. I thought she sold you this house."

Rosemary dropped the spade in a basket full of gardening tools. "Oh, her. Yes, I'm not very good with names. And I certainly did not hear that she was missing. But that's not unusual. We don't like to get involved in town gossip."

"It's more than just gossip. Our dog dug her up over there in the woods," he said, pointing toward the trees just beyond their backyard. "And the police say she was shot twice. Murdered."

Rosemary stared at Danny, but the sunglasses hid her expression. Her ruby red lips remained pursed and were in stark contrast to her ghostly white skin. "That's a shame."

"Yeah, I'll say it is. I mean, who would do such a terrible thing?"

"I'm sure I don't know," Rosemary muttered before turning and wandering toward her front porch.

"Although I did hear that she had a few enemies. I'm sure the police will want to talk to them. Your husband wasn't exactly a fan of hers, was he?"

This stopped her in her tracks. She slowly turned back around. "Excuse me?"

"I saw, in fact, my whole family saw Damien arguing with Wendi Jo while we were coming back from trick-or-treating on Halloween night. It got pretty intense."

"I'm sure if my husband was upset with this woman, he had a good reason."

"Right. How upset do you think he got?"

Hayley's stomach churned as she watched Rosemary slowly remove her glasses. The whole blank, Stepford Wife fake smile slowly faded. Her brown eyes seemed to darken until they were almost coal black. She glared at Danny, no longer pretending to be the utmost example of calm and civility.

"You ask too many questions," Rosemary sneered.

"I'm guessing the police will, too," Danny said, refusing to back down.

"Get off my property," Rosemary barked before spinning around and hurrying into the house.

Danny ambled back over to Hayley. "Believe me now?"

Hayley shuddered. Although she didn't approve of Danny's methods, she couldn't argue that Rosemary Salinger's sudden turn had been disturbing. Maybe he was onto something.

"Come on, you better drive me to work," Hayley said, circling around the car to the passenger's side.

"Why can't you drive yourself?"

"Because you're going to need the car to take the kids to school," Hayley groaned as she pointed at the school bus, red lights flashing, picking up some kids on the corner and driving off.

"Sorry," Danny said sheepishly.

Chapter Twelve

Hayley knew she was in for it when Danny burst through the back door armed with a manila folder stuffed with pages. She had just taken a meat lasagna out of the oven to cool, which she had made for dinner, and the kids were upstairs finishing their homework. She had been looking forward to a quiet evening with a glass of wine and maybe an episode of *NCIS* with her imaginary boyfriend, Mark Harmon, that was stored on the TiVo. But no, Danny was single-handedly going to make sure she wasn't going to have a moment's peace this evening after the kids went to bed. She could see it written all over his face.

Danny waved the folder in front of her face. "You are never going to guess where I have been!"

"I'm not even going to try," Hayley said with a sigh.

"The Jesup Memorial Library!"

"You're right. I never would have guessed that. When was the last time you actually read a book?"

"High school, I think. Mark Twain. It was *Tom Sawyer*, maybe *Huckleberry Finn*, I can't really remember. Who faked his own death and sailed down the river with an escaped slave?"

"I believe that was *The Adventures of Huckleberry Finn,* but don't quote me. Do you even have a library card?"

"I wasn't there to check out a book. I spent all afternoon in the periodicals section researching."

"I'm afraid to ask, but here goes. Researching what?"

Danny set the folder down on the kitchen counter and grabbed a beer from the fridge. "I wanted to find out more information about the house next door and its history. People have been talking for years about all the strange goings-on that have happened there, and I remember my parents telling me about one family back in the 1970s who were so spooked by the evil spirits haunting it, they ran screaming into the night and left town and never came back."

"Everyone's heard those stories, Danny. I'm sure they're exaggerated."

"Didn't you see *The Amityville Horror?*"

"Yes, and it was a scary movie based on a news story that was later proven to be mostly made up. If I thought there was any truth to those rumors, why would I ever have agreed to buy this house right next door?"

"Because it was the only one we could afford," he said matter-of-factly, taking a swig of his beer.

Hayley couldn't exactly argue that point. He was right.

Danny picked up the folder again and flipped it open. He showed Hayley xeroxed copies of some newspaper articles. "It's right here in black and white. An article written in the *Bar Harbor Herald* back in 1978. The Radditz family bought the house but only lived in it for three months. They were constantly calling the police because they kept hearing prowlers, but it turned out no one was trying to break into the house. Then, a few weeks later, they reported seeing apparitions roaming the hallways. They overheard their daughter talking to someone in the middle of the night, and the daughter claimed she had a new friend, a ghost who was hiding under her bed. Finally, the parents couldn't take it anymore and just packed up and left. The house stayed abandoned for almost six years before another family bought it. They lasted two years and then it stayed empty another seven. Why is it that no one can live in that house for very long?"

"Maybe the Salingers will break the curse," Hayley offered.

"Or maybe the Salingers have been possessed by the evil spirits that inhabit it and are here to do their bidding. Maybe what's called for here is some kind of exorcism."

"Do you hear yourself right now, Danny?"

"Of course I do. And I'm determined to get to the bottom of it."

"Okay, Ghostbuster, but do it after dinner. I hope you're hungry. I made a huge pan of lasagna."

"Good, because I invited Sal over for dinner."

"Sal? My boss, Sal?"

"Yeah."

"Why would you do that without telling me?"

"You just said you made a huge pan of lasagna. We have plenty for one guest."

"That's not the point. I had a long day at the office, and now you expect me to entertain my boss?"

"Listen, I remember talking to Sal a few years ago at your office Christmas party, and he mentioned to me that back when he was a twelve-year old kid, around 1978, he was friends with a kid named Timmy Radditz, who lived in the house next door, and from what I recall, he spent the night there once and got so scared he called his parents to come get him."

"Sal never told me that," Hayley said, suddenly curious.

"Why would he? You're a total skeptic! You'd probably accuse him of making the whole thing up."

The doorbell rang and Danny dashed out of the kitchen to answer it. Hayley called the kids down for dinner and mixed Sal his favorite cocktail, a Cutty Sark and soda. She pulled Danny aside and ordered him not to discuss any of this unpleasantness about evil spirits and haunted houses in front of the children. Danny surprisingly complied, and so the dinner conversation was focused on a few local news stories the *Island Times* was currently covering, although the major story right now was the Wendi Jo Willis murder. Hayley served dessert, a simple cheesecake, which the kids quickly devoured. Gemma and Dustin were finally sent upstairs to bed, allowing Danny and Sal to settle down in the living room and get right down to business. Sal knew he had only been invited to dinner to discuss his childhood memories of the haunted house next door, but he didn't seem to mind since his wife was visiting her sister up in Hampden and he didn't want to be stuck at home eating warmed up leftovers when he could be enjoying Hayley's homemade lasagna.

"So what do you remember about that night, Sal?"

"I had heard the stories about a murder taking place at that house back in the 1940s right after it was built," Sal said, sipping his third whiskey.

Hayley figured they would have to drive him home.

"Yeah, the details about that are kind of sketchy," Danny said breathlessly. "I couldn't find much about it in the archived issues of the *Herald*."

"From what I was told, and mind you, it was years ago when I heard it from my uncle, who was still around at the time, there was some kind of Lizzie Borden situation. A disturbed young woman hacked up her whole family. . . ."

Hayley gasped. "I never heard that! How awful!"

"It was right around the time of the big Bar Harbor fire, which destroyed a lot of the town back in the 1940s. The murder got buried after that because people were more interested in reading about the super-rich families like the Rockefellers and the Astors and the Vanderbilts, who used to come here all the time, who lost their huge mansions in the fire. That grabbed all the headlines.

"Obviously this street was spared because homes like the one next door are still standing. There was a report that the girl who killed her family died up in an institution in Bangor. Took her own life, from what I understand. The bank foreclosed on the house and sold it to a new family that moved to Bar Harbor in the early fifties. That's when the first reports of the house being haunted started to surface."

Hayley leaned forward, enraptured by Sal's

supernatural tale. Maybe Danny was right. Maybe there was something to all these stories.

"My mother didn't want me spending the night there, but my father said she was being ridiculous and let me go. I didn't think much of it. I just wanted to play with Timmy's new Hot Wheels set. I remember his bedroom was in the attic, and I remember hearing strange sounds, and at one point when a banging woke me up, I saw a ghost staring at me from the doorway. . . ."

"Sal, are you serious?"

"Scared the living daylights out of me! I yelled bloody murder! Timmy shot up and nearly dove out of the window. I cried like a baby and begged Timmy's mother to call my parents, which she did. They weren't too happy driving over there after midnight to take me home."

"Is that all you remember?" Danny asked.

"Pretty much." Sal shrugged.

"So you agree the house is haunted," Danny said confidently.

"I wouldn't say that. Who can be sure?" Sal said, polishing off his drink.

"But based on what you remember, how can you not be?" Danny argued.

"I remember what happened the next day when Mrs. Radditz called my mother and apologized because Timmy's older brother, Aaron, confessed to throwing a white sheet over himself and trying to scare us."

Hayley couldn't help but burst out laughing.

"The ghost was his *brother*?"

"Yeah, a real cutup, from what I remember. Always playing practical jokes."

"Why didn't you tell me that part when you first told me the story?" Danny cried.

"Because I still heard strange noises in the night, which Aaron denied having had anything to do with, and there was a murder that happened there, so there is no way to say one way or the other if the house is haunted or not."

Danny slumped back on the couch, deflated.

Hayley prayed this would be the end of his crusade to expose the Salinger family as possessed, or at the very least, your run-of-the-mill homicidal maniacs. And frankly, given their recent behavior, Hayley was not a hundred percent sure he wasn't at least right about that part.

"How about another Cutty Sark?" Sal said, raising his empty glass. "Hayley, that lasagna was out of this world!"

Hayley had worked for Sal a few years now. She knew him well. And it was clear he was willing to play along with Danny, tell him whatever he wanted to hear, in order to get a free home-cooked meal.

Actually, she was rather flattered that her boss would go to such lengths to enjoy her cooking. She also couldn't help but chuckle at her husband, who was at that moment stewing on the couch, disappointed that his latest firsthand testimony was a wash.

Chapter Thirteen

When Hayley returned home from work the next day, she arrived to find an empty house. There was no sign of Danny or the kids. She set about making dinner, having thawed a pound of turkey meat, and grabbed some canned beans and tomato sauce and spices from the cupboard, along with a green pepper and onion from the produce drawer in the fridge to cook up a pot of chili. She was washing the pepper underneath the faucet when she happened to glance out the window to see Danny coming out of the Salinger house with Damien. She was startled at first. How on earth did Danny, after completely alienating Rosemary just yesterday with his veiled accusations in her garden, worm his way into the house for a chat with the patriarch of the family, Damien? But then, upon reflection, there was no reason to be at all surprised. Danny was a charmer and could talk his way into just about anywhere. Danny good-naturedly slapped Damien on the back as he trotted across the lawn toward the house. Once he was in the kitchen, Hayley stopped chopping vegetables and turned to greet him.

"You never cease to amaze me, Danny Powell," Hayley said, shaking her head.

"What?"

"How did you get to be buddies with Damien Salinger after his wife basically kicked you off their property yesterday?"

"All it took was a six-pack of beer and a disarming smile," Danny gloated. "My mother always said I possessed an undeniable charisma. That's why you married me, isn't it?"

"I admit, you can have a certain magnetism, but a little bit goes a long way . . ."

"Ouch. Anyway, he's also a Red Sox fan, so that coupled with the beer as a peace offering was what really broke the ice."

"You're never going to give this up, are you?"

"Not until we figure out what's really going on next door," Danny said excitedly. "We were sitting in his den tossing back a few beers and talking sports, and I happened to notice there was a copy of the *Island Times* on a side table and it was open to the page with the article on Wendi Jo Willis's body being discovered in the woods, like he had just been reading about it before I showed up. He saw me glancing down at the picture of Wendi Jo and got real nervous, and then quickly directed my attention to his gun cabinet in the corner, like he was trying to distract me. Turns out Damien is a real gun nut and has a huge collection and is very proud of it. But get this. It was this really nice piece of furniture made of birchwood and had something like a fifteen-gun capacity for ten rifles and five handguns, but there was this empty slot right in the middle where a pistol should have been."

"Maybe he only has fourteen guns," Hayley said.

"I thought about that so I came right out and asked him, and he told me he had fifteen guns, but one of the handguns was out getting repaired because the barrel was jammed."

"He could have been telling the truth," Hayley argued.

"Maybe, but he looked really spooked when I mentioned the missing gun and he hemmed and hawed before coming up with the jammed barrel excuse. I know people, Hayley, I've got a knack for reading them, and I'm telling you, he was lying. He was acting suspicious, and I think it may be because that missing gun was the weapon he used to shoot Wendi Jo."

"You don't know that for sure, Danny."

"I've got a pretty strong feeling, and it's only a matter of time before I gather enough evidence to nail him," Danny said, like he was a dogged cop on an episode of one of the *Law & Order* shows.

The back door slammed open and Dustin wandered into the kitchen. "Mom, when's dinner?"

"It'll be a little while. I'm making chili," Hayley said, noticing someone hiding behind Dustin, almost crouched down in order not to be seen. "Who's your friend?"

Dustin turned his head and stepped aside, revealing little Carrie Salinger, a blank expression on her face, clutching a DVD. "This is Carrie. . . ."

"Yes, I recognize her. How are you, Carrie?" Hayley asked, smiling.

Carrie stared at her, like she was some hideous scary witch, and didn't answer her.

"We're going to go up to my room and watch a movie before dinner, okay?" Dustin said. "Come on, Carrie."

Hayley glanced at the title on the DVD. "*Nightmare on Elm Street?*"

"Yeah, Carrie says it's awesome. She's seen it like a hundred times."

Hayley grimaced. "I'm sorry, but I think you're a little too young to watch that movie. It's pretty scary and gory from what I remember. . . ."

"Carrie's parents let *her* watch it!" Dustin protested.

"That may be true, and that's perfectly fine for them, but we have our own rules here and I don't want you watching an R-rated horror movie."

"I'm nine years old!" Dustin whined.

"Exactly," Hayley said firmly. "You have plenty of movies in your room you can watch with Carrie, but you're not watching this one."

Dustin whirled around to his father. "Dad . . ."

"Sorry, champ. I'm with your mom on this one," Danny said solemnly.

Hayley nearly fainted. She was shocked that Danny actually was backing her up. She reached out and gently took the DVD from Carrie, who glared at her so intently, it sent a shiver up Hayley's spine. She set the DVD down on the kitchen table. "I'm just going to keep the movie here until you're ready to go home, Carrie, and then you can pick it up on your way out, okay?"

"I watch R-rated movies all the time and I don't have nightmares," Carrie said quietly.

"Good for you, and that's okay if your parents allow it, but here I just feel—"

"Serial killer movies are my favorites . . ."

Hayley exchanged a glance with Danny, whose mouth had just dropped open. The girl could not be more than ten years old.

"I have a whole MySpace page dedicated to the world's most dangerous serial killers. I've even written letters to a few, the ones that haven't been executed for their crimes yet," Carrie said matter-of-factly.

"Oh . . ." Hayley had no idea how to respond. "Well, that's nice, but today I'm afraid you're going to have to settle for watching *Kung Fu Panda,* okay?"

"Whatever . . ." Carrie shrugged.

Dustin started to head out of the kitchen with Carrie following behind him when Hayley called out after him, "Have you seen your sister? She's not in her room."

Annoyed, Dustin turned back around. "I saw her earlier outside talking to Casper."

Hayley glanced out the window. On the front porch of the Salinger house, the older son Casper was stretched out on a wicker two-seater, wearing earplugs and listening to music on an iPod.

"Can we go up to my room now?" Dustin asked.

"Yes, dinner will be around seven," Hayley said.

Dustin led Carrie up the stairs. Danny waited until they were gone before he turned to Hayley and whispered, "She's so weird!"

Hayley didn't respond. She marched past him and out the door, crossing the lawn to the Salinger porch. Danny followed behind her like a puppy. She could hear heavy metal music blasting through the earplugs.

"Casper!" Hayley yelled.

He didn't hear her or chose to ignore her. She

tried yelling his name a couple more times before she gave up and reached out and wiggled the kid's foot. He jumped out of the wicker chair, startled. Noticing Hayley and Danny, he angrily yanked the earplugs out of his ear.

"What do you want?" Casper barked.

"Sorry, I didn't mean to scare you," Hayley said.

"Nothing scares me," he spit out, insulted.

"Okay . . . we're looking for our daughter, Gemma, and her brother said he saw the two of you together earlier."

Casper studied both of them as if he was considering how to respond and then nodded slightly. "Yeah, she was here. We played a game of hide-and-seek."

"Hide-and-seek? That's odd. Gemma's a little old for that game," Hayley remarked.

Casper shrugged. "She went to hide in the woods and I waited here something like five minutes before I started looking for her. But I couldn't find her . . ."

"What do you mean you couldn't find her?"

"Just what I said. I looked for her for almost twenty minutes and so I finally gave up and came back here to listen to some music," Casper said, almost sneering.

"Well, did she eventually come back?" Hayley asked, suddenly worried.

"Nope. I never saw her after that," Casper said, bored enough with the conversation that he put his earplugs back in.

Hayley clutched Danny's arm. "Where is she? Where did she go?"

"The sun's almost down . . ." Danny said, his face full of dread. "Come on . . ."

Danny led Hayley into the woods. Hayley tried to stay calm, but the memory of finding Wendi Jo Willis's body was so strong and alarming, she began to panic as she and Danny called Gemma's name over and over again. When the sun was finally gone and darkness encroached, Danny suggested they go back to the house and call Sergio. Hayley wanted to keep searching. What if Gemma had fallen and was hurt or unconscious and couldn't answer them? Danny insisted they go back to the house and round up reinforcements. When they returned to the yard, Hayley gasped and pointed at the kitchen window. They could plainly see Gemma standing at the counter. They raced inside.

Gemma had browned the turkey meat and was adding it to the pot with the rest of the other chili ingredients. "I'm so starving. I decided to finish making the chili myself!"

"Where have you been?" Hayley demanded to know.

"Lori Alley's house," Gemma answered, nonchalantly.

"What were you doing there?" Danny asked.

"Studying for a spelling test we have tomorrow. You said I could walk to Lori's alone after school as long as I let you know where I was."

"Which you didn't."

"But I did. I left you a voice mail on your phone," Gemma insisted.

Hayley snatched her phone out of her bag, and sure enough, there was a voice mail from Gemma that she had missed earlier.

Danny stepped forward. "So you didn't play hide-and-seek with that creepy kid from next door?"

"Casper? No. We just chatted for a few minutes when I was on my way to Lori's about his favorite heavy metal band. He sure likes Guns N' Roses. I had never even heard of them."

"That was all? No hide-and-seek?" Hayley asked.

"Mom, please, I'm twelve." Gemma nodded. "I left for Lori's."

Hayley shook her head. "Why would he lie to us like that?"

"He was probably just joking," Gemma said as she set the pot on the stove and turned on the flame. "He's kind of an oddball."

Danny, infuriated, glanced out the window. "He's gone inside. I'm going over there right now and have a talk with that punk. What he did was *not* okay!"

Hayley put a hand on Danny's shoulder. "Danny, just forget it. I don't want to stir up any more trouble with that whole ghoulish family."

"Thank you for letting me come over, Mrs. Powell," a tiny voice said.

They all turned to see Carrie Salinger staring at them from the hallway.

Quickly covering, Hayley smiled and took a few steps toward the little girl. "Is the movie over already?"

"No, Dustin's still watching it. I was bored. Nobody got killed. Have a good night," she said before walking past them like a zombie, an empty look on her face, as she picked up her DVD from the kitchen table and disappeared out the back door.

"Not exactly Shirley Temple, is she?" Danny cracked.

Chapter Fourteen

Hayley thought she had heard wrong when she picked up the phone while sitting behind her desk at the *Island Times* office. "I'm sorry, what did you say?"

"This is Nurse Tilly from the Bar Harbor Hospital, Hayley. I thought you should know that your husband was just brought in. He's been shot!"

A numbness swept through Hayley's body as she tried to stand up, but she stumbled and fell back in her chair. "I . . . I'll be right there."

She dropped the phone and grabbed the desk with both hands and struggled to her feet. Her head was cloudy and her only thought was *I have to get to Danny*.

Without alerting Sal who was working in his office, Hayley ran out the door to her car, which was parked just up the street. As she approached the driver's side door, she realized the key was in her bag underneath her desk. Instead of returning to retrieve it, she broke into a run in the opposite direction toward the hospital, which was located not too far from where she worked. By the time she bolted through the automatic glass doors that swung open, leading into the emergency room, she was out of breath and felt as if she might pass out from the shock of the news that she was just beginning to absorb.

Although she knew most of the nurses who worked at the hospital, she didn't recognize the woman behind the reception desk. She was rather rotund, with rosy cheeks and a severe perm underneath her white nurse's hat. Her name tag read NURSE JOLLEY.

"Excuse me. My name is Hayley Powell and I was told my husband is here," she said, looking around, half expecting to find him in the emergency waiting room.

"Yes, Mrs. Powell, he's with the doctor now, but since you are family, you can go up. He's on the third floor," Nurse Jolley said, smiling, but with a concerned look on her face.

"Is he all right?" Hayley asked desperately. "How serious is it?"

"I'm afraid you'll have to speak to Dr. Rose," Nurse Jolley said, with a sympathetic smile.

Hayley rushed to the elevator and took it up to the third floor where she spotted Nurse Tilly coming out of a room with a bedpan.

"Tilly!" Hayley cried.

"Hayley, thank heavens you're here," the usually perky Nurse Tilly squealed. "Your husband is in exam room three."

"Which way?" Hayley cried, swiveling her head around.

"Down there!" Nurse Tilly answered, pointing down a hall.

"Thank you!" Hayley dashed down the hall.

When she came upon exam room three, she knocked loudly on the door, but didn't wait for an answer before she rushed inside. She found Danny wearing a baby blue hospital gown sitting on a table while Dr. Rose, a pudgy, bespectacled African American man in a white coat, kneeled in front of him while bandaging his foot.

"Hey, babe!" Danny said with a big grin on his face.

A wave of relief now swept over her as she took in the sight of her husband looking perfectly healthy except for a wounded foot.

"What happened?" Hayley gasped.

Danny held up a finger. "In a sec, babe. How does it look, Doc?"

Dr. Rose stood up. "Try to stay off it for two weeks. I'll get you some crutches you can use when you need to get around."

"Thanks, Doc!" Danny said.

"I'll give you some time with your wife," Dr. Rose said while nodding to Hayley as he stepped out of the room and closed the door behind him.

"No need to worry, babe. It's just a little flesh wound. The bullet grazed the foot. It didn't go in all the way."

"Who shot you?"

Danny slid off the table and hugged Hayley, slightly embarrassed. "I did."

"You shot *yourself?*"

"Yes, it was an accident," Danny said sheepishly. "I was on the lawn raking leaves when I saw Damien Salinger come home. He had a gun with him and said it had been the one that was out getting repaired, so I figured if it was the murder weapon, I should get a closer look at it."

"And he just let you handle it?"

"Yeah, he was proud because he loves his guns and is a full-throated supporter of the Second Amendment."

"And then you shot yourself in the foot."

"I just grazed it! But it hurt like hell."

"Oh, Danny . . ."

"I was on the ground writhing around, yelling that I needed to get to the hospital, and Damien said he would bring me here, but before he did, he made sure to look around for the bullet . . ."

"Did he find it?"

"Yes, he found it in the grass near the driveway and he put it in his pocket. Only then did he help me to his car and bring me here."

"Is he still here?"

Danny shook his head. "No. Once the doctor said I was going to be okay, I told him he didn't have to hang around until you got here."

"Well, I'm grateful he took care of you and got you here safely."

Danny hopped forward on one foot closer to Hayley. "We need to get that bullet."

"What are you talking about?"

Danny gripped both of Hayley's shoulders to maintain his balance. "That bullet could prove that Damien shot Wendi Jo Willis if it's the same kind as the two bullets they took out of her body."

"Danny, we should just let the police . . ."

"If we don't act quickly they could get rid of all the bullets and the gun and then we'll never have proof he did anything!"

"I am not going to do this. Do you hear me, Danny? I am not breaking into the neighbor's house and that's final!"

Hayley stuck to her guns until the next day

when Danny invited Damien and his two kids, Casper and Carrie, over to carve pumpkins in the backyard. It was clearly a distraction, which would allow Hayley to slip across the lawn and sneak inside to search the drawers of the gun cabinet for a box of bullets belonging to the pistol in question. After serving lemonade and cookies to the budding pumpkin carvers, who watched Danny intently as he scooped out the pulp and seeds, Hayley sighed as Danny tried to signal to her that this was the time, it was now or never, their only chance. He was never going to stop, and as horrified as Hayley was, the possibility that their neighbor might be a cold-blooded killer finally drove her to the decision to go through with it.

"Where's Rosemary today?" Hayley casually asked as she brought back a paper plate piled high with more cookies shaped like little mummies and ghosts.

"She went to run some errands in Ellsworth," Casper said, disinterested but still laconically partaking in the pumpkin carving.

Hayley set the cookies down on the table as everyone focused on shaping their pumpkins with eyes, noses, and mouths with Danny's expert coaching. Hayley nonchalantly wandered away, and when she was confident there was no one looking, sprinted across the lawn to the house next door and slipped through the front door, which was unlocked. She turned back to see Danny distracting Damien by showing him how to carve the features by keeping the pumpkin in your lap and cutting clean up-and-down slices. Gemma and Dustin were also keeping Casper and Carrie occupied, and Hayley hoped that Danny hadn't enlisted the kids to help out in any way with this harebrained scheme.

Hayley knew, according to Danny's recollection from his last visit, that the gun cabinet was located in a corner in the living room. Once she found it, she dropped to her knees and opened the bottom drawers. She cleared away a few boxes that she knew were for a rifle, not a handgun. She only found one box of nine millimeter caliber. She opened the box to find a handful of bullets left. She was about to pluck one out and stuff it in her pocket when she noticed in the corner of the drawer a piece of metal. She had almost missed it because it was in the shadows, but as she pulled the drawer open all the way, she saw it was a bullet. The top was crushed and it was scuffed and had clearly been fired. This had to be the bullet Damien found in the grass after Danny accidentally shot himself with his gun. She picked it up, looked it over, and was just about to close the drawer and get out of the house when she heard a familiar voice behind her say, "What are you doing in my house?"

Hayley's heart nearly stopped and she closed her eyes and dropped her head.

Her worst fear had just happened.

She had been caught.

Hayley crawled to her feet, took a deep breath, and then turned around to face Rosemary Salinger, who stood across the room, clutching two shopping bags, glaring at Hayley, infuriated. This wasn't the Stepford Wife Rosemary that she had first met when the Salingers moved into the neighborhood. This was the cold, detached, angry-acting Rosemary she had last encountered. And there was no question that Hayley was very scared of *this* Rosemary.

Chapter Fifteen

"Rosemary, let me explain," Hayley said lamely, taking a step toward her.

"Damien!" Rosemary screamed, holding up her hands, warning Hayley to stay right where she was.

Seconds later, Damien raced through the front door with Danny close on his heels, hopping along on his crutches. Damien's eyes widened at the sight of Hayley standing in front of his gun cabinet. Danny audibly gasped, acting completely surprised to find his wife inside the Salinger house.

"Rosemary, I didn't see you pull into the driveway," Danny said, mustering as much innocence in his tone as he could.

"There was a starter issue with the car, maybe a low battery, so I dropped the car off at the mechanic and walked the rest of the way home," Rosemary said evenly.

"Oh," Danny said, trying to act casual, as he turned and smiled at Hayley. "Hey, babe, what are you doing here?"

Hayley sighed and shook her head. "You are unbelievable, Danny Powell! Selling out your own wife? You're the only reason I'm here and you know it!"

Damien looked confused. "What's going on? Why did you break into our house?" He then noticed the bullet Hayley was holding. "What's that in your hand?"

Hayley knew it was time to come clean. If the Salingers were planning on shooting them, they would have to come through her first to get to the gun cabinet. She slowly raised the bullet she had between two fingers. "I came for this. The bullet you took from the grass after Danny stupidly shot himself in the foot."

"The gun just went off," Danny said defensively. "I think there was something still wrong with it. You really should take it back to whomever fixed it!"

"Shut up, Danny!" Hayley yelled.

Danny obeyed, and looked down at the floor like a scolded child.

"You broke into our house for a bullet? Why?" Rosemary asked.

"We wanted to compare it to the bullets that shot Wendi Jo Willis," Hayley muttered.

Damien's mouth dropped open. "You think *I* shot Wendi Jo?"

"No, of course not!" Danny interrupted, nervously eyeing both Damien and Rosemary, fearing they might charge the gun cabinet, grab a couple of weapons, and shoot both him and Hayley on the spot.

"Yes," Hayley said matter-of-factly. "We saw you having a heated argument with her on Halloween. She was shot twice. You are obviously a gun aficionado."

"A what?" Danny asked, puzzled.

"A fan of guns, Danny!" Hayley snapped.

There was a long awkward pause and then both Damien and Rosemary burst out laughing.

"So . . . let me get this straight . . . You think I was the one who shot Wendi Jo just because I collect firearms? Half the men in the state of Maine own guns!" Damien said, trying to catch his breath as he giggled. "That's . . . that's hysterical."

"I don't think a woman shot dead in the woods not too far from here is remotely funny," Hayley said flatly.

Damien finally managed to control himself. "You're right. What happened to Wendi Jo was a tragedy, and I feel sorry for her family, but I had nothing to do with it."

"So what were you two fighting about?" Hayley asked.

Rosemary stepped forward and slipped her arm through her husband's in a show of support. "We had every right to be angry with her. When we bought this house, Wendi Jo was representing the seller and she convinced us to use her cousin for the inspection. Well, he failed to disclose that the house needed a whole new roof, and we paid the full asking price. She purposely withheld that information in order to make a fast sale and her full commission. It was wrong and when Damien found out about it, he confronted her over the phone and threatened legal action! That's when she showed up at the house to try and talk him out of it and he chased her off with the ax."

It made sense, but Hayley still wasn't ready to let them off the hook just yet. "What was rolled up in the tarp that you were dragging across the lawn to your work shed?"

Damien looked honestly perplexed.

A light bulb seemed to go off in Rosemary's head. "Did you think it looked like a woman's body?"

"Yes!" Danny shouted. "And I saw Damien cutting it up with his power saw in his tool shed!"

"Come with me," Rosemary said calmly.

They followed her to the door leading down to the basement. Both Hayley and Danny stopped suddenly at the top of the stairs, fearing they might be walking into a trap, but Damien put a reassuring hand on both their shoulders from behind. "It's fine. We're not monsters. I promise."

Hayley wasn't so sure, but by now her instincts were telling her they were in no danger, so she took a chance and headed down behind Rosemary.

In the basement, there were about a dozen mannequins in various states of dress, a sewing machine station, and piles of fabric on a rack of metal shelves.

"I'm an amateur dress designer. My dream is to one day be a contestant on *Project Runway*. I adore Heidi Klum!"

Hayley perused the various dresses that some of the mannequins were wearing. "You're really good. I'd wear one of your dresses."

"Thank you," Rosemary said brightly.

It was the first time Hayley had seen a genuine smile, and Rosemary did indeed have a lovely, non-threatening smile.

"Rosemary had ordered some new mannequins, and so instead of just dumping some of the old ones I decided to cut them up for kindling to use in the fireplace this winter. I had wrapped one up in a tarp and left it outside because it was going to rain and I didn't want it to get wet."

Everything was making sense, and Hayley got a dreadful feeling in the pit of her stomach that they had made a terrible mistake.

Danny wasn't quite there yet.

"I'd still like proof that the bullets from your gun weren't the same kind that were used to kill Wendi Jo Willis," he demanded.

They all trudged back upstairs and Damien picked up the phone and called Sergio. Rosemary offered to make coffee, but Hayley and Danny politely declined. Within five minutes, Sergio was at the Salinger front door. He examined the gun for perhaps five to ten seconds before he handed it back to Damien.

"It's not the same gun or bullets," he said confidently.

There was another awkward silence. Hayley felt nauseous.

Rosemary scowled at them and asked, "Was there anything else?"

Hayley wanted to slap Danny upside the head for dragging her into his paranoid fantasies about haunted houses and neighbors possessed by evil spirits. She had been rightfully skeptical and should have remained the adult in the room, but Danny could be pretty persuasive, and because of that, she was now supremely embarrassed. "We should probably go check on the kids and see how they're coming along with their jack-o'-lanterns."

Hayley and Danny waved good-bye and then sheepishly retreated out the door. When they got back to their house, the kids were just finishing up carving their pumpkins.

"Look how talented you all are!" Hayley exclaimed. "Gemma, I see you've made Harry Potter again this year, and Dustin, that's the best Batman you've done yet." She turned to Casper and Carrie who were proudly showing off their own creations. "Casper, who is that supposed to be?"

"Freddy Krueger," Casper said, smiling.

"Oh . . . yes, I can see it now . . ." Hayley said before turning to inspect Carrie's carved pumpkin.

"Do you recognize him, Mrs. Powell?" Carrie asked, more excited than Hayley had ever seen her before.

"He does look familiar . . ." Hayley said, studying the face.

"Charles Manson!"

Hayley slowly backed away. "That would have been my first guess . . ."

The Salinger family may not have turned out to be homicidal maniacs, but that didn't make them any less strange.

Chapter Sixteen

Hayley was bending over an open kitchen drawer tearing off a piece of plastic wrap when Danny, already off his crutches, wandered into the kitchen and spotted a freshly baked pie cooling on top of the stove.

"Looks delicious," he said. "What kind is it?"

"It's a chocolate banana cream spider web pie," Hayley said. "It took a long time for me to make the chocolate on top look like a spider's web, but I think it came out great."

"I bet it tastes great, too," Danny said, reaching for the spatula lying next to it to cut himself a piece.

Hayley quickly snatched the spatula away from him and slapped the back of his hand with it. "You don't get any!"

"What? Why?"

"Because I didn't make it for you and I'm still mad at you," Hayley growled, setting the spatula down and then covering the pie with the plastic wrap.

"Look, so I was wrong about the neighbors. But

you have to admit, any rational person would have assumed the same as me. Look at them. It's obvious they're a little off. They don't act normal."

"No, Danny, you're the one who doesn't act normal. You got this whole family all worked up over nothing, and now, thanks to you, I could go to jail for breaking and entering!"

"They're not going to press charges," Danny scoffed.

Hayley picked up the pie. "Well, I'm just hoping this little peace offering helps calm the tensions between us."

"You only made the one pie?" Danny asked, crestfallen.

"Get it through your thick skull, Danny! I'm punishing you for starting a feud with our new neighbors! You're not getting any pie. Do you hear me?"

Hayley stormed out the door with the pie, crossing the yard to the Salinger house. With her heart beating faster as she approached the door, she took a deep breath and rang the bell.

After about a minute, the door flew open and Damien Salinger appeared, grimacing, clearly not happy to see her. "What do you want?"

Hayley held out her pie. "I made you a dessert for tonight. It's a chocolate banana cream pie with a spider's web topping and it's dairy-free and gluten-free so Casper can enjoy it."

"Carrie hates bananas," Damien said.

"Oh, I'm sorry, I guess I should have asked . . ."

"We don't want a pie from you. We don't want anything from you except for you to leave us alone!" Damien barked.

"Damien, I am absolutely mortified and embarrassed about what happened, and if there is anything I can do to make it up to you—"

He cut her off. "Do you realize I could have you arrested for breaking into my house?"

"Yes, I'm keenly aware of that possibility, but I was hoping—"

"I want you to get off my property! I don't want anything to do with you, or your husband, or your nosy kids who like to spy on us through the windows! And if you don't stay off my property, I'm going to file a lawsuit and claim harassment!"

Damien slammed the door in her face. Defeated, Hayley quietly walked back to her own house, carrying the pie. As she entered the front door, she set it back down on the stove. Danny was standing by the refrigerator, shoveling vanilla ice cream in his mouth directly from the carton with a spoon. "Didn't go well?"

"Don't talk with your mouth full, Danny," Hayley said, seething.

"Look on the bright side, babe," he said, giving her a wink. "At least we have one of your delicious pies to eat tonight at dinner."

He set down the carton of ice cream, and like a hungry seagull circling an unsuspecting fish, hovered over the pie and picked up the spatula.

Hayley wasted no time grabbing it out of his hand again and whacking him on the arm. "If you dare touch this pie, you'll be sleeping on the couch for the next six months!"

"Come on, Hayley!" Danny moaned.

She shot him a stern look so he knew she was dead serious.

Hayley was humiliated by what had transpired

with the Salingers, and she put the blame squarely at Danny's feet. They were no more murderers than her own family. But that still left the burning question. With the Salinger family finally and unequivocally in the clear, then who did shoot Wendi Jo Willis and bury her body in the woods?

Bar Harbor Cooking
by
Hattie Jenkins

I am quite sure by now that most of you have had your fill of sugary treats. I, for one, do not indulge in all that business when Halloween rolls around every year. But when this chilly weather settles in upon us for the next five months, I do admit to craving some good old-fashioned comfort food. And let me tell you, there is nothing more comforting than my delicious Easy Chicken and Dumplings. Trust me, my recipe, handed down by my grandmother, is a real keeper.

While I was puttering around my kitchen looking for the ingredients for this traditional fall/winter staple, I could not help but recall a memory from years past about a dear old friend of mine, Liz Caldwell, that involved chicken and dumplings.

Liz had been a spinster most of her life, until the day she met Pat, a Pennsylvania transplant who had been hired by the post office after the regular mailman for the past fifty-two years, Arthur Fielding, passed away from old age. Pat was personable and funny, and Liz looked forward to him showing up at her front door every day with her mail. Well, it didn't take too long for that spark to blossom into a romance, and the two were eventually married on a crisp fall day in 2006.

As with most couples who meet later in life, both Liz and Pat came into the marriage with a little extra baggage. Hers was in the form of her collection of ceramic cats and his was his mother! Apparently, Pat couldn't stand the thought of leaving his poor mother, Eileen, alone after all their years living together outside Pittsburgh, and Liz, although reticent about the whole situation, was just so darn happy to finally be married, she agreed to let his mother move to Maine and live with them.

It started out smoothly enough as the couple settled into married life, and Liz told her confidantes in town that it was actually a blessing to have her newly installed mother-in-law around to help with the cleaning and cooking since both Liz and Pat had full-time jobs. But pretty soon a disturbing trend seemed to emerge every night at dinnertime. Pat simply adored his mother's chicken along with her made-from-scratch dumplings, and so Liz held her tongue when Eileen served it practically every night of the week. Week after week. Her new husband didn't seem to mind or even notice the repetition and he consistently dove into the dish with child-like abandon and enthusiasm. Since Liz's culinary skills were spotty at best, she decided it would not be helpful to criticize.

But let's face it, after a few weeks of

eating the same meal every night, anyone is bound to go a little stir-crazy. And sadly, Liz did. After three weeks, she politely but forcefully suggested that it might be nice to incorporate a steak or a nice piece of fish into their weekly rotation. Her mother-in-law stared at her as if she had just asked her to cut off her own hand. But after a few tense moments, Eileen smiled and nodded, and then turned on her heel and walked away. Liz, who had been holding her breath, finally exhaled, proud of herself for finally speaking up and, more importantly, being heard.

Well, the next night when Eileen called the newlyweds to the dining table, Liz was shocked when her mother-in-law plopped down two piping hot bowls of chicken and dumplings in front of them. Pat gleefully dug in, not even bothering to lift his head from his bowl as he greedily slurped it up. Liz even caught Eileen smirking at her as she popped a generous piece of chicken into her mouth.

Something snapped inside Liz and she stood up, picked up her own bowl of chicken and dumplings, circled around the table, and dumped it all over Eileen's head. Well, needless to say, Eileen began screaming bloody murder and wailing at her son to do something, but Pat just had this surprised look on his face, and then after a few tense moments, just went back to eating.

Liz left the table, collected her ceramic cats, packed a bag, and walked right out the front door, never to be heard from again. Rumor has it she moved to Pittsfield where she met a nice mechanic who appreciated her limited cooking skills. As for Pat and his mother, they're still living together, and once a week, like clockwork, I see Eileen at the grocery store, stocking up on chicken and dumpling fixings. I hear she even crocheted an apron that says THE WAY TO MY SON'S HEART IS THROUGH HIS STOMACH, but to be honest, I've never seen her wear it so I can't say it's true although I'd say the betting odds are pretty good.

Hattie's Easy Chicken and Dumplings

Ingredients:

4 tablespoons butter
1 medium onion, diced
1 cup sliced carrots
1 cup sliced celery
1 teaspoon salt
1 teaspoon pepper
¼ cup all-purpose flour
4 cups chicken broth
3 cups cooked chicken, rough chopped
2 teaspoons poultry seasoning
1 teaspoon garlic powder
1 teaspoon onion powder
1 bay leaf
1 cup heavy cream
2½ cups Bisquick baking mix
1½ cups milk
salt and pepper, to taste

In a large pot on medium/low heat melt your butter. Add the diced onion, carrots, and celery. Season with the salt and pepper. Cook for about 10 minutes or until the veggies soften and begin to turn brown.

Add your flour into the cooked veggies and stir to coat. Add the chicken broth, chopped chicken, poultry seasoning, garlic powder, onion powder, bay leaf, heavy cream and stir well.

Turn your heat up to medium/high and bring to a boil.

In a separate mixing bowl mix your Bisquick and milk together.

Using a tablespoon, scoop generous spoonfuls of the dough and add to the boiling pot until all the dough is gone.

Lower the heat to a gentle simmer and cover pot for 20 minutes. After 20 minutes remove the lid and flip the dumplings and continue cooking for 10 more minutes.

Remove from heat and let rest for 5 minutes before ladling scoops of chicken and dumplings into bowls. Serve with salt and pepper to taste.

Chapter Seventeen

The following morning on her way to the office, Hayley decided to drop the spider web's pie off at the police station for Sergio and his officers to enjoy. It was also the perfect opportunity for her to get caught up on any progress in the Wendi Jo Willis investigation.

Sergio gleefully dove into the pie and was happy to oblige as they sat in the chief's office. "Her married boyfriend, Buster, is in the clear. He has an airtight alibi. He wasn't even on the island. He and his wife, Kathy, were in Portland at a Rustic Overtones concert."

"Did he have an idea who might have wanted to harm Wendi Jo?" Hayley asked.

Sergio moaned as he took another healthy bite of the pie. "Oh, that's the *best* pie I've ever tasted, Hayley . . ." He chewed some more and swallowed. "Yes, he did."

Hayley was dying of curiosity. "Who?"

"Her mother . . ." Sergio managed to get out between bites.

"*Dottie?*"

Sergio nodded.

"But that's ridiculous!"

"He said the close mother-daughter relation-ship was a joke! They despised each other!"

"What did they fight about?"

"According to Buster, everything. But their biggest row was about selling Dottie's house. Wendi Jo was worried Dottie couldn't take care of herself anymore, and so she wanted to sell her house and check her into a senior assisted-living facility and Dottie cried, 'Over my dead body!' Maybe after she thought about it, Dottie decided it would be over Wendi Jo's."

Hayley was not inclined to buy into the theory of Dottie as the killer, especially considering Dot-tie's fragile, almost feeble condition, and the fact that her daughter, hardly a waifish model, was about three times her size. "Are you saying you think Dottie shot her own daughter twice, killing her, and then had the physical strength to drag her body into the woods and bury it?"

Sergio sat back in his creaky chair and stretched out his arms, clasping his hands behind his head, as he yawned and said, "No, I'm saying Buster thinks so. But Dottie could have forced Wendi Jo at gunpoint into the woods and shot her there to avoid having to drag the body."

"Even if that's what happened, you would still have to believe Dottie had the strength to dig a big deep hole, roll Wendi Jo into it, and shovel a mountain of dirt back into the hole to cover up the body? Really? A frail, old woman?" Hayley asked incredulously, standing up from her chair. "I just can't imagine it."

"I know, it does not sound very plausible," Sergio admitted.

"We have to be missing something!" Hayley said as she paced back and forth in Sergio's office at the Bar Harbor Police Station.

"*We?*"

Hayley stopped suddenly. "I mean you, of course. I'm just a concerned citizen who just happens to want to know what happened to poor Wendi Jo Willis."

"I hope this does not become a habit, Hayley."

Hayley raised an eyebrow. "What do you mean by that?"

"It has not been lost on me that you have been very interested in this investigation, questioning people, showing up here to pump me for information. This is not going to become your new calling, is it? Playing amateur detective?"

"Of course not, Sergio! I have a life, you know. This is a one-time thing. I promise. And I have only questioned maybe one or two people about the murder."

Sergio eyed her skeptically. "I will not even show you the complaint I received about you hounding your new neighbors."

"That was Danny! He got me all worked up with his scary ghost stories, and I may have gone a little too far, and I fully regret my behavior . . . and *his!*"

"Other than you witnessing an argument between Mr. Salinger and Wendi Jo over a bi-curious house inspection, there was no evidence that he ever—"

"I don't mean to interrupt, Sergio, but a bi what?"

"What did I say?"

"Bi-curious house inspection? How can a house inspection be bi-curious?"

"Unfairly prejudiced! The fix was in! She hired a relative to do it in order to hide the fact the roof needed to be replaced!"

Hayley pondered this for a moment. "Biased! You mean biased!"

"Yes, whatever! That family is completely innocent!"

English was Sergio's second language.

Sergio sighed, frustrated. "And I have very few clues to go on except the locket you found at the scene. I took it to Bar Harbor Jewelry and showed it to Mr. Linscott, but he said he sells dozens of those lockets a year and had no idea who it belonged to."

"May I see it again?" Hayley asked.

Sergio picked up his phone and pressed a button. "Stuart, go to the evidence drawer and bring me that locket from the Willis crime scene, would you, please?"

He hung up.

"I thought you would have an evidence room not just a drawer," Hayley remarked.

"This is Bar Harbor, Hayley, not New York City."

A few minutes later, one of Sergio's younger officers, Stuart, popped in and handed his boss a plastic bag with the locket inside. He was a large young man with a baby face and had doughnut sprinkles on the sides of his mouth. He licked frosting off the fingers of his free hand.

Sergio stared at him and shook his head. "Your lunch break is in twenty minutes, Stuart."

"Got it. Thanks, Chief," he said, before nodding

and smiling at Hayley and ambling out of the office.

Sergio unzipped the bag and removed the heart-shaped silver locket. "It was already dusted for fingerprints, but we didn't find a match in the database. The only thing we're sure of is that the one print we found on it did not belong to Wendi Jo."

Hayley carefully examined the locket. As she turned it over in her hand, Stuart raced back into the office with a box of doughnuts. "Would either of you like a doughnut?"

His sudden appearance startled Hayley and she dropped the locket. It smashed on the floor and broke in half. They all stared down at it in shock.

A nervous Stuart spoke first. "I have a chocolate glaze and one with cream filling left. I realized I should have offered before when I brought in the . . . locket."

"Get out of here, Stuart!" Sergio growled.

Stuart scooted away.

Hayley bent down to pick it up. "Wait, Sergio, it's not broken. It just popped open. And look at this. . . ." She handed Sergio a tiny picture that fit perfectly inside the locket. It was an old photo, at least from the 1970s, of a young couple clearly in love. The man was in a white military uniform, most likely the Navy.

"Do you recognize them?" Sergio asked.

Hayley shook her head. "The woman looks familiar, but I'm certain I've never seen the man before."

Sergio squinted at the photo. "Do you think that's Dottie Willis?"

"Her features are too sharp to be Dottie . . ."

Hayley suddenly had an idea. "Can I borrow this photo?"

"I'm afraid not. I can't let any evidence leave this office until the case is closed."

Hayley took the photo from Sergio. "Then can I borrow your xerox machine?"

After copying the photo of the young couple, Hayley scurried out of the police station, hopped in her car, and drove straight over to Bar Harbor Jewelry where she knew the owner, Irving Linscott, sold silver heart-shaped lockets. Mr. Linscott was a chatty one, and it was common knowledge if you went shopping for a wedding ring or came in to get a necklace repaired, you were probably going to be there for at least an hour and a half while Mr. Linscott regaled you with his long, drawn-out, seemingly endless stories. Still, Hayley found him to be a jolly old man with sparkling eyes and a sweet demeanor. He just told boring stories.

Some bells jangled as she hurried through the door and she found Mr. Linscott, who some said resembled Santa Claus with his white beard and red complexion, helping a young man pick out an engagement ring for the girlfriend to whom he was about to propose. "Back in 1988, I think it was, I had a young man in here just about your age, and he was going to propose to his girlfriend and wanted to make it special so he had his uncle, who was a police officer, pull her over one day when she was driving home from work, and he approached her car and said, 'Sorry, ma'am, I'm pulling you over because you are a suspect in a theft crime.' And the woman says, 'I have never committed any crime in my life!' And then her boyfriend gets out of the back of the squad car, and his uncle the cop points to him and says, 'I believe you stole this man's heart!' And then the man got down on one knee and proposed. Well, good thing she said yes, because then the uncle gave her a ticket for speeding!" Mr. Linscott guffawed as the young man stared at him, smiling politely, before asking as he pointed to a ring behind the glass case, "Can I take a look at this one?"

"Most certainly," Mr. Linscott said, opening the case and removing the ring. As he handed it to the young man, he was still chuckling over his story. "I got another one that's even crazier. You just hold on while I deal with another customer."

The young man nodded, not sure if he wanted to stick around to hear it.

Mr. Linscott ambled over to Hayley. "Well, I haven't seen your pretty face in ages, Hayley. I think the last time was about two years ago at the Fourth of July parade. I have a funny story about that day—"

"Mr. Linscott, I'm sorry, I don't have a lot of time. I just need you to take a look at this."

She handed him a copy of the photo. He studied it carefully.

"Someone lost one of those heart-shaped silver lockets you have here . . ."

"My best seller in the whole shop."

"I recently found one and there was this picture inside. I know it's a long shot, but I was hoping you might be able to tell me if you have ever seen this photo or recognize the people in it."

"Sure do. I was the one who cut down the photo to fit inside the locket. That's her husband, Nate. He died in nineteen ninety-seven, but this picture was taken on their wedding day, must have been back in the early seventies maybe seventy-one or seventy-two. She brought it in about six months ago. I remember the day she came in because, well, it's a funny story—"

"Mr. Linscott, *who* is it?"

"Beatrice Lumley."

It took a moment for Hayley to recognize the name and then it dawned on her. Of course. That's why the woman in the photograph looked so familiar. She had just seen her recently. Beatrice. One of Dottie Willis's best friends with whom she played cards every week.

Chapter Eighteen

Beatrice's eyes widened in surprise. "You found my locket? That's wonderful news! I could not imagine what could have happened to it! It has such sentimental value. You see, inside there is an old picture of me with my late husband, Nate, and when I couldn't find it the other day, I was beside myself with worry—"

"I know. The locket accidentally opened, and I saw the photo. Your husband was very handsome."

"Thank you," Beatrice said, standing expectantly in the doorway of her modest home tucked away at the end of Hancock Street, not too far from the *Island Times* office. "Would you like to come in for some tea?"

"Perhaps another time. I have to get back to the office."

"I see . . ." Beatrice said, smiling, glancing at Hayley's empty hands. "So do you have it with you?"

"No, that's the thing. Police Chief Alvares wouldn't let me return it to you just yet on account that it was found so close to the crime scene."

The blood began to slowly drain from Beatrice's face. "What crime scene?"

"In the woods behind our house where poor Wendi Jo Willis was found shot and buried."

"I see. How on earth did my locket wind up there?"

"I was hoping you might be able to tell me!"

"What would I know about any of that nasty business?" Beatrice wailed, suddenly nervous, her hands fidgeting.

Hayley shrugged. "It's just odd that of all the places for your locket to show up . . ."

She let the suggestion hang there until Beatrice, who now was on the verge of some kind of emotional breakdown, blurted out, "I must have lent it to Wendi Jo! Yes! Now I remember! She was going on a date, and had coveted my necklace with the locket, so I let her borrow it for the occasion! Wendi Jo must have dropped it before she was killed. Yes, that's it. That's what must have happened!"

Beatrice nodded, happy with her explanation although Hayley didn't buy it for a second. And Beatrice, whose eyes were fixed on Hayley's skeptical face, couldn't help herself. She pointed at Hayley with a crooked finger. "What? You don't believe me? You think it was *me* who shot Wendi Jo? I had no ill will toward her! We never had a negative word between us! And I don't appreciate you accusing me of murder!"

"I'm not saying anything of the kind," Hayley said calmly and deliberately, which made Beatrice even more flustered than she already was.

"I swear to you, I have never fired a gun in my life and I am not about to start now! I despise guns! Rifles, pistols, all kinds! When Nate was alive, he loved to shoot cans in the backyard! It used to drive me crazy! All those loud shots ringing in my ears! Just a few weeks ago, I had to adjust my hearing aids so I wouldn't have to listen to all the loud banging!"

Hayley raised an eyebrow. "You heard shots recently?"

Beatrice's face froze momentarily as she realized she had probably just said too much. "Yes, but it wasn't out in the woods!"

Hayley stepped forward. "Where was it, Beatrice?"

Beatrice rang her hands together and hemmed and hawed before finally admitting, "Up in Ellsworth. There is a private firing range just outside of town on Route 3 and I accompanied a friend who just happens to be a proud card-carrying member of the NRA and wanted to do a little target practice."

"May I ask who this friend of yours is?"

"No, you may not, Hayley! That's none of your business frankly! People are entitled to a little privacy, and so it's not up to me to tell you anything about her hobbies!"

"*Her?*"

Beatrice was about to have a full-on meltdown at this point, but instead of dissolving completely in front of Hayley, she simply stepped back inside her house and slammed the door shut. Hayley then jumped in her car and drove straight to Ellsworth. She knew where the shooting range was located, and when she arrived, she found a lanky, sleepy-eyed young kid, around fifteen, sitting behind the counter next to a computer.

"You have to be a member to be admitted," the kid said, scratching the heavy acne on his face.

"I'm from the Maine Department of Fishing and Wildlife, which includes jurisdiction over hunting and firearms, so I know you have to be over eighteen to be working at a business with firearms," Hayley said sternly, folding her arms, glaring at the kid, who suddenly looked scared.

"I'm just watching the counter until my dad gets back," the kid tried to explain, forgetting to ask Hayley for any proper identification.

"Where is he?"

The kid appeared to be on the verge of tears. "He just went to pick up sandwiches at Subway. He's been gone like ten minutes!"

"I came here to check your membership to make sure everyone is legally licensed. If you can help me with that, maybe I will forget reporting your father," Hayley said.

The kid whipped the desktop computer around so Hayley could see the list of members who had been using the shooting range in the last month. As she scrolled down, she came across a familiar name.

Dottie Willis.

She looked up at the kid whose eyes were nearly bulging out of his head, he was so nervous about getting arrested. She had him right where she wanted.

"Do you know this woman?" Hayley asked.

"Dottie? Sure do. She's in here all the time. But she has a permit to carry. I made a copy of it my-self to put in her membership file."

"When was she last here?"

"A few weeks ago. She came by with the Granny Gang," the kid said, shaking his head and grinning. "Sometimes she brings along some of her old lady friends. They have lunch up here in Ellsworth, do some shopping at Marsden's, and then swing by here to watch Dottie shoot. There's Betty, Evie and . . . Mary, I think."

Beatrice, Ethel and Mildred.

But close enough. And it was all Hayley needed to start putting the pieces together that formed a clear picture of what really happened to Wendi Jo Willis.

Chapter Nineteen

Hayley rang the bell next to the front door of Dottie Willis's house, but knew she was not at home. She turned around and zeroed in on a flowerpot on the porch floor. She remembered Dottie mentioning that she kept a key underneath it just in case Wendi Jo stopped by when she was not at home. She crossed over to it, bent down, and lifted the pot. Sure enough, there was a rusted metal key. She set the flowerpot down a few inches to the right, scooped up the key, and let herself inside the house. She knew she was breaking the law, but she also knew Sergio was working on a warrant, and that would take time, and if the owner of the shooting range, or his son, somehow tipped off Dottie, then she might have time to get rid of the murder weapon before the police got their hands on it.

The house was eerily quiet, and Hayley had not informed Sergio when she called him with the information she had discovered that she planned on breaking into it. But she prayed that she would have enough time to do a quick search and maybe find the gun in question before Dottie arrived home. After looking around downstairs, Hayley hustled up the creaky stairs to the bedrooms, opening drawers and dropping to her hands and knees to check under the bed. Finally, she focused on the closet in Dottie's room, and suspecting the gun might be in a shoebox, opened a few that were stacked on the top shelf. Unfortunately, all the boxes were filled with shoes, as advertised.

She crossed to the nightstand next to the bed. She opened it to find a couple of novels and a notepad and pen for writing. She circled around the bed and opened the nightstand drawer on the other side. It was empty. That's when she noticed that the bottom was raised higher than the drawer in the matching nightstand on the other side of the bed. She knocked on it and it sounded hollow. It was a fake bottom. She pressed down on one end and, it popped up, and she was able to remove the fake bottom to reveal a pistol underneath. Bingo!

She grabbed a washcloth from the bathroom and came back and lifted the gun out of the drawer with it in order to preserve any fingerprints. She rushed out of the bedroom and down the stairs, freezing on the bottom step as the front door swung open, and Dottie entered the house, her "Granny Gang" behind her, Beatrice, Ethel, and Mildred.

"What are you doing in my house?" Dottie yelled.

She realized that it was the second time someone had asked her that question in the span of two days.

Hayley held up the gun covered with the white washcloth. "I came for this. It's over, Dottie. I know it was you who shot Wendi Jo."

"Pray tell, why? Why on earth do you think I would kill my own daughter?" Dottie scoffed, turning to her pals for support. They all shook their heads, acting disgusted by Hayley's preposterous ideas.

"Because Wendi Jo wanted to sell this house and put you in an assisted-living facility," Hayley said. "She would get a big fat commission on the sale and she wouldn't have to worry about taking care of you anymore. When you refused to go along with the plan, she began pushing the issue. . . ."

"I told you she was onto you!" Beatrice cried.

"Shut up, Bea!" Dottie hissed.

"Anyone who knew Wendi Jo knew she was stubborn and aggressive. Once she got something into her head, she just couldn't let it go. And she was determined to get you out of this house and out of her hair. But the thing is, Wendi Jo didn't get her ornery and headstrong personality from her father. No, she got it from you! You're just as tough and tenacious as she is, even more so, and there was no way you were going to allow her to take away your freedom. It must have all come to a head that night when she was last here, and in a fit of rage, fearing she was going to convince people you were too frail to look after yourself, you shot her! Twice!"

Dottie glared at Hayley, then clapped her hands, applauding her. "What a lovely performance, Hayley! So believable and impressive. But there is one big flaw in your fascinating tale. My mind may still be sharp, but look at me. Do you honestly think I have the physical stamina to move my daughter's body from here? Of course not! I have arthritis in

my hands and a bad back! I couldn't lift a Maine
coon cat let alone my overweight daughter!"

"You're right," Hayley said, nodding. "You could
not have moved Wendi Jo's body to the woods . . .
alone."

This caught the attention of Beatrice, Mildred,
and Ethel, who suddenly shrank back from Dottie,
who stood firm, relishing the confrontation, unin-
timidated by Hayley's musings.

"You had help from the Granny Gang, as the
boy from the shooting range in Ellsworth referred
to you all," Hayley said.

The mention of the shooting range caused Mildred to gasp.

Dottie shot her an admonishing look to keep
quiet.

"I'm right, aren't I? You were all best friends,
willing to do anything in order to protect each
other. None of you could stand the fact that Wendi
Jo was going to ruin her mother's life, your din-
ners out, your weekly card games, by putting her
in a home."

"I could never kill anyone!" Ethel gasped.

"I believe you, Ethel. But Dottie could. And
once it became clear that she had shot Wendi Jo,
you did find the strength to help her cover up the
crime. You all worked as a team to move the body
to the woods and bury it, hoping it would never be
found. It was there that Beatrice dropped her
locket, probably when she was helping dig the
hole in the ground."

"Dottie, what are we going to do?" Mildred
cried. "She's going to go to the police!"

"Relax, Mildred! No one knows she's here. She's

not going anywhere," Dottie said, speaking in a very calm and measured tone.

"What? No, we can't! Not again—" Beatrice wailed.

"What do you mean *again*? You barely got your hands dirty! But as for me, I have no problem making sure all of this stays a secret, no matter what has to be done."

Hayley unwrapped the washcloth and held the gun out.

Beatrice, Ethel, and Mildred all raised their hands in the air.

"It's empty," Dottie said, cackling. "There are no bullets. I got rid of them all after I shot Wendi Jo."

Hayley lowered the gun. "You were right about me not going anywhere, Dottie. But you were wrong about no one knowing I'm here."

"What are you talking about?" Dottie spit out.

Hayley pointed toward the front door, which was still ajar from when the Granny Gang first arrived. The flashing blue lights of a squad car parked out front caught their attention and all four women deflated at the sight of Police Chief Sergio Alvares marching up the footpath toward the house.

Chapter Twenty

When Hayley arrived home after witnessing the arrests of Dottie and the Granny Gang by Sergio and a few of his officers, there was a large moving truck pulling away from the Salinger house. Damien, Rosemary, and their two kids, Casper and Carrie, watched the truck disappear around the corner before they began loading their station wagon with a few remaining boxes and suitcases.

Hayley pulled into her driveway, got out of her car, and gingerly walked across the lawn toward the Salingers. When Damien noticed her approaching, he frowned and then turned to his wife and children, growling, "Get in the car."

"You're moving?" Hayley asked.

Damien nodded. "We rented a place up in Waterville. Rosemary has family there. Hopefully the neighbors won't bother us so much."

"Again, I can't tell you how sorry I am . . ."

"Just don't be so quick to judge the next family that moves in next door to you . . ." Damien said, shaking his head.

"I wish you were going to be around long

enough to let me make it up to you. We normally don't act like this, but sometimes my husband gets these wild ideas in his head . . ." Hayley tried to explain before noticing that Damien appeared unsympathetic to her cause and didn't care to hear anymore. "But there is no excuse."

"They're not so wild . . ." Damien murmured.

"I beg your pardon?" Hayley asked.

"Don't get me wrong. You, your husband. and your kids are a *big* reason we're moving, but I'd be lying if I said there weren't . . . other reasons."

"Like what?"

"The kids were always hearing strange noises, like moaning, or people whispering when they were trying to go to sleep at night, and Rosemary swore she saw a woman in the attic when she was moving some boxes up there . . . and well . . . I'm sure it was nothing . . . Anyway, good-bye, Hayley. I wish I could say I was going to miss you."

Hayley took the dig in stride because she knew she deserved it. She leaned down and waved at Rosemary, who sat upright in the passenger seat, staring straight ahead. "Good-bye, Rosemary."

Rosemary didn't answer and refused to make eye contact.

Hayley tried with the kids sitting in the back seat. "Be sure to let us know how you're doing!"

Casper was busy reading a comic book while Carrie stared at her with those cold dead eyes that always sent a shiver up Hayley's spine.

Damien turned his back on her, slid into the driver's seat, slammed the door shut, and then backed the station wagon out of the driveway and roared off down the street, happy to be leaving Bar Harbor behind for good.

Hayley couldn't help but feel a twinge of relief that the Salingers were moving out of town. Granted, she and her own family had practically driven them out, but the fact remained they were an odd brood, more than a bit unsettling, and perhaps now a friendlier family might move in, and pretty soon they could be having festive Sunday block parties and barbecues. That is, if anyone would be willing to ignore the house's checkered past and the spooky stories swirling around it.

As Hayley returned to her house to start dinner for her own odd brood, she turned around to take another look at the house next door, abruptly deserted once again. Something caught her eye up in a second-floor window belonging to one of the three bedrooms. A woman in what looked like a long flowing gown from another period, her long hair blowing as if she was standing near a fan, stood there with a haunted look on her face as she raised a hand toward Hayley.

Hayley gasped, rubbed her eyes, and looked again.

The woman was gone.

No.

She was not going to buy into this nonsense anymore.

The house next door was definitely *not* haunted.

And that's what she would keep telling herself.

Whether she actually believed it or not.

Bar Harbor Cooking
by
Hattie Jenkins

Sorry my column is so short today, but I have to drive up to Ellsworth to shop for some Thanksgiving decorations at Walmart. I also have to make a stop at the Hancock County Jail to visit some dear friends of mine.

As I'm sure most of you have heard by now, the terrible murder of our most successful local real estate agent Wendi Jo Willis has finally been solved. Wait, let me amend that statement and say *one* of our most successful local real estate agents. I don't need that loud-mouthed Liddy Crawford calling me at the office to complain.

Well, needless to say, I was shocked to find out the perpetrator was none other than her own mother, Dottie Willis. And if that wasn't awful enough, that malevolent old bat even roped her best friends into helping her! I knew Dottie had a temper. In fact, I witnessed firsthand one of her legendary tantrums that time her ball went in the gutter on our bowling league night. But Lordy, I never thought she was *that* bad! Thank God she never played bingo with us at the Ladies Auxiliary.

You all know I am never one to gossip, but I heard through a very reliable source that when Dottie and her accomplices were being carted to the courthouse for their arraignment, Dottie had a sudden "heart episode" and she is now resting comfortably at the hospital in Ellsworth with a handsome guard posted outside her private room while her best friends are rotting in a jail cell awaiting trial. I'm not saying Dottie faked her ailment in order to improve upon her living conditions, but you have to admit, it is highly suspicious. And we all know she was the mastermind of the whole insidious plot, so it just doesn't seem fair to Beatrice, Ethel, and Mildred.

That's why after I'm done shopping I'm going to go play cards with the girls at the county jail. They sent word that they needed a fourth since they're no longer on speaking terms with Dottie. I also thought I would surprise them with a pan of my delicious homemade Fall Apple Cobbler. The girls have been starved for something sweet. The most they can expect at the end of a meal in jail is a jiggling blob of bland green Jell-O. So I got permission from the county sheriff to bring my cobbler for them to enjoy. And don't worry, I didn't bake my cobbler with a hidden hacksaw for those Golden Girls to use to break out. Sorry, just a little jail humor. I couldn't resist.

Hattie's Fall Apple Cobbler

Ingredients:

8 tablespoons butter (1 stick), melted
1 cup granulated sugar
1 cup self-rising flour
1 teaspoon cinnamon
½ teaspoon salt
1 cup milk
1 can apple pie filling

Preheat your oven to 350 degrees.

Pour your melted butter into a 2-quart baking dish.

In a large mixing bowl add your sugar, flour, cinnamon, and salt. Mix to combine.

Stir the milk into the flour mixture and stir to combine.

Pour the mixture onto the melted butter. Do not stir.

Spoon apple pie mixture evenly over the top. Do not stir.

Bake in the preheated oven 40 to 45 minutes or until crust rises and top is golden brown.

HALLOWED OUT

Barbara Ross

Chapter One

"**O**ver my dead body!" My mother, my sweet, petite, unfailingly polite mother, raised her voice and crossed her arms over her chest.

"No, madam," Harley Prendergast replied. "Over hers." He pointed dramatically to a spot on the floor in my mother's front hall near the archway that led to the living room. As far as I could tell from my vantage point on the porch watching the interaction through the open front door, there was nothing on the old oak floorboards except a few late-morning sunbeams.

Mom's habitually perfect posture became even more perfect as she pulled herself up to her full height, which wasn't much. "I'm not discussing this with you further, Harley. Go find someone else to bother."

Harley reflexively stood taller, too. At six-four, broad-shouldered and paunchy, he loomed over her. But he seemed to grasp that he'd met his match. "I'll be back," he vowed. "You'll come around."

"You'll certainly be welcome back." Mom smiled

and let her arms drop to her sides. "As long as it's for another purpose."

Despite his size, Harley pivoted neatly toward the open front door, nodded as he passed me on the porch, and exited down the steps.

"What was that about?" I asked as I came through the door.

Mom, who seemed to be studying the lines on the floor, looked up. "Harley's shilling for stops for his Halloween Haunted House Tours and he claims we have a ghost."

"Here? In town?" My family was widely known to have a ghost, two in fact. But legend had it they resided at Windsholme, the abandoned mansion on the island where our family ran our authentic Maine clambakes during the summer tourist season. But a ghost at the house in town, the old sea captain's house on Main Street my parents had bought in the 1980s? I had never heard of such a thing.

"Come into the kitchen," Mom said. "I have time for another cup of coffee before I leave."

My mother was an assistant manager at Linens and Pantries, the big box store in Topsham, Maine. The store had put out its Halloween merchandise two weeks earlier, immediately after Labor Day, and was ramping up for the coming holiday season.

Mom poured each of us a cup from the coffeemaker on the counter while I fetched milk from the refrigerator. "Harley claims the story goes like this," she said when we were seated at the kitchen table. "The captain who built this house, Samuel Merriman, was engaged in the China trade, taking kerosene to Canton and returning with loads of tea. The round trip usually took eight months, to make the crossing, leave the cargo in New York or Boston, and finally return here to Busman's Harbor."

Mom pushed a hank of blond hair, only recently tinged with gray, back behind an ear and took a sip of her coffee. People say I look like her. I can't see it, except for the most obvious things, coloring and stature.

"One day," Mom continued, "while Captain Merriman was at sea, a sailor came here to town telling the tale of a Busman's schooner that had blown sky-high in Canton harbor when the kerosene it carried was somehow ignited. But the sailor had no details. He didn't know the name of the captain or ship and was vague about the date when the accident had occurred.

"Samuel's wife, Sarah, was worried sick when she heard this. As she calculated the dates, her husband and his ship would have been in Canton about when the sailor said the explosion happened.

"So she went up to the cupola." My mother's house had an enclosed cupola on its mansard roof. "And she stayed. She wouldn't come down. The housekeeper begged her, and then her children did. The cook sent up food that returned only nibbled on. Friends, family, neighbors came, and finally the minister, but she ignored all entreaties."

"Was it her husband's ship that exploded?" Poor Sarah Merriman. I imagined her anxiety in those long-ago days when loved ones went to the other side of the world with scant opportunity to communicate. To think she had walked the same halls of the house I grew up in.

"At last, a mast was spotted on the horizon, headed to Busman's Harbor," Mom continued. "The news spread through town. Now, surely, Mrs. Merriman would come down. But she said no, she'd wait until she saw the ship with her own eyes.

"Finally, Captain Merriman's ship sailed into the harbor. When she spotted it, Mrs. Merriman stood up and ran down the stairs, from the cupola to the third floor, from the third to the second, and then from the second to the first. But her legs were weak from disuse and she was running too fast. She tripped on the carpet at the top of the stairs and landed in the front hall, her neck broken. She never saw her husband."

We were quiet for a moment. "That is an awful story," I said.

"Such piffle," Mom responded. "Harley needs more stops for the haunted house tour. I'm sure he's across the street at the Snugg sisters right now telling them some made-up story about what happened at their house."

"Probably." I had to agree with Mom's likely explanation. The town of Busman's Harbor had struggled for years with Maine's pitifully short summer season. Sure, we got leaf-peepers from the end of September until mid-October. And the nearby Maine Coast Botanical Gardens generated a fair amount of business for the town from Thanksgiving to New Year's with their massive outdoor lighting display. But from the middle of October to Veteran's Day, tourist dollars remained stubbornly out of reach.

Until this year, when the tourist bureau had the idea for a weeklong, town-wide Halloween celebration. Why should Salem, Massachusetts, 150 short miles to our south, get all the visitors? We didn't have witches, that was true, but we did have ghosts, and we had Harley.

In a town where nearly everyone had to hustle to make a living during tourist season, Harley made the rest of us look like pikers. He and his wife, Myra, owned The Lobsterman's Wharf Motel on the east side of the harbor, and Kimbel's Souvenir Shoppe on the west side. All day long, seven days a week, from Memorial Day to Columbus Day, Harley drove his trolley back and forth, picking up passengers at each of the hotels on the east side, depositing them downtown, and then ferrying them back again when their feet hurt and their money was spent. That he happened to pick up and drop off in front of Kimbel's, the shop he owned, was a mere coincidence. Or so he would have you believe. During the summer, at night, he met groups of tourists downtown who were willing to part with $19.99 apiece ($14.99 for seniors, $9.99 for children under fifteen) to take them on his haunted house tour. That most of the places they toured were not houses, and were also, in most peoples' opinions, not haunted, was a detail. Everyone had a good time.

Now, in mid-September, Harley was getting his ducks in a row for the Halloween tour. He couldn't use some of his usual stops. Herrickson Point Light, for instance. There was no reason to drive people all the way out there in the fall. Even with extended daylight savings time, darkness came early when you were on the eastern edge of the time zone. The tour members wouldn't be able to see anything and it would be freezing. That's why he needed Mom's house. Or someplace like it. A convenient location, a tragic story. But I could tell by the look on Mom's face as she sipped her coffee, Harley wasn't going to get it.

"Have you ever heard my Mom's house is haunted?" I was seated at the counter at Gus's restaurant, the only person in the place aside from the proprietor. In the off-season, my boyfriend, Chris, and I ran a dinner restaurant in Gus's space, which we would reopen right after Columbus Day. The idea for the restaurant had been Gus's. He wanted to give me an incentive to stay in town over the winter, and also to offer a dining space where the community could gather. But the old curmudgeon had never shared his restaurant with anyone and, even as we prepared to open for our second season, he didn't find it easy. He was dawdling, cleaning the already gleaming coffee machine, reluctant to let go and let us work.

"Your mother's place? Of course I've heard the stories."

Really? "I don't mean on the island," I clarified. "I mean, have you ever heard about her place here in town being haunted?"

Gus shook his white-haired head. "Nope. Can't say as I have."

"Harley wants to put it on his Halloween Haunted House Tour."

Gus blew air out through his lips, rattling his jowls. He wasn't fat. In fact, he was lean and tough like an old buzzard, but his skin was loose with age. "Harley. She might as well give in now. He's relentless."

"She really doesn't want to do it." I took my

coffee cup to the sink behind the counter and washed it.

Gus took off his white apron and walked to the center of the front room, passing me as he did. "This place is haunted." He gestured, his hands indicating the space.

"The restaurant?" I squinted at him, trying to decide if he was teasing. "You might have mentioned that, seeing as how I've been sleeping upstairs for over a year." I lived in the large studio apartment over Gus's place, which was convenient when Chris and I staggered up to bed after a long night of running the restaurant.

"Ayup. 'Tis. You know the restaurant was used as a warehouse by bootleggers bringing in booze from Canada during Prohibition."

I did. The previous fall a desperate man had used the trapdoor in the floor that had been installed by the bootleggers to enter the restaurant.

"What you don't know," Gus continued, "is one of 'em was killed here. Gunned down in cold blood."

"Again, you might have mentioned—"

Gus ignored me, warming to the story. "The demand for real, honest-to-goodness hard liquor with the labels still on it was intense up and down the east coast of the United States during Prohibition. Canada had it, both made on its soil and imported from Scotland and Ireland and everyone wanted it.

"Booze came over by car and in trucks, but as that proved increasingly difficult, it came by ships. Big ships working for the Canadian distilleries and distributorships anchored out at sea just over the three-mile mark, in international waters. It was called the rum line. The old-timers said it was like a city out there; there were so many lights. Smaller boats would head out from the New England ports to buy the liquor and bring it back. In the beginning, the smugglers' boats were faster than anything the U.S. Coast Guard owned. They could outrun the authorities every time. That's why they were called rumrunners."

"Wait. The boats were called rumrunners, or the people who ran them?"

"First the boats, and then the men who captained them. The most famous rumrunner in Busman's Harbor was Ned Calhoun. Distribution of the liquor once it came ashore was almost exclusively the province of organized crime, but a few of the rumrunners were freelancers. Ned was a local lad, a fisherman, thirty years old and devilishly handsome. He was fast and daring, a legend. He made plenty of money for his services and he spread it around, buying from town merchants, giving to the Widows and Orphans Fund. He was regarded as a bit of a local Robin Hood. And when he fell in love with Sweet Sue, the prettiest flapper in town—"

"Okay, now I know you're kidding. Sweet Sue? Come on."

Gus put one hand up, oath-taking style. His eyes opened wide and his formidable white eyebrows flew up his forehead in a look of pure innocence. "Suzanne Kinney, from the Kinney family. They're still here in town. You can check it out."

I chuckled. "Okay." Then I nodded for him to go on.

"Where was I? Yes. Ned decided, why simply be the transport? He was leaving the booze around the harbor in warehouses that belonged to the gangsters. Their crews would pick it up and take it to the cities where it would change hands once again. Ned didn't see why he couldn't get in on this piece of the business, too. So when he'd go out to the rum line, he'd buy the booze his gangster masters wanted, but he'd also use his own ill-gotten gains to buy a few cases for himself. He sold it along the coast from here as far down as Portland. Demand increased. The money increased and pretty soon Ned had enough business, he didn't have to work for the gangsters anymore. He rented this place." Again, Gus gestured around his warehouse-turned-restaurant. As warehouses went, it was on the small side. It was easy to see why Ned would have chosen it to get his start.

"Things went okay for a while," Gus continued. "Ned and Sweet Sue were living high on the hog. They had a car, something practically nobody in town did except the doctor, the postman, and the merchants for deliveries. They bought a big sea captain's house on Main Street."

"Please, not my mother's house," I interrupted. "I'm trying to get Harley off her back, not give him a new tale."

"Not your mother's house. Down at the other end. The Fogged Inn."

"Whew." The Fogged Inn was a B and B in an old sea captain's home on the far end of Main Street. It had recently changed hands. I didn't know the new owners well enough to guess whether they'd be up for hosting a haunted house tour.

"But, since this is a ghost story," Gus continued the tale, "you've probably guessed, it didn't work out. Ned and Sue attracted too much attention.

The gangsters couldn't allow this local yokel to get rich off the alcohol trade; too many others might try the same thing, destroying their monopoly. So one night, when Ned sailed back from the rum line and entered his warehouse through that trapdoor right there—" Gus pointed to the door in the floor of the restaurant, which was, in fact, not visible because it was behind the bar, which somewhat undercut his gesture. "When he came through the door, Al Capone's men were waiting with their Tommy guns, and rat-tat-tat-tat. They shot him."

Gus paused so I could take it in, but since I'd been expecting this dramatic turn of events, I motioned for him to speed up the story. He looked disappointed but went on. "He managed to gasp out his dying words. 'My only aim was to help my fellow citizens of Busman's Harbor. Tell Sweet Sue I'll always love her.' And then he died. Right here, on the floor.

"Sweet Sue never recovered. She never married. They say she sat in the window of that big old house, wearing her wedding dress every day for the rest of her long life."

"Now I know you're kidding." *Really, bringing Miss Havisham into it.*

"Every word is true. At least, as the story was told to me. I didn't arrive here in town until thirty years later."

"So who's the ghost? Ned Calhoun, or Sweet Sue, or . . ." If it was Sweet Sue, I could send Harley after the new, and hopefully naïve, proprietors of the Fogged Inn.

"Ned, of course. A handsome, young man like that, cut down in his prime. He became more brave, a better captain, and more charitable with every retelling of his story. And then people started seeing him."

"In this restaurant?"

Gus nodded. "Right here in this restaurant."

"Gus, I've been coming here since I sat in a high chair. For the last year I've lived here and worked here. And I have never, ever heard this story."

"What story?" My boyfriend, Chris, walked through the kitchen door, ready to continue the work of setting up our restaurant.

"The story of Ned Calhoun," I answered.

"The rumrunner?"

"You know about him?"

Chris shrugged. "Of course. You don't?"

"Not until five minutes ago."

Gus took his red and black plaid shirt-jacket off the hook by the door. "I can see my work here is done. I'm going to skedaddle."

And then he did.

The next morning I was hard at work in the clambake office on the second story of my mother's house. The office had been my dad's when he ran the Snowden Family Clambake Company, and the big, old mahogany desk, the olive green metal file cabinets, and the prints of sailing ships made me feel comfortable and protected, like Dad was watching over me. Le Roi, the big Maine coon cat who ruled our island in the summertime, sat on my desk, purring. He was staying at Mom's for the off-season and gave no sign that the change from out-door cat with an entire island to rule over to indoor cat perturbed him in the slightest.

The doorbell rang. I looked out the window

into the street. Harley's trolley was stopped at the curb in front of the house. Mom was at work, thank goodness. I went downstairs and opened the door.

"Julia."

"Harley."

"May I come in? I'll only take a moment of your time."

I stepped aside so he could enter the front hall.

Harley cleared his throat. "I was hoping you might help me persuade your mother to let me add her house to the Halloween Haunted House Tour." He looked me in the eyes, but warily. He knew it was a big ask.

"Harley, I'm sorry, but Mom's a firm no. It's getting into her busy season at the store. She's a private person. She doesn't want trolley-loads of people trooping through her house." I should have stopped there. I should have known better. When you've said what you have to say, shut up. But instead, I kept going. "Besides, Harley, my parents bought this house thirty years ago. None of us had ever heard about Captain Merriman's wife falling down the stairs until you showed up yesterday. And I guarantee we've never seen her."

"Oh, really." Harley's eyes traveled to a spot on the front hall floor, where I noticed for the first time during our conversation, that the upstairs hall rug was sitting, doubled over on itself near the archway between the hall and the living room, exactly where Harley had indicated Sarah Merriman had landed and broken her neck. I'd come in the kitchen door and gone up the back stairs. I couldn't swear the rug was in the upstairs hall when I'd gone by it, or even walked over it, earlier that morning. I'd been on autopilot. That trek was my morning commute.

"Did you know Gus's place is haunted?" It was an absolutely transparent ploy of changing the subject.

Harley stepped back, brow furrowed in concentration. "Ned Calhoun!" he said at last. "Ned Calhoun and Sweet Sue. How could I have forgotten about them? You're right. I'll talk to Gus right away."

What had I done? "What about the Fogged Inn?" I tried to divert him. "That's where the ghost of Sweet Sue hangs out."

"You're right! I'll add them, too. As soon as I talk to Gus."

I swallowed. "I'll talk to Gus. The venue belongs to me and Chris at night."

"I can see it now." Harley bounced on the balls of his feet with enthusiasm, a little-boy movement that looked ridiculous for such a big man. "We'll act out the scene. You can be Sweet Sue and Chris and Gus can be Capone's men. We'll have to recruit at least one other guy. Then you and Chris can serve hot cider and some kind of cookies or something. It will be a nice break on the tour. We'll put you right in the middle. The best slot."

This was getting way out of control. "How many nights are you doing this tour? I don't think we can shut down the restaurant."

"The tour lasts seven nights, starting Saturday, a week before Halloween. You open for dinner at six o'clock, right? It gets dark at five-thirty. If you push back opening time by an hour or so, the tour will be in and out of there before you know it."

"I don't know. It sounds like a big commitment. I have to talk to Chris. And Gus, too."

"Of course, of course. You can confirm with me as soon as you've talked to them. If it doesn't work out, I can always ask your mother again."

That felt vaguely like a threat.

Harley bounced on the balls of his feet again. "I've had the most marvelous thought. I know exactly the person who can play Ned Calhoun. Spencer Jones. He's a professional actor who works at the Barnhouse Theater every summer. I'll call him right away. I'll make all the arrangements. Costumes, props, the works. You figure out what refreshments you want to serve. This is going to be terrific."

He turned to leave, as enthusiastic as a puppy who'd just spotted his owner.

"Was Sweet Sue even present at the murder?" I shouted at his back as he retreated down the steps.

"Poetic license," he called back. "We can't put on this show without Sweet Sue."

Chapter Two

And so it was that six weeks later, a group of us gathered at Gus's for a dress rehearsal. It was in the quiet of the afternoon, my favorite time at the restaurant. Gus was done serving for the day and the place was, as always, spotless.

As I'd anticipated, Gus and Chris had balked when I told them about Harley's plan.

"I don't want a lot of tourists trooping through the place," Gus had insisted, which I admit, was an unusual position for a restaurateur. Gus catered exclusively to locals. If he didn't know you, or if you didn't come in with someone he knew, you weren't getting served.

Chris and I didn't observe Gus's rule about strangers. Chris's objection to two haunted house tour was the late start to dinner service for the week. Our restaurant was popular with lobstering families and retirees, both groups notoriously early supper eaters. I pointed out the delay in opening was only for one week. We were closed Tuesdays and Wednesdays. It was a bye-week for the New England Patriots, which meant business would be down in our bar on Sunday.

"So it's really only Thursday, Friday, Saturday," I concluded, looking as appealing as I could.

"What happened to Monday?" Chris asked, though in a teasing tone that told me he was softening.

"Okay, I'll give you Monday." I went in for the kill. "The main reason I want to do this is to get Harley off Mom's back. She really, really doesn't want to be involved."

"Well . . ." He wavered and I knew I had him. Chris and Mom been skeptical of each other in the beginning. My mother thought Chris, with his rangy body, green eyes and dimple in his chin, was "too handsome for his own good." And despite the fact that she'd lived in town almost as long as he'd been alive, Chris had viewed Mom, the descendent of a wealthy summer family that owned a private island, through the usual locals-versus-summer-people lens. Lately, however, they'd settled into a tight alliance, driven by a grudging respect on each side and their mutual love for me.

"You'll be here," I'd assured both Gus and Chris, "every evening to make sure nothing goes wrong." That had gone a long way with each of them, especially Gus, until they heard that not only would they be present, they would be wearing costumes and participating in the "reenactment."

More conversations had followed, challenging my persuasive skills, but in the end, they'd agreed.

Harley and his wife, Myra, were the first to arrive. My sister, Livvie, her husband, Sonny, and their almost eight-month-old, Jack, came in next. Jack was strapped into his stroller and Livvie made no move to take him out. I'd tried to get Livvie to portray Sweet Sue, but she'd used the "Jack card." I didn't see how that prevented her from playing the role, especially since she was able to be present at the dress rehearsal, but she held the line and I gave in.

Sonny had agreed to be one of Al Capone's men. He walked in with his costume on a hanger he held over his shoulder. No way was he walking through town dressed like a 1920s-era gangster.

I was already in my costume. Like the ones the guys were using, it had come from a Barnhouse Theater production of *Guys and Dolls*. The Barnhouse was our regional summer playhouse. The bulk of the costumes used in its productions were rented, but the costumers supplemented them with clothes solicited from local and summer people. I had a gorgeous, shimmering, flapper dress accessorized with a long onyx necklace, a felt cloche, and a beaded handbag. I loved it. I'd been back in Busman's Harbor for almost two years and had put on a dress only for funerals, so I enjoyed the chance to get spiffed up.

While Chris, Gus, and Sonny went up to my apartment to change into their costumes, Harley, Myra, and I walked through the layout of the open front room of the restaurant. Myra would ride the trolley with Harley, looking after guests and helping him herd them around and stay on schedule.

"We'll put the cookies, pumpkin bread, and cider on a long table over there," I said, "to keep people away from the counter and the kitchen." On one side of the big room, open to the area where Gus and Chris cooked, there was an old-fashioned counter with a linoleum top and wide chrome sides and round stools with red leather seats. "You'll come in the front door, down the stairs with the guests." Gus's restaurant was below street level, built on stilts on a rock over the back harbor, the working part of Busman's Harbor.

"Ned Calhoun will come up here." I pointed to the trapdoor, which had been hidden behind the backbar and nailed shut. Chris and Gus had "liberated it" that morning. A year earlier when Chris and I had started the dinner restaurant, Gus had agreed that if we were going to be a place for locals to gather in the evening over the long winter, we had to have a bar. However, he'd insisted it had to be built in a way that allowed it to be removed over the summer when Chris and I were occupied with other things. We'd agreed, and that flexibility had come in handy for this endeavor.

Chris and Gus had untethered the bar and backbar and rolled them on their castors to the back of the space. Then the three of us had clustered the bistro tables in the corner so the tour members would have a ringside seat when Ned Calhoun rose up through the trapdoor.

Harley rubbed his hands together. "Ah. Café seating. This is perfect."

"Where's the actor who's playing Ned Calhoun?" I asked.

"Spencer's already in position under the trapdoor, awaiting his big entrance," Harley answered.

It was chilly out and I imagined the poor guy crouched on the boulder under Gus's, ten feet or so above the cold Maine water.

At that moment, Livvie shrieked. I stared at her, my heart beating wildly. Then she doubled over with laughter. I turned and saw Chris, Gus, and

Sonny in their costumes, exiting the stairs from my apartment. Their three-piece suits and fedoras made them look like idiots. Sonny's dress shirt strained across his barrel chest and Gus's hat was so big it wobbled around his head, nearly covering his eyes. Chris's pants ended far above his ankles, leaving six inches of bare calf visible over the top of his spats. None of them looked happy.

Most hilarious of all, each of them carried a pint-sized Tommy gun that was obviously plastic and obviously a toy. The big men in their too-small clothes with their tiny guns was too funny. I couldn't help myself. I laughed, too, until my sides hurt. Myra giggled and soon the guys joined in, the tension broken by the absurdity of the situation.

Harley wasn't amused. "Let's get to this," he barked. "Myra and I have more venues to visit." He looked at the men. "Okay. You're there. You're there. You're there." He pointed to the area stage right of the trapdoor, away from the audience. Chris, Gus, and Sonny got in position. "And Sweet Sue, you're there." He pointed to one of the café tables in the front row.

"I'll tell the story. When I get to the part about Ned Calhoun coming up through the trapdoor, Myra will send a text to Spencer. He'll enter." Harley looked at me. "Sweet Sue will scream, terrified of what she knows is going to happen." He turned to the guys. "And you three will gun him down. Spencer does his death scene. Got it?"

It was pretty simple. We all nodded.

"Okay. From the top." Harley started the tale. When he got to the part about the ambush, Myra typed something into her phone. A few seconds later, the trapdoor flew open and "Ned Calhoun" emerged. I screamed my loudest, most full-throated scream. Chris, Gus, and Sonny lunged forward. They pulled the triggers on their plastic guns, which made the most unconvincing burp-urp-urp sounds. That set Livvie off again. She broke up, and then I did, and then we all did. Except Harley, who scowled.

And Spencer, who like the professional he was, went on with the show. "They got me," he shouted, clutching his heart. He lurched, and twisted, and fell quite thunderously to the floor. He was older and heavier through the middle than I'd imagined the handsome rumrunner Ned Calhoun to have been, but at least his costume fit. I wondered if he'd brought his own.

"I am but a poor fisherman, trying to make my way in a violent world," Spencer intoned, dragging himself across the floor in my direction. "All I only ever wanted was to help my town." By this time he was at my ankles. "And to love you, Sweet Sue. To love you forever and to give you everything you deserve. Never. Forget. Me," he gasped out with his dying breath. "I will always love you." And then clunk, his head fell to the hardwood floor.

The laughter had died by this time. I had to hand it to Spencer. It was one heck of a death scene. We were silent for a moment.

Harley cleared his throat. "I have some notes." Spencer opened his eyes.

"Here's my note," Chris replied. "I'm wearing my own pants next time."

"And my own hat," Gus added.

"I think I have a dress shirt somewhere." Sonny looked over at Livvie, who nodded.

"What are we going to do about these ridiculous guns?" Chris asked.

"I don't think we want more realistic-looking machine guns, do we?" Livvie said. "There will be children on this tour. Right, Harley?"

"Children, adults, seniors," Myra answered. "In the summer, at least, we get a nice age range. Fun for the whole family."

"But these guns"—Chris gestured with his plastic prop—"made us laugh. They're going to make anyone laugh."

"Burp-urp-urp-urp," Jack babbled from his stroller, right on cue.

"How about this?" It was the first time Spencer had spoken out of character. His natural voice was a good deal higher than the one he used for Ned Calhoun. "When I emerge and Sweet Sue screams, we douse the lights. The room goes black. That will give folks an extra thrill. Then we play a recording of real machine guns, or at least a more convincing sound effect. The lights come up. I do my death scene. Et voilà! We're done."

Harley smiled and nodded along as Spencer talked. "I knew you'd have a solution, Spencer," he said. "You're a real professional."

"Thank you." Spencer stood up and gave a little bow. "By the time the curtain goes up tomorrow, we'll be more than ready."

"Thank goodness," Harley said. He looked at Myra. "We need to get going. Add finding the right gun noise recording to the task list. Thanks, everybody. See you at showtime."

"Remember the old theatrical expression, 'Bad dress rehearsal, great opening night,'" Spencer said. "Tomorrow's going to be fabulous."

Chapter Three

But the next day didn't go smoothly. At five-fifteen I was at Gus's, accepting the two loaves of pumpkin bread and platter of lemon ginger cookies that Livvie, who made all the desserts for our little restaurant, had baked for the enjoyment of the trolley tour's participants.

"Are you coming back for the show?" I asked.

Livvie laughed. "No, thanks. I've seen it. Break a leg."

My cell phone rang. It was Harley.

"Julia, the worst has happened. The worst."

"What's wrong?" I mentally cataloged situations Harley might consider "the worst." Perhaps he hadn't sold any tickets for tonight's tour.

"It's Myra. She's come down with the flu."

"That is bad. Give her my best wishes for a speedy recovery." Did Myra have any health issues that would exacerbate the flu? Harley seemed over-the-top upset.

"I will, I will, but that's not why I called. I need you to ride on the trolley with me tonight."

"Me? Why?"

"I can drive, and I can narrate the tour, but I can't do all that and keep an eye on the customers."

"Are they liable to be unruly?" The idea had never occurred to me.

"No, not at all, unless the Halloween crowd is very different than the one we get in the summer. I need someone to hostess, make sure everyone's happy, that they don't get up and walk around. That sort of thing. So naturally I thought of you."

"I'm not sure I follow."

"You're the hostess at your restaurant and at the clambake. You know what to do. Besides, I happen to know you're available."

"What about my costume?" I wasn't giving up on that beautiful flapper dress.

"Put a coat on over it. But get over here. I need you at the trolley stop in fifteen minutes."

I ran up to my apartment, threw on the dress, the necklace, and some makeup. Providently, one of the few pieces of clothing I'd kept from my New York City life was a black trench coat, which I put on over the dress. On my way out the door I left the cloche in Gus's powder room so I could put it on quickly before my big scene. Chris had come into the restaurant earlier to do as much prep as he could for our delayed dinner start, but then he'd gone back out. I texted him.

HAVE GONE TO RIDE TROLLEY WITH HARLEY. WILL BE BACK WITH HIM FOR PERFORMANCE. SEE YOU THEN. BREAK A LEG. LOVE, ME.

There was already a small crowd milling around when I rushed up to the trolley parked in front of

Kimbel's. Harley stood on the trolley step, collecting money, giving change from an old-fashioned change belt, and joking with the people gathered around him.

"Here's my lovely assistant now," he called out when he spotted me crossing the street. "It must be time to get started. All aboard, all aboard."

We piled onto the trolley. It was only half full, though Harley seemed unconcerned. Perhaps attendance would build through the week as it led up to Halloween. The passengers settled into their seats clumped in groups. Harley pointed me to a seat at the very back next to a big white cooler and I sat down.

He stood at the front and addressed us. "Ladies and gentlemen, welcome aboard the Haunted House Tour. We'll head out toward our first stop in a moment. A few rules. Do not move about the trolley when it is underway. Keep your hands, heads, and any other appendages inside the trolley at all times." As he said this, Harley looked meaningfully at two teenaged couples sitting in the back across from me. Slumped in their seats, they muttered and joked, no doubt at Harley's expense. They did seem the most likely to stick their heads out the window, but it was twilight on a fall day. The windows of the trolley were pulled up and I doubted anyone would open them.

"We have bottles of water in the back. If you want one, put your hand up and my co-host, Julia, will bring it to you. As advertised, we'll also be stopping midtour for something warm to drink and light refreshments." Harley paused and looked around the trolley. "Our first stop is not a haunted house at all, but the Busman's Harbor cemetery where we're going to hear about the most famous of the many ghosts associated with our peninsula." With that, Harley sat down and started the trolley. Everyone settled into their seats and we headed out of town toward the highway.

The cemetery was about halfway up the peninsula that ended at the harbor. I could see why Harley had placed it first on the tour. It would be important to get there before full darkness if the tour members were to see anything. Harley pointed out local landmarks as we rode along. I tuned him out and studied the tour members. In addition to the four teenagers in the back with me, there was a group I took to be a mother with her two sons, one a teenager, the other an adolescent, who sat in two middle rows, the mother and the younger boy together, the older boy in front of them.

A slender woman sat by herself in front of the mother and sons, leaving an empty row between them. Like me, she was dressed in a belted trench coat, only hers was the more traditional beige. A haunted house tour seemed like a strange choice of activity to do alone, but I silently cheered her on. *Do what you want. Go where you want,* I thought.

There were two women traveling together, whom I took to be mother and daughter, given the solicitous way the mousey, younger woman helped the older woman onto the trolley. The older woman barked at her, "Not there, Elizabeth. No, no, over there," until they finally settled on their seats in the row behind Harley.

Opposite them, also in the front row, perfectly

positioned so he could lean across the aisle and talk to Harley, was another singleton. This one I recognized: Clyde Merkin.

Every small town had a know-it-all, and Busman's Harbor had quite a few, but nobody knew more than Clyde. At least in Clyde's opinion.

Even now, as we pulled up to the cemetery, Clyde leaned forward to give Harley advice about how to negotiate the turn and ease the trolley through the cemetery gates, never stopping to consider that Harley had driven his trolley thousands of miles and Clyde had driven it none.

Despite Clyde's help, Harley successfully made the turn into the private road that led up the hill to the cemetery. The pavement was in terrible repair and the wooden seat of the trolley whacked me with every bump.

Harley pulled to the side of the road across from a particularly well-known grave and motioned for us to get out. He led us across the lane and we stood around the large marble marker emblazoned with the words UNKNOWN MERMAID.

The unknown mermaid was one of the few legends or ghost stories in our town that was demonstrably true. Not the ghost part, of course, but that such a person had existed. The proof was the headstone our little group clustered around.

Harley stood at the front and told the story—or tried to.

"One winter day in 1901, the lighthouse keeper at Herrickson Point Light walked into Westclaw Village to get supplies and pick up his mail."

"February 18, 1901 to be precise," Clyde said. He was not a tall man, and at first it was hard to see where his voice had come from. But then the teenagers shuffled out of the way, and there Clyde was, his bald head fringed with sandy blond hair that had half gone gray. He had on an L.L. Bean jacket that was unzipped to show his plaid shirt and khaki pants, which were belted above the navel.

"Yes, thank you, Clyde." Harley wrested back control. "On his way the lighthouse keeper passed a beautiful woman in the finest clothes walking in the opposite direction. There was nothing out there but the lighthouse and the point, so he asked if she was lost. She said no and went on her way."

"The lighthouse keeper's name was Samuel Herrickson," Clyde added.

"Thank you, Clyde." Harley didn't look happy. I could tell Clyde was messing with his rhythm.

At that point, Sarah, one of Dan and Darla Small's four teenaged daughters, rose out from behind the headstone. The Smalls were six of the most gorgeous people anyone had ever seen—tall and blond, tanned, long-limbed and healthy-looking with perfectly symmetrical features, straight, bright-white teeth, and big, dark-lashed gray eyes. The sight of one was arresting. When the six, parents and daughters, were together, it was impossible not to stare. The parents owned and ran the ice cream shop on the town pier, just across from the Snowden Family Clambake ticket kiosk, so I saw a lot of them. And still I stared.

All the Small daughters had taken a ton of ballet. Sarah, the second oldest, emerged ethereally from behind the Unknown Mermaid's headstone, one long leg extension at a time. Her costume, a Gibson girl bodice that slowly dissolved into shredded sleeves and shirt, only added to her beauty. Despite my perky flapper dress, I had momentary costume envy.

Sarah danced prettily in front of the headstone while Harley continued the story. "When the lighthouse keeper returned to the point, he didn't see the woman. The next day, he and his wife found her body, brought in by the tide."

"Actually, it was his sister, not his wife," Clyde said. "Samuel didn't marry until 1907."

Harley shot him a murderous glance. Sarah lay down on the grass and two other Small daughters danced out from behind the big headstone, dressed as the lighthouse keeper and his wife (or sister). They pantomimed exclamations when they found her. The lighthouse keeper checked Sarah's pulse while his wife (or sister) listened to her heart. Then they held each other and cried.

"She had stones in the pockets of her overcoat, but had left no note," Harley told us. "The labels of her expensive, fashionable clothes had been cut out. The people of the village tried to puzzle out the identity of the dead woman." So far, despite Clyde's interruptions, Harley was holding the crowd's attention pretty well. Given that a quarter of them were teenaged boys, and the Smalls were, it cannot be said enough, gorgeous, he didn't have to work too hard.

"The townspeople looked far and wide," Harley said. Plie-ing in fourth position, the lighthouse keeper and his wife (or sister) put hands to their brows and looked around. "How did she get to town? No one admitted to having driven her down the peninsula from the train station, and none of the conductors claimed to have seen her. Since the dead woman clearly had expensive clothes, the townspeople thought she must be a member of a summer family or at least someone who had been a guest of one. How else would she know about the little village or the direction of the point?" Harley paused so we could all think about that.

"But when the season came and the summer families returned, no one claimed to have known her. She'd been buried in the lighthouse keeper's family plot and the citizens of Busman's Harbor chipped in to erect the stone you see here. People see the Unknown Mermaid regularly, both here in the cemetery and at the old keeper's cottage at Herrickson Point. Sometimes from the point, they see her swimming in the waves, free from whatever the cares were that drove her to her fate."

The three Small sisters did a pretty little step-step-turn and took a bow. The tour members clapped appreciatively.

Beat that, I thought as I got back on the trolley.

The two teenaged couples asked for bottles of water, which I fetched for them. But, instead of re-turning to the bench at the back Harley had as-signed to me, I sat down next to the single woman. She had watched the performance at the first stop with a look of studied determination, not cracking a smile. Hers seemed like a strange attitude for a person who would want to go on a haunted house tour alone.

"Hi. I'm Julia Snowden," I said.

She looked over at me but didn't smile. "Carla." No last name. Even in the low light of the trolley, I could see she had luxurious, long brown hair, held back by a pair of large barrettes, and large brown eyes. She appeared to be in her late thirties or early forties.

"What attracted you to the tour?" I tried to draw her out.

"You know, ghosts, dead people, people from the past." She waved a loose hand, implying all that was out there. She had a slight accent, soft and sibilant. I couldn't be sure, but I thought it might be Spanish.

"Ah." I didn't know where to go from there. "Do you believe in ghosts?" seemed too intimate a question for someone who to all appearances did not wish to be engaged. We rode in silence back down the peninsula to the second site on the tour.

Harley parked the trolley on the street and shepherded us into the old stable behind the Snugg sisters' B and B. The stable was normally choc-o-block full of stored outdoor furniture and various castoffs from two generations of Snuggs. Someone had cleared enough space for the tour members to crowd in.

Harley started his story about a stable boy, an orphan taken in by the sea captain, who had built the house. The stable boy had died after being kicked in the head by a horse. He roamed the barn still, looking for his parents. The tale didn't hold together particularly well. Why was he looking in the stable for his parents? All the people who had claimed to have seen the ghost were conveniently out-of-towners who had stayed at the inn.

More saliently, Fiona and Viola Snugg, known to one and all as Fee and Vee, had lived across the street from my parents' house for my entire life. I'd had the run of their place and treated it as a second home. I had never, ever, heard a story about a stable boy ghost or any other ghost.

In a dark corner, the teenagers snickered and poked each other as Harley told the tale. The two boys taking the tour with their mother were politely attentive, but nowhere near as engaged as they'd been out at the cemetery. The older boy's eyes kept wandering back to the B and B.

"I've never heard this story," Clyde said. His tone implied that if he hadn't heard it, it wasn't true. For once, I agreed with him.

As if sensing he was losing his audience, Harley hustled us back onto the trolley. I introduced myself to the mother and her two sons and sat down next to the older boy. After all, if I was supposed to be the host, I should host.

"I'm Julia," I said, leaving aside the last names, having learned my lesson with the recalcitrant Carla.

"Joyce Bayer," the mom said, providing her surname and proving you should never try to predict what people will do. She put her hand over the back of my seat so I could shake it. "This is Will." She indicated the younger boy sitting next to her. "And this is Kieran." She pointed to the older boy sitting next to me, who smiled.

There was no time for more conversation because we were at our next stop, a big Victorian on Main Street much like my mother's. We all got off. The daughter in the mother-daughter duo helped her mother up the front steps. We crowded into the front hall, tracking grass from the cemetery and dirt from the stable on our shoes.

Harley's story, I had to admit, was a good one, about the sea captain builder of the house who was killed when he was washed overboard in a storm. His ghost returned to his beloved home to find his widow had taken up with a new man. The ghost so terrified his successor that the man ran out of the house screaming, vowing never to return.

I thought the story was pretty good, but the giggling teenagers were clearly unimpressed. One of the boys asked if he could use the bathroom in the house, and I was grateful my mother hadn't caved to Harley's pressure to use her home. I assured the kid our next stop was a restaurant, with restrooms.

Harley herded us back onto the trolley. I sat in front of the mother-daughter combo; the only two I hadn't introduced myself to, aside from Clyde and the group of four teenagers. "I'm Marge," the older woman said. "This is my daughter, Elizabeth."

"Hello, Elizabeth." I got a shy nod of the head. Evidently the daughter couldn't speak for herself.

Settling into my seat as we drove toward Gus's, I was relieved the next stop would supply a little drama, and snacks. It was six-twenty. We were only five minutes behind schedule. *Showtime.*

Chapter Four

We all trooped down the stairs and entered the front room of the restaurant. The place smelled great from the warm cider, which was out, along with the pumpkin bread and lemon ginger cookies, on a long table that blocked off the counter and kitchen area. In my absence, the guys had really outdone themselves. They had piled boxes artfully around the room, with straw and bottles of Canadian Club and other whiskeys tumbling out of them. The whole effect was warehouse-cum-speakeasy. It looked great. Most of the lights were off except for the ones over the café tables and the two exit signs, which glowed dimly. I noticed two speakers among the boxes, the sound system for the machine gun noise, no doubt.

"Ah, the story of Ned Calhoun," Clyde said.

Harley stared daggers at him for naming the ghost before he could. I hoped Harley didn't think it was part of my job as host and customer-wrangler to keep Clyde quiet, because I didn't think I could.

I hurried into the restroom to shed my trench

coat and put on my cloche. When I came out, the tour members were all seated at the café tables with their snacks. I sat at the table with the RE-SERVED sign, now strategically placed under the light switch.

Harley stood up and started the tale. He made Ned Calhoun sound even more like a Robin Hood for the town than he had in his original telling. Clyde tried to interrupt a couple of times, but Harley talked right over him and he shut up.

When Harley got to the part about Sweet Sue, he gestured to me. I smiled coyly, crossed my legs, and batted my eyelashes. The group smiled back appreciatively.

When Harley mentioned Capone's men, Chris, Gus, and Sonny charged out the door of our apartment into the restaurant. They looked a hundred times better than they had in the dress rehearsal. Chris wore his own black dress pants. Sonny had supplied his own shirt, which fit, and Gus wore what I assumed to be his own fedora. The Tommy guns still looked small and plastic, but the hoodlums wisely kept them at their sides. They came off as intimidating as they were meant to be.

Harley worked up to the dramatic moment. "Not knowing Capone's thugs were in place, Ned innocently returned to his waterfront warehouse to meet Sweet Sue." As subtly as possible, Harley pressed the screen on his cell phone, sending the text to Ned Calhoun.

Seconds later, the trapdoor flew open. I opened my mouth and gave my most full-throated scream. Spencer's head emerged as he climbed the stairs under the trapdoor and I doused the lights. There was a terrific boom, which left my ears ringing. For a split second, I thought, "Wow, that gun sound effect is much more realistic," but no sounds of machine gunfire followed. Something was terribly wrong. I quickly flicked on the lights.

There was a horrified gasp. It might have been me who made it. It might have been somebody else; it might have been all of us collectively. The actor, Spencer Jones, lay as still as a mannequin on top of the open trapdoor, his legs bent at the knees, dangled over the stairs. He had been shot squarely in the forehead.

Chris and Sonny ran toward Spencer. "Nobody move!" I shouted. I knew from unfortunate experience the police would want to talk to all the witnesses.

Nobody did move for a second, and then all of them, including Harley, got up and ran for the stairs, screaming out into the night and leaving Chris, Sonny, Gus, and I staring at one another in stunned silence.

Chapter Five

Chris, his fingers pressed to Spencer's carotid artery, looked at me and shook his head. I took my cell phone out of the beaded handbag and pressed 911. In Maine, the state police Major Crimes Units investigate all suspicious deaths that occur outside Portland and Bangor, the only cities big enough to have their own detective squads. In response to my emergency call, the local Busman's Harbor police would get here first, secure the scene, and connect with the state police and the medical examiner.

"Stay on the line," the 911 dispatcher commanded. "Is there an active shooter at your location?"

I looked from Gus to Chris to Sonny. "I—I don't think so."

"You're not sure?" she clarified.

"Unless he's hiding. No one is shooting now."

"Are there weapons at your location?"

Two plastic toy guns were on the floor where Chris and Sonny had dropped them. "Gus, put that down." I pointed to his machine gun. He dropped it. "There are toy weapons on the floor here," I told the dispatcher. "Please don't shoot us."

Almost immediately, there was a blaring of sirens and sound of vehicles braking in the street. Above us, the front door banged open.

"Identify yourselves!" I recognized the voice of my childhood friend, Jamie Dawes, calling from up the restaurant stairs. Jamie had recently become the second-newest member of the Busman's Harbor PD due to the presence of a new hire.

"Julia Snowden!" I called out.

"Christopher Durand!"

"Bard Ramsey, Junior!" The last time I'd heard Sonny use his given name was at his wedding to my sister.

"Gus Farnham!"

There were a few moments of silence.

"Four people total? How many weapons?"

"Four people, plus one dead body. Three toy plastic machine guns. No working weapons," Chris called back.

"Put the toy guns on the floor, where we can see them when we approach," Jamie directed.

"Already done," Chris answered.

"We're coming down." Jamie's long legs appeared on the stairs followed by the shorter, squatter ones of his partner, Pete Howland. When they came into view, their guns were drawn. The four us of stood with our hands up while they searched both restrooms, the coat closet, the dining room, the pantry, and the walk-in refrigerator.

Howland went up the stairs to my apartment while Jamie went to the kitchen door of the restaurant, unlocked it, and stuck his head out. He said something, undoubtedly to other officers who were searching Gus's little parking lot, and then shut the door.

"Clear," Howland announced when he came down the steps a minute or two later. A minute or two that felt like an eternity. The police holstered their guns. Jamie moved toward the body. Chris and Sonny stepped back, allowing him access. He bent his blond head and did the same things they'd done, checking for a pulse and a heartbeat, though it was obvious Spencer Jones was dead.

"Tell the EMTs they can leave," Jamie told Howland. "He isn't one for them." He turned toward us. "Why don't you all sit down?" Jamie pointed toward the second room of the restaurant, the dining room. "This is going to take a while." He pulled out a cell phone and walked away from us, presumably to report in to the Major Crimes Unit. Gus led us to a table in the dining room, strategically placed out of the sightline to the body.

Chris reached for my hand under the table and gave it a reassuring squeeze. "How many reservations did we have for tonight?"

"Plenty, it's Saturday."

"I guess the cop at the door will turn them away," he said.

"Those who don't look up Main Street and see all the cop vehicles and draw their own conclusions," Sonny put in.

When Jamie finished his call, he came over to where we sat.

"Do you know the victim's name?" he asked.

"Spencer Jones," I answered.

"Why is he half-in half-out of the trapdoor? And why are you all dressed like that? And what's all this?" He pointed into the front room toward the cups of now-cool cider and the remnants of pumpkin bread and cookies left on paper plates on the café tables.

"It's a long story," I said. "You might want to sit down yourself."

He pulled up a chair, turned it around, and sat, resting his hands on its back. "Okay."

Chris, Gus, and Sonny stared at me. Clearly, since I'd gotten them into this mess, it was up to me to explain. As succinctly as possible, I told Jamie about the haunted house tour, Ned Calhoun, and Sweet Sue. When I got to the part where the tour group arrived in the restaurant, he said, "Let's save the next part for individual interviews when Major Crimes gets here."

"Sergeant Flynn is half an hour out," Howland called from the other room. "Same with the medical examiner." Our local, part-time, medical examiner was a family practice doctor. This scene was clearly above her pay grade.

Jamie nodded his acknowledgment and turned back to me. "Who was on this ghost tour? The state police will need statements from everybody. "

"Uhm, Carla."

"Last name?"

"I don't know. Harley may know. He may have taken credit cards or reservations or something. A mother and two sons. Joyce Bayer, Kieran, and Will."

"The sons are minors?" Jamie asked.

"Kieran looks like he's in high school, Will in middle school," I answered.

"Local?"

"I don't think so. They seemed like tourists. I've never seen them before."

"Who else?

"A mother and daughter. Marge and Elizabeth."

"Last names? Never mind. Is the daughter a minor?"

"I'd put her in her early to mid-thirties."

"So no. Local?"

"Again, I've never seen them."

"They looked a little familiar to me," Gus put in. "I think they might live somewhere in a neighboring town, close enough that I've seen them before."

"But you don't know their last name?" Jamie asked him.

"Didn't know their first names until thirty seconds ago," Gus answered.

Jamie turned to me. "Who else?"

"Two high school-aged couples. I don't know first or last names, but I'm pretty sure they're local."

"Dwayne Cox, Jimmy Bartlett, Kelly Brown, Molly Carroll. They all go to Busman's Harbor High," Sonny said to Jamie. "Dwayne and Jimmy play on the football team." It didn't surprise me Sonny would know this. Friday night high school football was every bit as big a deal in small-town Maine as in any other rural area. Sonny and Chris had played in high school and they both kept up with the team.

Jamie nodded. "I know who they are." He made a note. "Is that it?"

"Clyde Merkin was on the tour," I answered. "He—"

"We're familiar with Mr. Merkin." Jamie's tone was bland and professional, but I doubted he'd come across Clyde Merkin while he was involved in some criminal enterprise. More likely Clyde had stopped into the Busman's Harbor police station to tell them how to run an investigation, or maybe even the department itself.

"What about the victim?" Jamie asked. "Any of you know where he's from?"

"Harley hired him," I answered. "He was a professional actor who works at the Barnhouse Theater during the season. Other than that, you'd have to ask Harley."

At that moment there was the sound of a door opening above. "Officer Dawes!" a male voice shouted. "You down there? There's a guy up here says you want to talk to him."

"Does he have a name?" Jamie called back.

"It's Harley Prendergast."

"Mr. Prendergast." Jamie stood to greet Harley. "Officer."

The formality was driven by the circumstances. I was sure they'd called each other as "Harley" and "Jamie," every time they'd previously met in their lives.

Jamie pulled over another chair. "Join us."

Harley did, creeping past the body and looking green around the gills, though he didn't come to within twenty feet of it.

"Why did you leave the scene, Mr. Prendergast?" Jamie asked.

"I, er, thought you might need information about the people who were on the tour, so I returned in my trolley to my home to retrieve it." Harley waved a manila folder with some pieces of white printer paper poking out of it.

In my opinion, Harley had fled out of terror,

like every other tour participant, but I kept that to myself.

Jamie, too, seemed doubtful. "You drove your trolley all the way out to Eastclaw Point?" The Prendergasts lived all the way down one of the two points that sheltered our harbor. From the air, they looked like lobster claws, thus Eastclaw and Westclaw Point. It was a ten-mile journey to the Prendergast house, and the trolley didn't go above thirty miles an hour. Harley normally left the trolley parked at the Lobsterman's Wharf Hotel and drove his Hyundai home from there.

"I was so flummoxed, I forgot to stop and pick up my car," Harley explained.

"And what about on the way back? Did you stop and pick up your car then?"

A flush crept up Harley's neck. "I didn't. The trolley is parked with the emergency vehicles in front of the restaurant."

Jamie frowned. "And what about the tour members? Did you take them in the trolley when you left here?"

Harley shook his head. "By the time I got to the street door, they had all run away. I could see some of them in the lights on Main Street."

"I'll leave it to the Major Crimes Unit detectives to question you about what you saw and heard in this room tonight," Jamie said. "I'm more interested in what you can tell me about the other participants, and most importantly, about the victim."

Harley opened the manila folder and straightened the first page of printer paper. "There were eleven people on the tour, in addition to Julia and myself." He cleared his throat. "Ms. Carla Santiler."

"Local or tourist?" Jamie asked.

"Tourist," Harley answered.

"Traveling alone or with companions?"

"Alone. She was one of two singletons on the tour."

"Do you have an address for where she might be staying locally, or a phone number?" Jamie pressed.

"A cell phone number. Her credit card info included a billing zip code in Saint Petersburg, Florida."

"Is that info on there?" Jamie indicated the piece of paper. When Harley nodded, Jamie said, "I'll need you to give that to me when we're done."

"Yes, yes, of course," Harley replied. "That's why I printed it." He cleared his throat. "Next, Joyce Bayer, and her sons, Kieran and Will."

"Same questions," Jamie said. "Tourist or local? Do you know where they're staying and how to reach them?"

"Tourist definitely," Harley answered. "Credit card zip code is Montclair, New Jersey. I didn't take a phone number, but I have an e-mail address. They walked to the trolley stop, so I'd guess they're staying right in town."

"Thanks. Next?" Jamie said.

"Marge Handey and her daughter Elizabeth. Marge paid, so I have her info, but not the daughter's. They live locally, in Brunswick. I have a cell number."

Brunswick, a lovely college town, was a forty-minute ride down the coast. So Gus probably had seen Marge and Elizabeth around.

"Dwayne Cox, Jimmy Bartlett, Kelly Brown, Molly Carroll," Harley continued.

Jamie nodded. "Yep. I know them."

"And besides Julia and me, one other local. Clyde Merkin."

"We're familiar with Mr. Merkin," Jamie repeated.

There was the sound of heavy footsteps coming down the stairs into the front room. The crime scene techs or the medical examiner, maybe both. There was a murmur of voices from the front room and the flash from a camera.

Jamie, who'd listened momentarily, returned his attention to Harley. "What can you tell me about the victim?"

"His name is Spencer Jones. I've known him for years. He's been one of the equity actors the Barnhouse Theater hires for the season. He's taken several of my tours, including the haunted house tour. Naturally, I thought of him when the Halloween tour came up."

The Barnhouse Theater was typical of the kind of regional, seasonal little theaters found in resort areas. The theater was an actual former dairy barn that had been refitted. The company squeezed four productions into our short summer, rotating them every three weeks. Typically there was a serious play, a comedic play, a cabaret of some sort, and a big musical to cap off the season. Most of the parts were performed by talented locals and summer people who participated year after year, but three or four "New York actors" came in every summer to play the major roles and teach the kids at the children's camp, another way the theater made money. I rarely got to see any of the productions, given the Snowden Family Clambake was open every night all summer long.

"Do you know where Mr. Jones lived when he wasn't here in Maine?" Jamie asked Harley.

Harley shook his head. "I had a cell phone number for him. That's how I called him. I honestly don't know where he was when I reached him."

"Do you know where he was staying when he was in town this week?" Jamie asked.

"No."

"Do you know where he usually stayed when he came for the summer? Perhaps his landlord has more information about him."

"No, sorry. I'd meet him downtown. We'd chat. We exchanged cell phone numbers. That was it."

"Do you know how he got to Gus's tonight? Should we look for a car somewhere nearby?"

Harley looked at his lap and sighed. "I honestly don't know."

Jamie pushed his chair back. "All right. This was helpful. I'll see if I can find the other tour members locally and look for contact information for Mr. Spencer. I'm sure the state police will want to speak to each of you when they get here. If you could wait, we would appreciate it."

"Do you mind if we all go up to Chris's and my apartment?" I asked. "It's more comfortable up there."

Jamie glanced through the archway into the front room. "The medical examiner is here. Why don't you give him some more time to work without you all walking through? I'll come back soon and give you the all-clear."

Chapter Six

Eventually, Jamie told us we could head up to our apartment. "Please, don't talk to one another about the events of the evening. The state police will want your individual perspectives."

So we waited. And waited. Occasionally, I glanced out the little bathroom window, the only one that looked over the street. There were cop cars, an evidence van and, most incongruously, Harley's trolley. An official car from the Major Crimes Unit arrived and then left. The medical examiner's van left.

Gus fell asleep, his head leaning on the back of the couch, mouth wide open. He opened the restaurant at five every morning, feeding the lobstermen and other early risers. It must have felt like the middle of the night to him. Sonny sat next to Gus, watching a college football game on our old TV, the sound turned off. Harley perched, knee jiggling, at the little table where Chris and I ate our infrequent meals at home. Chris went over and started a game of two-handed gin rummy with him to keep him occupied. I put on a pot of coffee.

I searched on my laptop for information about Spencer Jones. He seemed to work a regular circuit. New York in the fall, mostly off-Broadway, but with the requisite three appearances on *Law & Order*, as a criminal, a dad, and a judge, aging through the roles. He worked in regional theaters in Florida in the winter and spring, and then came up to Maine in the summer. There had been a few other guest appearances on TV and some small roles in movies, a few commercials, but as far as I could tell, the movement from Maine to New York to Florida to Maine again had been his pattern for years. Why would anyone have wanted to kill him? It was confounding.

Finally there was a knock on the door downstairs. "Sergeant Tom Flynn! Can I come up?"

"Of course." I went to the top of the stairs, happy Flynn had been assigned to the case. He'd started off a stranger in our little town. He'd almost arrested Chris and he hadn't understood why his boss had put up with my "help" with a few past murders. But eventually we'd become friends; especially during the time he dated a friend of mine. That hadn't worked out, but the warm feeling between us remained. I exhaled with relief. We were in good hands.

Tom came up the stairs and stood in the middle of the apartment's only room. He had close-cropped brown hair and a body toned by strict diet and hours in the gym. He was in his mid-thirties, a little older than me.

Chris, Sonny, and Harley stood to greet him. Gus was still out cold.

"You're on your own?" I asked. "No Lieutenant Binder?"

"There's another apparent homicide in Waterville. You're stuck with me." The three Major Crimes Units in Maine, South, North, and Central, where Flynn worked, covered vast territory. He looked at each of us. Well, he looked at Chris, Harley, Sonny, and me, and then he looked at the top of Gus's head on the back of the couch. "I apologize. I know you've been waiting a long time. We had multiple things we had to take care of. If you don't mind, I'd like to interview each of you, formally and individually, at the station."

"Right now?" Harley glanced at his watch. It was after midnight.

"Yes, please," Flynn answered. "And Mr. Prendergast, if you could leave your trolley here, we'll get you a ride home. We'd like to search it."

"Of course, of course," Harley said.

Chris put a hand on Gus's shoulder and shook gently. Gus came to with a great deal of snorting. He and Harley accepted a ride to the station with Flynn because it was late and cold and dark. Sonny took his pickup. Chris and I said we'd walk the few blocks. Downstairs in the restaurant the scene was still busy. Before we went out the kitchen door I noticed the remains of the pumpkin bread and cookies on the long table where they'd been served and on plates, partially eaten, on the bistro tables. Someone, thank goodness, had turned off the heat under the cider. Gus would have a fit if that stuff was still there when he showed up in the morning, even if the restaurant couldn't open.

It felt good to be outside. Busman's Harbor's ugly, brick town-hall-firehouse-police-station was a few short blocks away, and as we walked over the harbor hill, the town was dark and silent. Chris set a brisk pace, but I dawdled a little, holding him back. I thought Flynn would have the sense to interview Gus first and have someone take him home, but I wanted to ensure it.

As we neared the station, the activity level picked back up again. Though the town hall and the firehouse were dark, lights glowed from inside on the police side of the building and the parking lot was full. When we walked into the station, a uniformed state police officer took our names. "I'll let the sergeant know you're here." As I'd hoped, it looked like Gus was already inside the multipurpose room the state police used when they were in town.

Gus came out and Jamie volunteered to drive him home, though I knew his shift must be long over. Harley went in next. I fiddled with my phone, looking for early reports of the murder on statewide media, which I didn't find.

Sonny went after Harley who came out of the multipurpose room looking exhausted. Jamie was back from running Gus home and drove Harley to his car.

That left Chris and me alone on the hard bench by the empty receptionist's desk. I sagged into his muscled chest. It was so comforting and warm. His rhythmic breathing so relaxed me, I would have dozed if Flynn hadn't come out of his office to get him. Sonny grunted, "G'night," on his way out the glass front door.

Finally it was my turn. I went through the door to the multipurpose room as Chris sat down on the hard bench outside to wait for me. As I expected, Flynn very professionally walked me through the whole story. The plan for the haunted house tour, the plan for what was to happen at Gus's, and my participation as the host on the trolley. "So Mrs. Prendergast canceled at the last minute?"

"Harley said she had the flu." I hesitated. "You don't suspect her, do you?"

"It's too early to suspect—or not suspect—anybody." He asked about the dress rehearsal. Had I spoken to Spencer Jones?

"Hardly at all."

"Hardly?"

"I can't remember anything either of us said that was meaningful. I remember being impressed with how he played the death scene. And impressed with his ideas about how to fix the performance after the disastrous rehearsal."

Then Flynn led me through the events that night at Gus's, again asking detailed questions. I was starting to lag. The late hour had finally hit me.

"Do you own a gun?" Flynn asked.

"No."

"Does Chris own a gun?"

"A hunting rifle." The answer would be the same for many of the men in town.

"Does Chris keep a rifle or any other gun at your apartment?"

"I assume you asked him that."

"I did."

"The answer is no. The rifle is locked up in his cabin. Are you done at the restaurant?"

Flynn answered my question with a question. "Do you and Chris have somewhere else you can stay tonight? The more we get done, the sooner it gets done, the sooner we're out of your hair. And Mr. Farnham's."

I imagined Gus had given Flynn a piece of his mind about all the people and fuss at his restaurant. "We can stay at my mom's. What took you so long to come to question us?"

"I . . ." Flynn's brown eyes slid sideways. He was deciding whether to tell me. "I had to do the death notification."

"So you found the next of kin? That was quick."

"Your friend Officer Dawes found contact information for Mr. Jones's agent in a database on the Web. We called the agent, who had a home phone number in addition to the cell. When we called that number, a man answered and said Jones's wife and their two boys were on a vacation in Busman's Harbor, Maine, staying at the Snuggles Inn."

"Joyce Bayer, and Kieran and Will? Those boys saw their father shot!" The idea was horrifying.

"They did. I was the one who confirmed he was dead. It wasn't fun, I can tell you that."

"Her name is Bayer. I never put it together." Poor Joyce. Poor boys. Poor Flynn. What a mess.

"She never took her husband's name, which is his real name, not a stage name, by the way. Evidently, Ms. Bayer and Mr. Jones have been separated for a long time. The guy who answered the home phone is a live-in boyfriend. She claims them coming here and the victim being here was a coincidence."

"But you don't believe her."

"Seems like one heckuva coincidence."

* * *

Chris and I walked back through the silent town to Mom's house.

"You were in there for a long time." Chris kept his voice low.

"I was on the whole tour, so we had more ground to cover than you did. Did Flynn ask you a lot about the dress rehearsal?"

In the glow of the street lamp, I saw Chris nod. "Yep."

We reached Mom's house and climbed the stairs onto the front porch. I opened the big, mahogany door, which was never locked, let us into the front hall, and flicked on the light. I locked the door behind us, just for tonight.

The Oriental carpet from the upstairs hall lay in a heap on the floor. I pointed it out to Chris. "That's exactly where Harley said Sarah Merriman fell down the stairs and broke her neck. Mom says the upstairs rug ends up there all the time."

Chris raised his eyebrows. "Maybe the place *is* haunted."

"Stop kidding around."

"Who says I'm kidding?"

He picked up the rug and we crept up the stairs. At the top, we lay and straightened the rug and then kissed good-night. My old room still had a twin bed in it, so he was going to sleep in Livvie's old room, which also had a twin bed. It had been decorated aggressively in pink and princesses for my niece Page by my mother back when my father was dying and Livvie and Page had spent many, many nights at the house. At eleven years old Page was rapidly outgrowing the decor, but it always cracked me up to think of Chris sleeping in there.

I tread quietly back and forth to the bathroom, hoping not to wake my mother and scare her to death. When I climbed into bed Le Roi jumped in next to me, the force of old habits. His loud purring lulled me to sleep.

Chapter Seven

Chris was gone by the time I got up. It was a clear, crisp day and he needed to get on with the fall cleanup and closing of summer homes that were a part of his landscape business.

Mom was at the kitchen table drinking coffee when I came down. "Chris told me what happened," she said. "Are you all right?"

"I'm okay, I guess. It was pretty awful. The poor woman staying at the Snuggles saw her husband killed. Their sons saw it too, which seems even worse."

Mom shivered. "I didn't want the tour to come through my house, but I never imagined anything like this."

"We can't be sure it was someone on the tour who shot him."

"Who else could it have been? Other than the tour group it was you, Chris, Gus, Sonny, and Harley. It wasn't one of you."

I guessed she was right. The kitchen door to the restaurant had been locked. No one could have gone out it. If it was opened from the inside, it had to be relocked from the outside with a key.

"There's coffee in the pot," Mom said. "I have to get to work." She went to the back hall to fetch her coat. "By the way, the upstairs rug was on the floor in the front hall again this morning."

"I know. Chris and I put it back last night."

"No, I mean when I came down this morning, it was there."

"Has this thing with the rug happened before? Before Harley told us about Sarah Merriman, I never saw it."

"Yes, very occasionally in the last couple of years, but not so frequently as it has this fall. In the past I assumed it was Page and her friends fooling around, but it's started to happen when they're not around." She gave me a kiss on the forehead, an unusual display of affection, which I knew must flow from her concern about me. "Take care of yourself. Be good. Stay out of trouble."

After she left, I took my coffee mug and walked to the front of the house. There was no misplaced carpet on the front hall floor, but that wasn't what I was after. I stared out the front window at the Snuggles Inn across the street. The leaves were off the trees and Sonny had taken the screens off Mom's front porch earlier in the month, so the view of the B and B was sharp in the bright morning sunlight. Gingerbread molding snaked across the eaves of the now-empty front porch of the Snuggles. I couldn't stand to think about the poor woman and unfortunate boys staying there. I took my mug back to the kitchen sink and then headed out the front door.

* * *

"Julia. How lovely to see you. Come in, come in." Vee Snugg answered the door. She and her sister, Fee, were both in their seventies, neighbors beloved by our family and honorary great-aunts to Livvie and me. Vee looked glamorous as always, her snow-white hair swept back in a chignon. She wore a brown tweed skirt, a brown sweater set pinned with a gold brooch and, as she did for any task in any season, hose and high heels.

"Is Joyce Bayer here?"

"You've heard." Vee led me into the big, old-fashioned kitchen, a place as comfortable for me as my own home.

"I was there."

"Oh, my. I hadn't heard."

"I was working with Harley on the tour."

"The tour group came here you know, to the old stable."

"I was with them."

Vee pursed her lips. "I've lived in this house for decades and I never heard that story about the stable boy."

Indeed. With Harley, poetic license was more like poetic armed robbery. "Where are Mrs. Bayer and the boys now?"

Vee cocked her head toward the swinging door that led to the dining room. "In there, pushing food around their plates. She's anxious to leave, but Sergeant Flynn has asked them to stay. He has to interview them again. As you can imagine, last night she was in no fit state, either to give her own statement or to be present when her boys were interviewed."

"I want to talk to her. Do you think you could distract the boys?"

"Surely. We'll bake." Baking was Vee's response to any kind of stress.

I went through the swinging door, followed by Vee. As she had said, no one had eaten much breakfast. The older boy, Kieran, gazed out the window toward the harbor, while the younger boy played a game on a cell phone. Joyce Bayer stared at her plate. I studied the boys, trying to see a resemblance to Spencer Jones. I didn't see it, except maybe Will around the eyes.

"Mrs. Bayer, may I talk to you?"

She looked up and I could see the toll the events of the night before had taken. Her brown eyes were red-rimmed, and deeply circled. Her sharp nose was raw, her curly, brown hair disheveled. The night before I had judged her to be in her mid-forties. This morning she looked much older.

"Of course. You're Julia, right?"

"C'mon, boys, and bring your plates," Vee said. "I'm going to teach you to make banana bread."

Will, the younger boy, looked at his mom, who nodded it was okay to go. Kieran heaved himself out of his chair and followed.

I sat down next to Joyce. "The detective told me Spencer Jones was your husband. I am so sorry this happened to you and your boys."

"Thank you. It is horrifying. Neither of them has cried. I think they're both in shock. I'm so worried about what this has done to them." She hesitated. "And devastated about Spencer. We weren't together anymore, but he was a part of my life for more than twenty years, and we had two beautiful children together."

"Did you really not know Spencer was here?" I asked it as gently as I could, hoping it didn't sound like an accusation.

"I didn't. No one was more shocked to see him lying there than I was. I'd caught a glimpse of him coming through the trapdoor before the lights went out, but, honestly, I didn't recognize him. It was so fast, and he was the last person I expected to see in the last place I expected to see him."

"So you really didn't know he was here." I said it as a statement, meant to reassure her.

She misunderstood me. "I can see why you would be skeptical. That detective certainly was." She put her hands together on the tablecloth and turned toward me. "It might be a coincidence, but I don't think it was." She lowered her voice. "I think Will somehow found out his dad was going to be here and wanted to see him. It's the only thing that makes sense. Spencer was never very present in their lives even when he and I were together. His work caused him to be away a great deal. When the boys were little, we traveled with him, but once Kieran started first grade, I stayed behind in New Jersey. Spencer was only consistently with us four or five months a year, and even then, if he was in a play, he was gone by the time the boys got home from school, out way after their bedtime, and still asleep when they left in the morning.

"Will, in particular, has been longing to see his dad, and he was the one who initiated this whole trip. I honestly couldn't understand why a thirteen-year-old boy would think going to Maine for a haunted house tour was the coolest thing in the world. But I knew from experience with Kieran, once they become teenagers, if they want to have anything to do with you, you have to be grateful."

"You haven't asked him?"

"No. We were all so tired and shocked last night. I wasn't sure. I'm looking for the right moment. If it's true, I think he and I have to have the conversation before we talk to the detective again. And I need to know if Kieran was in on it."

"What an awful thing, for him to scheme to see his dad and this happens. I am so sorry."

"Thank you."

"You and Spencer were divorced?"

"No. Never officially. We've been separated for seven years, though given how rarely he was home; the marriage was effectively over long before that. One of the ridiculous things about this situation is that I've been looking for Spencer. I wanted to serve him with divorce papers. We never got around to it. The separation was never formal; he just didn't come home one fall after he left here. But now, I have a new partner, someone I want to marry, so I was eager to get officially divorced."

"Spencer didn't have regular visitation with the boys? You weren't in touch?"

"Sadly, he wasn't interested. It's been hard on our sons. I'm lucky they like Scott. He's great with them. They're at an age when they need a man in their lives."

"Will you stay in town long?"

She shifted in her chair. "I want to go home as soon as we can. We need to do these interviews with the police and then sign statements. And I guess, once the medical examiner is through, it's my responsibility to figure out what to do with the body. Spencer's parents are dead, and he and I are still legally married. I want my boys to see their dad treated with respect." She lifted a paper napkin to her eye as a tear escaped.

My heart went out to her. "My mom lives right across the street," I told her. "I'm staying with her until the police say it's okay to return to my apartment, which is in the same building where the shooting took place. Please let me know if you need anything. Anything at all."

"Thank you. Everyone has been so kind. I feel just awful about how everything has turned out."

I left through the front hall, avoiding the kitchen, where the sounds of chatter and the scraping of a spoon on a bowl told me the boys were occupied.

Chapter Eight

As soon as I left the Snuggles, I got a text from Flynn that my statement to the police was ready for me to review and sign. There being no time like the present, I headed down the street in the direction of the police station.

On my way down the walk to the station house door, I ran into Marge and Elizabeth, the mother and daughter who'd been on the tour.

"It's you," Marge said.

"It is me," I agreed. "Are you here to give your statements?"

"We just did." Marge turned back and pointed toward the glass door. "So long, so tedious." Then she seemed to remember it wasn't entirely about her. "And such a terrible thing to have happened, of course."

"Of course."

"Anyway, we were here for hours. Hours! That sergeant insisted we had to be interviewed individually, and by him. Even though we were in the same place and saw, and didn't see, exactly the same things. Now we have to drive back to Brunswick. By the time we stop and pick up groceries on the way, the day will be done. Done, I tell you."

I didn't know what to say to this. Silently, I tried out "What a shame," which didn't seem to fit, and "I'm so sorry." But what was I apologizing for?

Fortunately, Marge didn't seem to notice my lack of response. "We've got to go," she said. "Got to go. We cannot wait to leave this all behind us. It's been nice to meet you, Julia, but I hope we never see each other again." Marge grabbed Elizabeth by the elbow and dragged her toward the parking lot.

By this point, I was truly speechless. I hoped Marge didn't get her wish, because if I never saw her again, that meant there wouldn't at some time in the future be a trial. And if there wasn't a trial, that might mean the killer had never been caught.

As I watched them go, I realized it had been my second meeting with Elizabeth Handey and I had yet to hear her utter a single word.

"I don't think she did it."

Flynn looked up from his laptop, furrowing his brow as he did. "Mrs. Handey?"

"Joyce Bayer. I think she's shocked to her core by the murder, and I think she's too much of a mother to murder their father in front of her sons."

"You've talked to her, then." He sat back in the metal folding chair, arms across his broad chest.

There was no sense in denying it. "I visited her at the Snuggles. I thought she might need some company, or support."

"Your friends the Snuggs strike me as the very essence of comforting and supportive."

"I don't think it was her." I dug my heels in.

"Yet you admit it was a tremendous coincidence that after a long separation Mrs. Bayer happened to be in the place where her husband was murdered."

I wanted to tell him the visit had most likely been engineered by her younger son, but then I remembered Flynn hadn't yet formally interviewed either Joyce or her boys. How they came to be in Busman's Harbor wasn't my story to tell. "I'm here to review my statement."

"I'll get it."

While Flynn was gone, I waited in the uncomfortable metal folding chair across from the folding table he used as a desk.

"Got it." He waved the papers fresh off the printer in front of me. I took them and reviewed what I'd said. All seemed to be in order, so I signed them.

"What else is new?" I asked him. Sometimes, depending on the case, he would tell me.

"Ballistics reports and a preliminary medical examiner's report is what's new. Jones was killed with a single bullet to the brain from a Remington 22 Viper hypervelocity bullet shot from a Smith & Wesson 43C 22 caliber J Frame revolver."

I stared at him blankly.

He grinned. "You have no idea what I just said."

"I heard some numbers, and also the letter. *J.*"

"Mr. Jones was killed with a single shot from a small revolver."

"A small revolver? It sounded like a cannon."

"The high-velocity ammunition would have added a little volume, but mostly it was loud because it was fired from right next to you."

"Right next to me!" I could feel the color drain from my face.

Flynn held up a hand. "Maybe not literally next to you, but from the area where the tour participants sat."

"So it was a member of the tour group who shot him."

"Most likely, unless someone snuck in and got in place before the trapdoor opened. But they would have to have hidden near, almost in, the tour group, and no one I've spoken to so far saw anyone who wasn't on the tour."

Flynn's certainty about the trajectory of the bullet eliminated Chris, Sonny, Gus, and Harley from suspicion. Not that I ever thought it was one of them, but it was good that Flynn had no reason to consider any of them. "Have you found the gun?" I asked.

"No. It's nowhere on the site. Whoever shot Jones must have taken the gun."

"Wouldn't they need to get rid of it?"

"One would think. The killer was a great shot."

Spencer had only been visible for a few seconds before I'd turned out the lights, and he'd been on the move. To place that bullet in the middle of his forehead in the dark seemed remarkable.

"Have you interviewed everyone from the tour group?" I asked.

"Not quite. I talked to the four teenagers, along with Mrs. Handey and the daughter this morning. Clyde Merkin's on his way in. I'll talk to Ms. Bayer and her boys this afternoon. I interviewed you,

Chris, Gus, Sonny, and Harley last night, so almost everybody."

"You left someone out."

"Ms. Santiler. She's unaccounted for. She was registered at the Bellevue Inn and supposed to stay there overnight, but she retrieved her car from the valet less than half an hour after the incident. He saw her throw a suitcase in the trunk and leadfoot it out of the parking lot."

"She's on the run."

"Maybe," Flynn conceded. "Or maybe simply unnerved by the murder. Mr. Prendergast gave us her credit card number. If she uses the card we'll find her soon." He shifted in the uncomfortable chair, which made me aware of how much my backside hurt. "Did you talk to Mrs. Handey and her daughter on the tour?"

"I introduced myself, but not much more. I talked to them a little bit when I met them on the walk on my way in here."

"What did you think? Mrs. Handey gave me a hard time about interviewing her daughter one-on-one. She wanted to be present."

I thought back over the whole of the trolley tour and the chat on the walk this morning. I had assumed Elizabeth was shy, and with a mother like Marge, could barely get a word in edgewise anyway. But maybe my assumptions were wrong. "Do you think the daughter is impaired in some way?"

"You mean mentally? No. She was clear and straightforward once I got her away from her mother. I think the younger Ms. Handey is almost pathologically shy, but I don't think she has any intellectual challenges."

He glanced at his watch. "Mr. Merkin is due any minute."

I stood. "I'll go along then. Can I move back into my apartment?"

"Yes. We weren't done in time for Gus to open the restaurant this morning, but it's clear now."

"Thanks."

Clyde Merkin came down the walk toward the station as I left. "Julia! How are you doing? Wasn't that something last night?"

"I'm okay, Clyde. Still a little shaky, if I'm honest."

"Yeah. That'll be the shock. Were you meeting with Sergeant Flynn?"

"I just signed my statement. I was interviewed last night."

"I'm going in for my interview now. Of course, I'm an eyewitness, like you are, or maybe more like an *ear*witness, since the lights were out when the shot was fired." Clyde shifted his weight from one foot to the other and continued to muse.

"In that sense, I'm not only a witness to the event, I'm something of an expert witness." He paused so I could take that in. *Of course he was.* He went on. "I'm an expert on firearms. I shoot at the range every Saturday, and I've trained my ear to recognize every gun that's fired. I could tell you the caliber, the make and model, sometimes even the type of bullets."

"I'm sure Sergeant Flynn will be grateful." I wasn't going to mention the ballistics report was already in, or the slug pulled out of Spencer Jones by the medical examiner.

"In this case," Clyde said, "I can state positively the weapon was a Glock, a nine-millimeter." He gave me a self-satisfied smile.

So help me, I took the bait. I shouldn't have, but I did. Flynn had mentioned lots of numbers, but none of them had been a nine-millimeter. "That's funny," I said. "Sergeant Flynn told me not five minutes ago the ballistics report said the gun was a Smith and Wesson revolver, twenty-two caliber."

Clyde looked nonplussed, if only for a second. "Well, well. A revolver. There was only the one shot, so I couldn't be expected to . . . A twenty-two, huh. It's a miracle it killed him. Though if it was a tour member who shot him, we were at quite close range. Well," he said, recovering, "I wouldn't have heard many twenty-two revolvers at the range because *it's a lady's gun.*"

That did it for me. I might not know a soldier's gun from a soldering gun, but a lady's gun. *Really?* "Bye, Clyde. I've got to run."

He, however, wasn't deterred. "Still, it was a lucky shot."

Or a very skilled one. I didn't bother to say it.

Finally, he was done. "Bye, Julia. Wish me luck. I'm off to the firing squad. Ha, ha, ha."

Clyde disappeared through the glass door to the station, and I took off down the street.

Chapter Nine

Gus was in the restaurant when I got back there, mumbling as he removed spoiled food from the walk-in. The trapdoor was closed and what blood there had been was on the underside. There hadn't been much that I remembered. Spencer must have died instantly. A lucky shot, Clyde had said. A highly skilled shot, Flynn believed. Either way it was shot in the dark.

I got to work right away, throwing away the left-over pumpkin bread and cookies, pouring the cider down the sink and scrubbing the pot. I had starting moving the tables back to their regular positions when Chris arrived.

He gave me a side hug and a kiss on the cheek. "I've come from signing my statement," he said.

"I did mine about an hour ago."

"I still have to go down there," Gus called from across the room. "I wanted to get my place put together and ready for tomorrow before I went."

"It's too late for us to open tonight," Chris said to me. Harley had removed our stop from the tour,

permanently, though he was determined to go on
with the rest of it. Chris and I had agreed we'd reopen the restaurant as soon as we were allowed.

"I know. I'll put a sign on the door."

We went back to work. I finished with the tables
while Chris got out Gus's toolbox and nailed the
trapdoor shut. Gus stood over him as Chris worked.
"Good riddance," Gus said as Chris banged the last
nail in. "I am never opening that door again. Every
time we do, it's trouble."

Chris nodded and stood, dusting off the knees
of his jeans. Together the three of us moved the
bar and backbar into place and everything was
back to normal. Sort of.

I started to put on a pot of coffee when Gus
said, "You got any cold beer?"

We did and we all agreed we'd earned one. We
sat at the counter and relived the day before. It was
a way of processing what we felt, bonding over a
shared experience. I was so grateful to have these
two wonderful men in my life.

"Flynn said the gun was a twenty-two-caliber revolver," I told them.

"You don't say," Gus said. "A twenty-two."

"Have they found it?" Chris asked.

"No," I answered.

"It must've been ditched somewhere," Gus said.

Chris agreed. "The killer has to know that with
only sixteen people present, aside from the de-
ceased, the police will zero in on a suspect soon
and get search warrants for homes and cars."

"If it was ditched, it probably was around here,"
I said. "In the confusion, as everyone ran out."

"Are you suggesting we look for it?" Chris asked.

"The cops have been all over this place," Gus said. "They were still searching outside when I got here earlier."

"Did they search under the restaurant, around the pilings?" I asked.

"Ayup, a bunch of 'em were down there."

"What about the cave?" There was a cave and a tunnel, partially natural and partially man-made that went from the rock under Gus's to the Busman's Harbor Yacht Club nearby. During Prohibition smugglers had used it to drop off booze for the rich men who belonged to the yacht club, a kind of protection that ensured their work didn't get too much scrutiny. Probably Ned Calhoun had used it.

"Told 'em about it," Gus said.

That appeared to be that. We got back to work, but I admit, whenever I went outside, I looked around. After I took the last garbage bag out to the Dumpster in Gus's small parking lot, I stood on its seaward edge. The tide was dead low. In a few minutes it would turn and start coming in. Daylight savings time hadn't yet gone, but winter was coming. The sun was low in the west and cast a golden glare, throwing deep shadows from the exposed rocks and boulders.

I saw a glint in the distance. Could it be? I stepped to the kitchen door. "Chris, can you come out here?"

"Do you see that, glistening in the mud there?" I pointed, and his eyes followed my finger.

"You don't think that's . . ."

"Could someone have thrown it that far?"

Chris picked up a rock and pitched it, not specifically in the direction of the glinting object, but out over the harbor. The rock landed several yards beyond it.

"Hey, Gus!' Chris called, bringing the old man to the door. "Did the police have divers here, do you know?"

Gus shook his head. "Not today. I imagine they will tomorrow if they don't find the gun before then."

Before Gus finished speaking, I dialed Flynn's number.

Chapter Ten

The next morning I woke up in my own bed. The murmur of voices, clanging of dishes, and the smell of bacon told me Gus was open for business. I leaned over and shook Chris's shoulder. "Pancakes," I whispered.

He opened a sleepy green eye. "Breakfast," he agreed.

By the time we were showered and dressed, Gus's was pretty crowded. The lobstermen were gone and the working folk had taken their places. "Our" booth was taken, but Chris and I slid into an open one.

There was less talk around us about the murder than I expected. What snippets of conversation I did overhear seemed to follow along the theme that the victim was an outsider, the suspects were outsiders, and it was nearly none of the town's concern. I was glad Harley, Gus, Chris, Sonny, and I were not considered to be suspects according to the wisdom of the town. Nor were the four teenagers, or Clyde. But then, that was easier, wasn't it? If it was some dastardly person From Away.

We had our coffee and had placed our orders, blueberry pancakes for me, eggs over easy and hash for Chris, when Sergeant Flynn walked down the stairs into the restaurant's front room.

Chris's back was to him, but I saw Flynn and he saw me. I motioned him over. "Join us."

He looked around, taking his time to decide. "Don't mind if I do." Gus's menu hadn't changed in half a century and Flynn knew what he wanted. "Two eggs, soft-boiled," he told Gus when he came to take the order.

"Toast?" Gus asked, though he surely must have known the answer.

"No, thanks." Ordering accomplished, Flynn turned his attention back to Chris and me. "That was a lucky thing, you spotting the gun." He'd said as much to me the evening before when he'd interviewed each of us thoroughly about how we had found it.

"It was a lucky thing," I agreed. "The tide was dead low, and the sun happened to catch a glint off it."

"It could easily have gotten buried in the mud in the bottom of the harbor," Chris added. "Not many guns are silver these days. Most are the exact same color as the mud."

"Aluminum alloy with stainless steel," Flynn corrected. When the gun had come out of the water, not only was it silver colored, it had a robin's egg blue grip.

A lady's gun. Indeed.

Gus chose that exact moment to bring Chris and me our breakfast. He set down the steaming plates in front of us. I pushed around the butter on the pancakes so it would melt evenly and then drenched them in Maine-made maple syrup, the only kind Gus served. I always felt self-conscious eating in front of Flynn, and never more so than with a plate full of pancakes.

"You'll be interested to know," Flynn continued, "we traced the owner of the weapon. It is Mrs. Joyce Bayer of Montclair, New Jersey."

I fell against the back of the booth in surprise. "Have you arrested her?"

"The gun was reported stolen five weeks ago. Of course, she could have reported it stolen when it wasn't, preparatory to committing premeditated murder."

Suddenly I wasn't so hungry. "That's awful. I could have sworn it wasn't her. She seemed genuinely horrified by what her boys had witnessed."

"I agree," Flynn said. "She appears quite credible. But there's more. Not only had she drawn up divorce papers for the victim so she could pursue another relationship, through his union Mr. Jones had substantial life insurance policies."

"She's the beneficiary?"

"Her boys."

Which brought up the thing I was trying not to think about. "If you arrest her, what will happen to those boys?"

"I haven't arrested her, but I have asked her to stay in town to 'help us with our inquiries.' Her live-in boyfriend is on his way here. Depending on how long she stays, he'll either remain here with them or take the boys back so they can go to school. Mrs. Bayer wants everything to be as normal as possible for them."

"Hard for it to be normal when you've seen your father shot."

"Heard him shot," Flynn reminded me. "None of you saw it."

But the boys had seen the aftermath, as had we all. "Did you find the other woman from the tour yet, Carla Santiler?" I asked.

"Not yet," Flynn answered. "The local police in Saint Petersburg have a patrol car outside her house, in case she shows up there. She hasn't used her credit card yet. Harley had a cell number for her. It's turned off."

"That seems like a loose end."

"It's one of those loose ends that's keeping Mrs. Bayer out of jail."

Chris excused himself. It was another beautiful day and he had to get as much outdoor work done as possible before autumn turned nasty. Gus brought Flynn's eggs in two little eggcups on a plate. I sat with him while he ate. I asked if he was dating. My friend, Genevieve, had broken his heart and then sailed off to be a chef on a superyacht. He'd been slow to get back out there.

Flynn carefully tapped an egg with his spoon, then flipped the top off when the shell cracked. He studied the runny yolk, longer than I thought necessary. "Nobody special. I've been on a few fix-ups, but nothing I've wanted to pursue. How about you and Chris? Any announcements there?"

The path for Chris and me had been long and complex. Flynn knew some of the story but not all of it. "No announcements," I answered. "I'll keep you posted."

"Do that." Flynn finished his eggs, pulled a ten out of his wallet and left it on the table. "Back to the salt mines." He left me sitting alone.

* * *

After breakfast, I went back to my normal fall routine, which was work in the clambake office at Mom's house in the morning and then at the restaurant in the afternoon and evening.

When I got to Mom's, the upstairs carpet was in a heap near the arch between the front hall and the living room. I couldn't imagine my mother walking by without picking it up, so either she'd been very late to work, or the ghost of Sarah Merriman had replayed her fatal fall sometime between when Mom left and I arrived.

With the season over, the clambake work was about completing the accounts, getting ready to pay the taxes, and figuring out how much profit was left to distribute to Mom, Livvie, and Sonny, and me, as well as Quentin Tupper, our silent partner. It was tedious, but it had to be done, and I worked away, squinting at the little numbers in the spreadsheets open in my computer monitor. There was work being done on our island as well. Windsholme, the mansion built by my mother's ancestors, was to undergo a massive renovation in the spring. Working on that involved phone calls and decisions, some of which I could make quickly and some that had to be deferred until I could circle up with the rest of the family.

No matter what I was doing, I couldn't keep my mind entirely on my work. The events of the past two days constantly intruded.

I had to admit things looked bleak for Joyce Bayer. Her estranged husband was killed with her gun. As Flynn had said, she could have reported it stolen as a part of a plan to kill Spencer, though not a very good plan. Which brought on an even worse thought. What if one of the boys had taken the gun? Joyce suspected her son Will had discovered his father would be in Busman's Harbor, which is why he'd lobbied for the trip. What if his purpose wasn't a loving reunion with an absent father, but something much darker?

How could Will have known his dad would be in town? Our little Halloween pantomime wasn't like a show in a theater. There was no program, no list of the players anywhere. None of the stories in the local paper or the publicity the tourist bureau sent out would have contained the names of the actors.

Will and his dad could have been in touch without Joyce knowing about it. Spencer could have sent Will an e-mail or a text, or even made a phone call to say he'd be in Busman's Harbor. How much did mothers know about what their thirteen-year-olds were up to? But would Will, who seemed like such a nice boy, have murdered his father? Thirteen-year-olds could kill. That was a fact. Although I'd only met him briefly twice, nothing about Will had raised the palest pink of red flags.

Which left Kieran. He was older. More capable of taking on his neglectful father, perhaps. More angry? Had Will told Kieran he found their dad? Or had it been Kieran who found him? Joyce had guessed it was Will, but she wasn't sure. And most important, when had this been? Was it more than five weeks earlier, when the gun was reported stolen? Because that would certainly demonstrate intent—on someone's part.

Every time I heard a car door slam in the street, I got up and looked out the office windows toward the Snuggles, discommoding Le Roi whose preferred spot was purring in my lap whenever I worked on the office computer. The first several times, it was nothing—people parking to walk downtown, the Snugg sisters returning from the supermarket. Le Roi was clearly annoyed by all the back and forth, though he jumped back on my lap each time.

Finally, when my morning work was done and the computer powered down, I heard a car door slam. Dashing to the window, I saw a Saab parked on the street. A middle-aged man with curly black hair ran toward the Snuggles front porch. The door of the inn burst open and Joyce Bayer fell into his arms. Kieran and Will followed closely behind their mother and the four of them moved in for a group hug. The man glanced back at his car as the rest of them hustled him into the house. Even from my perch on the second floor, I could see the look of loving concern on his face.

As I closed my mother's front door, my phone pinged, indicating a text. It was from the police station. My statement from the day before, telling how I'd spotted the gun, was ready to be signed. It was a good time for me to stop by, since my clambake work was done and Gus was still serving lunch at his restaurant.

When I got to the station, the door to the multi-purpose room was open and all the lights were off. "Is Sergeant Flynn here?" I asked the civilian receptionist.

"Flew to Virginia." Jamie's voice came from somewhere behind the partition that separated the receptionist area from the bustle of the office. Then he appeared.

"Virginia? In the middle of an investigation?"

Jamie cocked his head toward the doorway of the empty multipurpose room and we went inside. "Carla Santiler walked into a police station in Arlington, Virginia, this morning. She told the officer on duty there that she thought the police in Maine might be looking for her as a witness. She told him she was so terrified by the murder she got in her car, drove off, and kept driving. She spent yesterday with a friend in Virginia, calmed down a bit, and realized she was a witness to a crime and police here for sure wanted to talk to her. Her friend talked her into going to the local station and accompanied her there for support."

"So Flynn's down there? He couldn't interview her on the phone, or have the local police do it?"

"He took off for the Portland Jetport almost as soon as he got in this morning. In this case, we have a limited number of witnesses and a limited pool of suspects. Every one of you sat in a slightly different place at Gus's and may have heard different conversations and observed different things during the tour. Flynn wanted to interview her in person, and it was faster to get him to her than to wait for her to get back here." Jamie glanced at the wall clock in the front of the room. "He may even be there by now. The Arlington police said they'd pick him up at Dulles."

"I guess. Anything else going on?"

Jamie shrugged. "Nope. Aside from this, it's a typical off-season. Pretty quiet."

Chapter Eleven

As I passed the Snuggles on my way to Gus's I spotted Will sitting alone on the front porch. He sat on the top step, his feet resting two steps down. He held his phone in both hands in front of him, but he wasn't looking at it. He stared off into space. I waved as I walked by, but he didn't respond.

"Will! Will!" I called.

He snapped to it and managed a small smile.

I walked down the sidewalk. "Can I talk to you for a minute?"

"Sure." He scooched over, making more room for me next to him.

"How's it going?" A neutral question.

"Better now that Scott's here. Mom's been crying a lot. I don't like that."

"Your mom is sad about your dad."

He rolled his shoulders in an exaggerated movement. "I guess." He was silent for a moment. "But I don't think that's why she's crying. I think she's scared."

My stomach clenched into a tight little ball. "Why do you think she's scared, Will?"

He turned to look me full in the face, bathing me with his warm, brown eyes. "She's scared I shot my dad."

His declaration took my breath away. I was afraid to ask the next question, but afraid not to ask it. "Did you? Did you shoot your dad, Will?"

His mouth dropped open and his brows flew up, opening his eyes wide. He was genuinely shocked I'd asked him directly, even though he'd been the one to bring it up. "No way!"

I tried to match his agitation and surprise with my calmness. "Have you told your mom it wasn't you?"

He shook his head. "She hasn't exactly asked me the question. I said she's scared I did it and she's afraid to ask. I don't want to freak her out by even bringing it up. We have to talk to that state police detective again. It was supposed to be today, but now it may be later or even tomorrow because he had to go out of town. The detective's going to talk to me and Kieran separately. My mom will be with me, and there's going to be a lawyer there, too. Mom says I have to tell the truth." He said it solemnly, like he was repeating something a grown-up had told him was *Very Important*.

"Why do you think your mother is scared you did it?" I asked.

"Two reasons. It was my idea to come on this trip. She thinks I knew my dad was going to be here."

"Did you?"

"Yes." He didn't hesitate, but he didn't elaborate.

"How did you know he was here?"

"I got a call that told me he was."

Again, it felt like an honest answer, but the barest bones of one.

"A call from your dad?"

"No, from a lady. She didn't tell me her name. She said, 'Your dad is going to be in Busman's Harbor, Maine, working on the haunted house tour from October twenty-fifth to the thirty-first. He told me to tell you he wants to see you.' "

"Was this on your cell phone or your home phone?"

"Cell, but the number was blocked. I already thought of that."

The police would be able to find out the number, once Will told them what had happened. "Did you recognize the voice?"

"No."

"Would you recognize it if you heard it again?"

"Yes. No. Maybe. I don't know." He sagged in on himself. "I'm sorry."

"It's not your fault. You didn't know what was going to happen. Anyway, after you got the call, you decided to come to see your dad."

"I hadn't seen him in like three years. If he wanted to see me, I couldn't take the chance—" Will's voice, deeper than a little boy's but still not an adult's, was husky with emotion.

"So you came up with this trip?"

"Yeah. I thought about sneaking off, maybe taking the train, but I knew Mom would lose her mind if I ran away."

The trip from Will's house would involve at least three trains, all leaving from different stations than the previous one had arrived at, and finally a bus to reach Busman's Harbor. The odds he could have gotten away with it, particularly once his absence was discovered, were slim.

"Then I thought maybe I would tell her that Kieran and I were going to see Dad; maybe she would allow that. But I knew she'd want to talk to Dad and ask a hundred questions about where we were staying and stuff. I had no way to reach Dad and I knew she didn't either because she was always complaining about it."

He shifted his bottom on the step. "So that's when I came up with the idea for the trip. I got all excited about it, and that got Mom excited about it. I heard her say to Scott, 'I don't know how many of these we have left with just the three of us.' Because they're getting married," he explained. "The hard part was getting Kieran to come. He thought the haunted house tour was a dumb idea, and he wanted to stay home with Scott." Will studied his shoe. "So I had to tell him. I had to tell him Dad would be here."

We sat quietly for a moment after that, each with our own thoughts.

"You said there were two reasons your mother was scared you'd shot your dad. What was the other one?"

"Her gun was stolen."

I feigned surprise. "Her gun was stolen? When?"

He shrugged. "Nobody knows. It's kept locked up in a box in her closet. She's been way too busy to go to the range, for, like, a long time. Years, maybe. About a month ago, she was getting out her fall clothes and she moved the box and she could tell there was nothing in it. Right away she asked me and Kieran and Scott if any of us had taken it. None of us had, so she and Scott reported it stolen to the cops."

"But you think your mother suspects you took it."

"She's scared I took it."

"The lock on this box, did it need a key or a combination?"

"Combination."

"Do you know it?"

"No—I swear. I didn't take it."

"Did Kieran take it?" Sometimes siblings knew things parents didn't.

"He wouldn't. I know he wouldn't."

"Do you keep your house locked?"

"Yeah, all the time."

In a dense metropolitan suburb, they would. Of course, I thought everyone should, not that I'd ever be able to convince my mother. "Did your dad still have keys to the house?"

"I guess. It wouldn't matter if Mom made him give them back; anybody could get in who knew the garage code. That's never been changed since we moved there when I was a little kid."

I nodded. It was a comforting thought for Will, that anybody could have taken the gun. But they'd have to know where it was in the house and what the combination was to the box. The Montclair police had undoubtedly concluded it was an inside job.

"My dad didn't steal my mom's gun to kill himself." Will said. "He wouldn't have that lady call me to come and watch him do it. He wasn't a great dad, but he wasn't a psycho."

The ballistics report hadn't indicated suicide. It said Spencer Jones had been shot by someone sitting near me. Someone on the tour.

"You're right," I reassured him. "The police don't think your dad's death was a suicide."

He let out a long breath, as if he hadn't exhaled fully since the murder.

I got up and walked down the steps, turning back so I could look Will directly in the eyes. "Tomorrow, or whenever this interview with Sergeant Flynn happens, tell the truth. Tell it like you told me here. Your mom won't be mad, I promise. It will all work out."

"Do you really think so?"

His eagerness broke my heart. "Yes," I said. "I do."

I was surprised when Flynn walked into the restaurant that evening just before we finished dinner service. He often ate with us if he was staying overnight in town. We were the only place open weeknights during the off-season besides the dining room at the Bellevue Inn, where he never could have eaten under the limits of his expense account. I was surprised he was back from Virginia.

"That was quick," I said as he took his accustomed seat, solo at the bar.

"I only interviewed one witness."

"Is she . . . back here in Maine?" I had no reason to suspect Carla Santiler of killing Spencer Jones, except that she ran and kept running.

"No. I questioned her and let her go on her way. I asked her not to leave her home in Saint Petersburg." He shrugged. "We'll see. It's not enforceable."

I gave him a glass of seltzer without him asking. No ice, no lemon, no lime. "Is she a suspect?"

"She's definitely a person of interest." He hunched over the bar, shortening the distance between us. "And for the most unbelievable reason. You will never guess it in a million years."

I picked up the gauntlet. "She's a suspect because she's a famous sharpshooter."

He laughed. "Guess again. Although she does have a concealed weapon license in Florida, so maybe."

"She's a suspect because she's a hired assassin who travels from town to town killing actors in local holiday celebrations."

"I have to admit, that's unbelievable," he conceded. "Guess again."

I went for the most obvious. "She's a suspect because she had an affair with Spencer Jones." He spent five months a year doing regional theatre in Florida.

"Warmer," Flynn encouraged, still keeping his voice low.

"I give up."

His eyes flashed in triumph. "She's a suspect because she and the victim are married."

"No!" I shouted, causing heads in the dining room to turn in our direction.

"Shush." He grinned in spite of his warning. "I swear. I haven't seen the documents yet. She's going to produce them, but Ms. Santiler firmly believes that she is Mrs. Spencer Jones."

My mouth flew open. I was as shocked as Flynn had hoped I'd be. He chortled in response to the look on my face. I had a hundred questions. "How long have they been married? Did she know about Joyce Bayer? Why was she in Busman's Harbor?

Why did she run? She must have known it would make her look guilty."

"She and Jones had been married for seven years. The marriage was breaking down, and one of the issues was not only his nomadic lifestyle but also the fact that, for the last three years at least, he didn't communicate well when he was gone. Didn't call, text, or e-mail, or even respond to such. Ms. Santiler claims she didn't know a thing about Joyce Bayer until a week ago when she got a mysterious phone call from a woman who told her about Ms. Bayer and the kids."

Another mysterious phone call. "She had no idea?"

"Jones had told her he was previously married, no kids."

"No kids means there's no reason to keep in touch with the ex-wife, a clean break."

"Exactly. No messy connections. The caller told her if she wanted to catch Jones in the act to come to Busman's Harbor and take the haunted house tour on its first night."

"So she did." I had wondered why she'd taken the tour on her own. The answer was one I couldn't have imagined.

"So she claims. The decision was spur of the moment, which is why she drove all the way from Florida. She did it in two days, and told herself every mile of the way she could turn around. But she didn't."

"It's a strong motive." I couldn't imagine the anger and hurt Carla Santiler must have felt to have been deceived in that way. And to have found out the way she did, from an anonymous phone call. I had no doubt the caller was the same one who had told Will Jones where to find his father. Flynn didn't know about that call yet, but he would hear about it firsthand in the morning.

"Ms. Santiler has a strong motive," Flynn agreed. "And she ran. But she also turned herself in. And she did none of the things you would do if you were planning a premeditated murder. She registered at the Bellevue under her own name. She didn't take Jones's name after they married," he told me as an aside. "And she paid for the ticket for the tour with her credit card. She easily could have paid Harley cash and we'd never have known who she was."

"Maybe it wasn't premeditated. Maybe when she saw him she got so mad, she—"

"Shot him with Joyce Bayer's gun?" Flynn chuckled. "I don't think so. Whoever did this knew five weeks ago what they were going to do."

I had to agree.

"Carla Santiler may have motive," Flynn continued. "But her existence gives even more motive to Joyce Bayer, especially if she learned her husband was a bigamist as recently as Carla Santiler did."

"I suppose." It gave even more motive to Will or Kieran too. Had Will told me everything he'd learned in the mysterious phone call?

I took Flynn's order. He always ordered fresh fish (haddock tonight), an undressed salad, and a vegetable. Then I got busy and Flynn ate, watching Monday Night Football on the television over the bar.

As I refreshed drinks, delivered desserts, and cleared tables, I thought about the two mysterious phone calls, one to Will Jones and the other to

Carla Santiler. Someone was determined they should meet. *If* each of them was telling the truth about the call. Carla could be claiming she got a call when she'd actually plotted the murder and called Will. Will hadn't mentioned his caller had an accent. I was sure he had received a call, but I wasn't sure he'd told me everything about it.

When Flynn was finished he asked for the check.

"Are you sure I can't tempt you with dessert? Livvie-made specials—bread pudding with caramel sauce or coconut cake." I knew it was pointless to ask, which made me all the more determined to do so.

"No, thanks. I'm headed back to the Fogged Inn. I didn't want to stay at the Snuggles with Mrs. Bayer and her kids there. I'm talking to them all again in the morning."

When Will would tell about the mysterious call he received.

Chapter Twelve

In the morning I woke up thinking about the mystery calls to Will Jones and Carla Santiler. The caller, if I assumed it was the same caller—and I did, because one anonymous caller was weird enough, much less two—had been cunning and manipulative. In the Bayer-Jones household she had targeted the youngest member, the one most likely to have a burning desire to see his absent father. With Carla Santiler, the mystery caller had played to anger, instead of longing. Carla was already mad at her husband for his lack of communication during his long absences. She was probably near the end of her rope. The caller had taken a knife, cut off the rope, and sent Carla into free fall.

I couldn't stop thinking about it as I worked in the clambake office. The sky was gray and the weather had turned colder. My mother had a strict policy against turning on the heat before November first, and I shivered as I worked. It was Tuesday, a short day for me because, at Chris's insistence, the restaurant was closed on Tuesdays and Wednesdays. "What part of 'off-season' don't you get?" he'd asked me back when the schedule was set. "I need the time to fix up my cabin, fix up my boat, get my deer."

At nine-thirty I heard voices from across the street and looked out of the window. Joyce Bayer and her boys headed toward her boyfriend's car. I felt better when I spied the roly-poly figure of Cuthie Cuthbertson accompanying the four of them down the front walk. Despite his harmless appearance, Cuthie was a brilliant defense lawyer and I was glad he and Joyce had found each other. The Snugg sisters must have made the connection. Cuthie got in his own car and both vehicles drove away. They would all be in for a long morning, full of questions about the theft of the gun and the mystery phone call.

I returned to my desk but couldn't concentrate. There were some important things about the mystery caller. How she'd targeted each household was important. So was the timing. Whoever it was had known for some time that Spencer Jones would be starring in our little show at Gus's place at the end of October. I was in the scene with Spencer and I hadn't known who he was until the day of the dress rehearsal.

Who did know? Harley did. And presumably Myra. Try as I might, I couldn't think of any reason either one of them would want to kill Spencer Jones. Who else knew? People Jones had told. That was the only answer.

I thought about the other people on the tour. The shot had come from our section of the restaurant. In that group, were there any more people with hidden connections to Spencer Jones?

I dismissed the two teenage couples immediately. Their motivation for taking the tour was to fool around and goof on Harley.

Clyde Merkin was a professional-grade know-it-all. It had seemed in character to me that he would want to know all about the haunted house tour and would have taken it on the first day. That way he could clear up Harley's "misapprehensions" and be able to tell everyone around town he'd been on the tour, what they'd be seeing, and what was wrong about it.

Harley had said he met Spencer downtown during the summer and became friends with him over a series of conversations. That certainly might have been true for Clyde as well. But if Clyde was friends with Spencer, that moved him even more to the center of the drama, and he couldn't have resisted talking about that. Unless he was the killer. It seemed like a long shot.

That left Marge Handey and her daughter, Elizabeth. I wasn't sure how they could have known Spencer, but it was worth figuring out. I found an address for a Mrs. Orville Handey in Brunswick, the only Handey listed. I assumed that was Marge. There was no address for Elizabeth Handey. Perhaps she lived with her mother.

No longer able to sit at my desk, I went to my mother's garage where I kept my maroon Subaru, pulled out, and pointed its nose toward Brunswick.

Chapter Thirteen

Marge Handey lived in a two-family house on a large corner lot in a neighborhood near Bowdoin College. The gray clapboards needed a coat of paint, but they still contrasted nicely with the dark blue trim around the windows and on the porch rail. I parked on the street and approached the house.

There was only one doorbell and I pushed it. Over the doorbell, there were two mailboxes, one over the other. The bottom one said HANDEY in big, block letters. The top one said JONES, equally bold.

My heart beat faster. Was this the place Spencer Jones rented when he played at the Barnhouse Theater in the summer? Did he rent seasonally? The name on the mailbox might indicate a more permanent residency. Maybe he rented the place year-round. Which might mean he had planned to stay here during his performances for the haunted house tour. Maybe he even called his landlady in advance and told Marge he would be in town. I had discovered a connection between the Handeys and Spencer. It hadn't even been difficult.

I thought about fleeing down the walk. If Marge Handey was Spencer Jones's landlady, this visit was better left to Sergeant Flynn. But at that moment, the front door flew open and Marge stood there. "Julia," she said, "what brings you here?"

I took a deep breath. *In for a penny, in for a pound.* "I'm still getting over what happened the other night." Of course I was; it had only been three days. It's not every day that you see someone gunned down in front of you. "I wondered how you and Elizabeth were doing."

"How kind of you to be concerned." Marge's mouth said "kind," but her eyes did not. She squinted at me, assessing. "I would say we're doing about as you might expect." She pulled her sweater tighter around her. "It's raw today. Come in."

All my instincts told me I shouldn't go inside. I stepped over the threshold into the front hall the two apartments shared, but left the door open behind me and went no farther. "Is Elizabeth here?"

Marge glanced at the staircase that led to the second floor. "She's got her own place, upstairs. I'm not sure if she's home. She works at Renys department store and her schedule changes all the time."

Elizabeth lived upstairs? The mailbox said JONES. Instinctively, I stepped back toward the open door. As I did, my eye fell on a small pile of envelopes on the narrow table in the hall. The top one was from the electric company. MRS. SPENCER JONES, the address read. APT #2.

My stomach dropped. Elizabeth Handey was Mrs. Spencer Jones! Of course she was. Jones had a wife for every town and every season, Joyce Bayer for New York, Carla Santiler for Florida, and Elizabeth for Maine.

My feet, which had momentarily frozen, moved again. I took another step back, but not quickly enough. Marge's gaze followed my own, spotting the pile of envelopes. Before I could react, she lunged at me, grabbing me by the throat and squeezing tight. My hands flew to my neck where I tried to pry hers away, grabbing at her hands, then her fingers. She kept up the pressure relentlessly. I couldn't breathe! I was afraid I would pass out. Then what would she do to me? My heart hammered against my rib cage.

"He ruined my daughter, deceived her! He was going to break her heart. He deserved what happened to him, every bit of it."

Marge was my height and considerably heavier, but I was younger and in better shape. I shook my body violently from side to side, trying to shake her off, but it only tightened her grip. I put both hands on her chest and pushed against her with all my might, trying to break her grip.

"Wheeze, gurgle, burg!" I rasped.

"Who knows you came here?" She looked deep into my terrified eyes. "No one, as I suspected. We'll hide your body and destroy your phone. We'll hide your car, like we did Spencer's. No one will *ever* know!"

I fought her in earnest then, overcoming any inhibitions caused by her age. I pushed, I slapped, I kicked, but she was surprisingly strong. Neither of us was getting anywhere.

Blam! A sound like a thunder crack caused us both to jump. Bits of plaster rained down around us.

"Mother, enough!" Elizabeth Jones stood on the stairs from her apartment, a hunting rifle in her hands, pointed at the ceiling. "This has gone far enough."

It was the first time I had heard her speak.

Marge Handey squeezed my neck one more time for good measure, but then dropped her hands.

"Get out of here," Elizabeth directed me, her tone deadly calm. "I'll take care of this."

I ran to my car and squealed away from the curb. I pulled around the corner, called 911, and told the Brunswick police what was happening. "She had a gun. She said she would take care of it. I don't know what she meant." My voice shook so hard, I worried the dispatcher wouldn't understand me. "Please don't hurt her," I begged. "She saved my life." Then I began to cry.

Before I was off the line, I heard sirens. Grasping the wheel and taking deep breaths to steady myself, I slowly backed up my car so I could see what was happening down the street. Time stood still. I could hardly breathe. "Don't hurt her, don't hurt her, don't hurt her," I mumbled.

Then, both Marge and Elizabeth came down the front walk with their hands up, followed by a half-dozen police officers. I was so relieved, I cried again.

I called Flynn and sobbed out what had happened. He practically threw me off the phone so he could get in touch with the Brunswick PD and fill them in. "Are you all right?" he asked. "Can you drive?"

"I think so." My voice didn't sound as confident as the words.

"Go immediately to the Brunswick police station," he commanded. Then, more gently, "They'll need to talk to you. I'll need to talk to you. Everyone will need to talk to you."

It was much later in the afternoon when Chris drove me to Mom's house. He'd rushed to the Brunswick police station immediately when I called him. I'd been so relieved to see him, I cried again. We'd left my car in Brunswick. The adrenaline had drained out of me and I was too shaky to drive.

Mom ran to greet me as soon as I came through the front door, hugging me, asking me questions and then hugging me again.

"Julia, what were you thinking?" Mom asked. The same question Flynn had asked me, though he'd been a lot louder and redder in the face. The same question Chris had asked on the ride home.

I answered them all the same way. "I didn't realize what was going on until I got to their house and saw the name Jones on the mailbox."

"Was it both of them? Were they in it together?" Mom asked.

"Flynn is still sorting through it. Marge and Elizabeth are season ticket holders at the Barnhouse Theater. Spencer and Elizabeth met at the opening reception three years ago. They dated and he proposed. He moved into her apartment at her mother's house."

"Of course he did," Chris interjected.

"Last summer, Marge became suspicious something wasn't right. She hired a private investigator and learned about the other two Mrs. Joneses. She confronted Jones, who confessed. He begged her not to tell Elizabeth and swore he was in the process of divorcing the other women. She agreed. Then she engaged him in a series of conversations where he revealed to her the phone numbers for Will and Carla, the garage code for the house in Montclair, the location of Joyce's gun, the combination for the gun box, and I'm sure a whole bunch of other stuff. Apparently, all this information was extracted as a form of blackmail. Marge threatened she would tell Elizabeth everything if he didn't provide the information she sought. Marge told Flynn that Jones seemed relieved to finally tell the whole story, to have someone who knew about his life. Marge tucked the knowledge away for later.

"When Labor Day came, Spencer did his usual disappearing act to New York. Marge suspected he'd made no moves to divorce the other Mrs. Joneses. Then he called, completely unexpectedly, six weeks ago, to tell Elizabeth he'd be back in Maine for a week at the end of October.

"Marge was furious. She believed Jones had 'ruined' her daughter and she wanted revenge. She went to New Jersey, stole Joyce's gun, and made the calls to Will and Carla. She hoped Joyce or even Carla would be blamed, most likely Joyce because of the gun. Marge didn't know Joyce had discovered it was missing and reported it stolen."

"And then she shot him in cold blood?" Chris's brow was creased.

"I'm not sure Flynn is buying her story. I think he's convinced Elizabeth was in on it, though both mother and daughter claim otherwise." As I said this, I remembered Marge had said, "*We'll* hide your body . . . *We'll* hide your car, just like *we* did Spencer's."

"I'm sure Elizabeth was involved," I said. "At a minimum, she's an accessory after the fact. Spencer had driven them all to Busman's Harbor the night of the murder. Elizabeth had an extra set of keys to Spencer's car. When everyone ran out of the restaurant after the shooting, one of them, Marge or Elizabeth, threw the gun into the water. They could have ditched it anywhere on the way home, but Marge wanted it to be found. She wanted the murder pinned on Joyce. Then they walked calmly to his car and drove home. No one was looking for the car then. No one even knew it existed. They caravanned out to the woods later and ditched it there."

"Isn't it easy, the question of who pulled the trigger?" Chris said. "Which one was the crackerjack shot?"

That shot, directly to the middle of the forehead, hitting someone who was climbing stairs, in the dark, was remarkable.

"They both belong to a gun club," I said. "Flynn will interview the members to see which of the two was more likely to have the ability."

My own feelings were complicated. Elizabeth was certainly involved, but I hoped she wasn't the shooter and hadn't known of Marge's plan ahead of time. Elizabeth had saved my life.

What would I do if my own beloved mother killed someone right in front of me? Help her hide the evidence? I would be sorely tempted, especially in the heat of such a moment. And I had more resources, more personal strength, and more independence than Elizabeth Jones. Though she'd had the strength she'd needed to end the murder spree, to stop the killing at one.

"Flynn will figure it out," Mom said. "He'll make them tell the truth."

"Either way, Joyce Bayer and her boys are off the hook," I said. That was one good thing about this awful turn of events.

Mom looked from me to Chris and back again. "My goodness, we're so into the story, we haven't moved from the hall. Come into the kitchen and have something to drink."

Just then, there was a terrific scrabbling in the hall upstairs, the thumps of four feet running at top speed. All three of us looked up in time to see Le Roi take a running leap onto the hall carpet, launching it over the stairs. The big Maine coon rode the carpet with a silly grin of supreme self-satisfaction as he traveled through the air, hanging above the stairs for a few seconds before both cat and carpet landed in a noisy heap on the front hall floor.

We all stared as Le Roi got up, shook himself, and strolled calmly toward the kitchen.

Mom laughed, and then I did, too, feeling the tension leave my body for the first time since the murder. Soon we were all hanging on one another, tears in our eyes, grateful for the relief, grateful for the touch, and grateful for answers.

RECIPE

Livvie's Pumpkin Bread

In the story, Julia's sister, Livvie, makes this pumpkin bread for the people on the Halloween Haunted House tour. In reality, it's a recipe I often made in the fall for my children when they were young. Made with canned pumpkin, it is simple and practically foolproof.

Ingredients

2 eggs
½ cup sugar
½ cup oil
⅔ cup canned pumpkin
1 cup whole-wheat flour
¾ cup white flour
⅓ cup molasses
½ teaspoon baking soda
½ teaspoon baking powder
½ teaspoon nutmeg
½ teaspoon cinnamon
1 teaspoon ginger
¼ teaspoon cloves

Instructions

Pre-heat the oven to 350 degrees. Beat eggs and sugar together. Add oil and pumpkin. Mix well. Add rest of ingredients and mix until well blended. Pour into greased 9x5x3 loaf pan. Bake for 50 minutes.

Dear Readers:

I hope you enjoyed meeting or revisiting Julia Snowden, her friends, and family in *Hallowed Out*. If you'd like to read more about them, there are seven Maine Clambake Mysteries and two previous novella collections, *Eggnog Murder* and *Yule Log Murder*. Both also include stories by Leslie Meier and Lee Hollis.

I was thrilled when Kensington asked me to write a Halloween-themed novella for *Haunted House Murder*. The question wasn't whether or not there were ghosts in Busman's Harbor, it was which story to tell. I had already written about one of the ghosts haunting Windsholme, the abandoned mansion on the private island where the Snowden family runs their authentic clambakes, in *Stowed Away*, the sixth Maine Clambake Mystery.

I found, writing about the off-season, I was more attracted to the ghosts to be found in town. I imagined, like most old resorts I've been to, Busman's Harbor offered an evening ghost tour. That's how Harley and Myra Prendergast appeared in my imagination. I already knew Gus's restaurant had been used by rumrunners during Prohibition from the fourth Maine Clambake Mystery, *Fogged Inn*. I was off to the races!

I hope you have enjoyed "Hallowed Out." I'm always happy to hear from readers. You can write to me at barbaraross@maineclambakemysteries. com, or find me via my Web site at www.maineclam bakemysteries.com, on Twitter @barbross, on Facebook www.facebook.com/barbaraann ross, on Pinterest www.pinterest.com/barbaraannross and on Instagram http://www.instagram.com/maineclam bake.

I wish a happy Halloween to all our readers. May you have jack-o'-lanterns, corn mazes, , apple cider—and not a single, solitary murder to spoil your wonderful night.

Very sincerely,

Barbara Ross
Portland, Maine